THE DISTANT
SOUND

THE DISTANT SOUND
GERT JONKE

a novel

TRANSLATED BY JEAN M. SNOOK

DALKEY ARCHIVE PRESS
CHAMPAIGN AND LONDON

Originally published in German as *Der ferne Klang* by Residenz Verlag, 1979
Copyright © 2002 by Jung und Jung, Salzburg und Wien
Translation and introduction copyright © 2010 by Jean M. Snook
First English translation, 2010

Library of Congress Cataloging-in-Publication Data

Jonke, Gert, 1946-2009.
[Ferne Klang. English]
The distant sound / Gert Jonke ; translated by Jean M. Snook. -- 1st English translation.
   p. cm.
Originally published in German as Der ferne Klang, 1979.
ISBN 978-1-56478-526-8 (pbk. : alk. paper)
1. Composers--Fiction. I. Snook, Jean M., 1952- II. Title.
PT2670.O5F413 2010
833'.914--dc22
              2010010331

Partially funded by the University of Illinois at Urbana-Champaign, as well as by grants
from the National Endowment for the Arts, a federal agency, and the Illinois Arts Council,
a state agency

The translator and publisher would like to thank the Austrian Federal Ministry of Education,
Arts and Culture for financial assistance toward this translation

www.dalkeyarchive.com

Cover: design and composition by Danielle Dutton, illustration by Nicholas Motte
Printed on permanent/durable acid-free paper and bound in the United States of America

INTRODUCTION

When the Austrian author Gert Jonke died in 2009 at the age of sixty-two, Angelika Klammer, editor at Jung und Jung, Jonke's Austrian publisher, commented that she considers *Der ferne Klang* (1979) to be his most important prose work.[1] It is the second part of a loose trilogy. The first, *Schule der Geläufigkeit,* appeared in English translation in 2008 under the much-debated title *Homage to Czerny: Studies in Virtuoso Technique.*[2] Fortunately, *Der ferne Klang* can be translated directly as *The Distant Sound.*[3] And the title of the third part *Erwachen zum großen Schlafkrieg,* if literally translated, will be "Awakening to the Great Sleep War."

As part two of the trilogy, *The Distant Sound* occupies a position analogous to the peak of a musical phrase, and if verbal density can be equated with louder volume, the book begins fortissimo. The first forty pages are the densest prose I have ever encountered. Feeling the need for feedback from other translators, I took the first four pages along to an intensive German-English translators' workshop at Translation House Looren in Wernetshausen, Switzerland, in November of 2008. The twelve of us worked on the first sentence of *The Distant Sound* for an entire morning. The first sentence is also the first paragraph in the original German. We felt that Jonke's sentence length should be respected, so we wrenched and tugged at the 122 German words, cutting out a redundant reflexive pronoun in the English, moving a few phrases around, but essentially leaving it as dense as we found it. And all agreed it was the densest prose we had ever seen. I continued on in this way, keeping my translation as close to the original as possible. After forty pages or so, Jonke switches back to the flowing style he used in *Studies in Virtuoso Technique*, and the rest of the novel contains only isolated sections that are as challenging as the opening.

Encouraged by that week in Switzerland, I entered my translation of pages 58–101 in the competition for the inaugural Austrian Cultural Forum Translation Prize, and was delighted that the panel of distinguished international judges awarded me the prize. In fact, they awarded two prizes, with the other prize going to Uljana Wolf and Christian Hawkey for their joint translation of Ilse Aichinger. During the award ceremony in New York, we were asked how we approached translating. I told the audience how I always stay as close as possible to the original, perhaps due to my experience as a translator of scientific texts, but Uljana, who is a poet, said that she translates, rather, from the "spirit" of the text. Her remark made an impression on me. I was still concerned about the first forty very dense pages of *The Distant Sound*, and it occurred to me that perhaps I should try Uljana's approach. Perhaps, for the first time, I had encountered a text so dense that I would have to use poetic license.

In retrospect, I can see that by seeking the advice of professional German-English translators, I had simply locked myself into the groupthink of people who, like me, had the advantage of knowing the source language. When I looked at my own work again for the first time in several months, it was obvious that I hadn't quite completed the transition from German to English. Instead, as in the old party game, I had sat down between two chairs. The more literal approach had preserved the specifically Germanic rhetorical modes of the original, rather than translating *these* into English as well. I did a trial revision of the first few pages of my translation, sent it to my editors at Dalkey Archive Press, and then, with their approval, I carried on.

Since Jonke's long sentences had worked in English translation before, and are indeed retained in many sections of *The Distant Sound*, I wondered at first if the problem was just the surreal imagery in the opening section. As an experiment, I rewrote the German of the first paragraph, changing as few words as possible, but substituting mundane subject matter. This is the opening paragraph as translated by the workshop:

> *Just now all the chimneys of the apartment building up ahead suddenly began to blow stirring music, at first in individual very deep blasts from their blowers puffed forth from the chimney hoods breaking forth randomly from all the flues, vehemently spitting too, sometimes erupting like belches, but astonishingly soon they had gathered together bit by bit to begin a disciplined darkly trumpeted fanfare, organized like a flawless funeral march almost in unison, just as if all the bass tuba players and contrabassoonists of our city and the surrounding countryside had hidden in*

the attic of this one building, perhaps for a secretly meeting exceptionally mysterious contrabassoonists' assembly, whose exemplary music making together was still blown out across the plain through the chimney pipes, out of the attic, out of all chimney stacks for a very long time.

And here is the workshop-vetted translation with substituted content:

Just now all the dogs in the neighborhood up ahead suddenly began to make a distracting noise, at first in individual very deep howls snarled forth from their doghouses breaking forth in snapping sounds from all the gardens, vehemently whining too, sometimes erupting like yowls, but astonishingly soon they had gathered together bit by bit to begin a disciplined darkly barked fanfare, organized like a flawless funeral march almost in unison, just as if all the wolves and coyotes of our city and the surrounding neighborhood had hidden in the park of this one neighborhood, perhaps for a secretly meeting exceptionally mysterious canines' assembly, whose exemplary barking together was still blown out across the plain through the doghouses, out of the gardens, out of all the streets for a very long time.

Well, that doesn't work either. So, clearly, while stretching the limits of our imagination, Jonke is also writing more densely than ever before, than anywhere else.

Next question: Why is such dense writing acceptable in German, but not in English? Why do German speakers keep reading, even if they call it *Gehirnjogging*, or brain jogging, while English speakers throw up their hands? From a purely grammatical standpoint, it may have something to do with the limitations of thinking imposed by the structure of language. English speakers are accustomed to having the finite verb close to the subject, as in: "She said she didn't want to go shopping until the weekend." German speakers are accustomed to waiting for the finite verb in any dependent or relative clause: "Sie sagte, dass sie nicht vorm Wochenende einkaufen gehen wollte." (She said that she not before the weekend to shop go wanted.) They are accustomed to long sentences.

A possible cultural explanation also springs to mind: German speakers equate dense writing with erudition. Their academic writing style requires that an essay begin with a philosophical discussion of the method used, a discussion that is often very densely written and has little to do with the actual subject matter of the essay to follow. This beginning can be skimmed, because the substance will come later. For that reason, or perhaps as a send-up of the academic style, Jonke could safely begin *The Distant Sound* with very dense writing that does not at first glance make much sense. The German-speaking reader will persist through this in the expectation that things will soon even out; the English-speaking reader may simply put the book down.

Another reason that Jonke could get away with opening his book in this way is that *The Distant Sound* was not his first novel; it was his tenth. He had won the inaugural Ingeborg Bachmann Prize in 1977,[4] and was an author in demand. His German-language readers knew the book would be, eventually, entertaining. Jonke had a dramatic bent, and frequently recast his prose as drama. His writing is all about performance. It is alive with different narrative voices. For example, in *The Distant Sound*, the appropriately flowing passage about "river control" is written in the form of a reminiscence, with the speaker prompting himself about the details by asking a series of twenty-two pseudo-rhetorical questions: "because hadn't the river always rolled through the country as good as gold"; "Hadn't it already happened many years ago"; "And hadn't people talked back then about a huge sum," and so on. Jonke gradually takes us right inside the speaker's mind. The main paragraph of this section begins with a concise sentence of fourteen words; the next sentence has 74 words; the next 209; and the next and last sentence has 1,676 words in the original German. It is easy reading, because we are caught up in the rhythm of this distinct narrative voice. As Fatima Naqvi has observed: "The plot is, as so often with Jonke, not the main point of entry into this text."[5] Jonke is not so much using language to tell a story, as he is demonstrating—as an entertainer—that he has a seemingly endless supply of narrative voices in his repertoire. The medium is the message.

The techniques Jonke uses are easily recognizable: theme and variations (it is a wash stand, no, a gymnast's horse, no, a burial mound); different speech patterns as different instrumentation (the blunt speech of the fairground cleaner, the sign language of the tightrope walker); the entrance of a new theme ("Oh, please, shut . . . Watch out!"). Jonke is quite capable of saying things in everyday speech: "they simply went in, forcibly invaded the place, if this way of saying it seems more suitable to you." But the distant sound is distant both because conventional language cannot capture all its nuances . . . and because our power of concentration comes and goes. Jonke shows heard speech decaying as our attention flags, and he takes us to the edge of dreams, where language becomes entirely bizarre.

Jonke was a visually oriented writer as much as a musician, and in his prose he occasionally creates optical illusions by bringing together two disparate objects, much in the way that our minds perceive the world: we are quite capable of looking at one thing and thinking another. In *The Distant Sound*, for example, Jonke brings together the image of an external landscape with the image of a ragged washcloth, and by applying the anticipated description of the one to the other, he continues his description as an extended metaphor. A little later on, he likewise brings the image of viola strings into close proximity with the image of high-tension wires. This unusual literary strategy is reminiscent of the compositional technique pioneered by the American composer Charles Ives, who is famous for capturing in an orchestral score the conflicting sounds of two marching bands practicing independently.

In fact, the similarities between Ives and Jonke are striking. Both of them delighted in combining things that are usually kept separate. Ives's experimentation with sound finds its counterpart in Jonke's experimentation with visual imagery. But Jonke also shares an extraordinary attention to acoustic detail with Ives. Both were classically trained, accomplished pianists. Each listened keenly to his environment and resolved to capture its sound as he heard it in his chosen art form. They opened their ears to what had always been there, but had been selectively screened out. And they innovatively expanded the scope of musical and literary composition. One could even say that what Charles Ives did for music in the first half of the twentieth century, Gert Jonke did for literature in the latter.

Think of Jonke's insistence in his opening paragraph on defining exactly the sporadic beginnings and various nuances of a certain sound, then how it develops, and how it fades away again. Charles Ives's compositions are characterized by the same insistence on accuracy:

> His keen ear caught the sound of untutored voices singing a hymn together, some in their eagerness straining and sharpening the pitch, others just missing it and flatting; so that in place of the single tone there was a cluster of tones that made a deliciously dissonant chord. Some were a trifle ahead of the beat, others lagged behind; consequently the rhythm sagged and turned into a welter of polyrhythms. He heard the pungent clash of dissonance when two bands in a parade, each playing a different tune in a different key, came close enough together to overlap; he heard the effect of quarter tones when fiddlers at a country dance brought excitement into their playing by going a mite off pitch. He remembered the wheezy harmonium at church accompanying the hymns a trifle out of tune. All these, he realized, were not departures from the norm. They *were* the norm of popular American musical speech. Thus he found his way to such conceptions as polytonality, atonality, polyharmony, cluster chords based on internals of a second, and polyrhythms.[6]

In fact, in the first part of Jonke's trilogy, the author prepares us for his radical departure, in *The Distant Sound*, from the traditional idiom, signaling his intent to experiment with a three-dimensional approach to literature. With imagery that, fittingly, comes from the world of music, the narrator of *Studies in Virtuoso Technique* describes the great discrepancy between the irresistibly seductive music that he has recently heard and the frustrating inadequacy of our notation system in its present state of development:

> I was attempting on a piece of notepaper to jot down from memory at least a few sequences of notes in their systematic succession and pitch from the phenomenon, its tone color was hopelessly indefinable anyway, since it was music performed on unknown, unmanufacturable instruments, a music that had to be thought. But not a single one of the notes or chords wanted to let itself be graphically arranged on the paper, and not because my memory was too weak [...] but because the tones simply could not be put down on a surface like a piece of notepaper in the traditionally used two-dimensional system of representation, the notes and tones in my memory could only conceivably have been represented at different elevations in the space above and below the piece of notepaper and also around it in an endlessly extended three-dimensional spatial system of coordinates for musical notation [...] (66)

In other words, Jonke is thinking of moving up off the page, of putting a tilt on his sentences. A linear string of words tilted up at one end will use less horizontal space, but, losing none of its contents, will gain in density as the angle of elevation increases. More and more information will be packed into a shorter and shorter space on the page . . . and the reader, unaccustomed to such condensed communication, may begin to suffer from information overload. In English translation, the first paragraph, as acceptable to the twelve translators, bears down on the reader with the force of 138 dense words per sentence. The revised version, which conveys essentially the same information, has been divided into five sentences. Some commas have been added. Some opaque imagery has been unpacked and clarified. Let's have the reader get the picture without getting a concussion.

Jonke provides us with a memorable image for increasing the angle of elevation to increase the force of a sentence. One of the fantastic vignettes in *The Distant Sound* describes a violinist who has had to abandon all thought of a traditional concert career because he tends to spin to the left. This uncontrollable tendency is caused by his violin trying to escape the bow as it approaches from the right. The solution, he finds, is "to hold the bow at a considerably steeper angle than before, bringing it down diagonally on the violin, very fast, from high up, as if he wanted to pierce the instrument and run it through with the bow like a sword."

Jonke has a refreshing sense of the foolishness of most human activities, an infectious appreciation of the absurd. One of his favorite targets is the figure of authority whose competence has become questionable, the dotty director of the conservatory in *Studies*, the mad psychiatrist in *The Distant Sound*. So we read with some satisfaction that the main character's mind goes blank when he is prodded by the psychiatrist to remember and recount the events of his last evening at home. After all, it did seem in the opening pages as if he was fighting his way through a fog. But then, surprise, surprise, once he has escaped from the asylum and is well free of the psychiatrist, it all comes back to him again, indeed with a recall that is close to perfect. The final pages of the book consist of almost exact quotations from the first pages, in all their complexity, thus forming a frame around the novel. Suddenly we see "the insignificant, idiosyncratic detail taking on a life of its own and becoming telling for a larger view of life in general,"[7] and we realize that this is yet another manifestation of Jonke's ongoing preoccupation with "The Presence of Memory," which is the subtitle of the first part of *Homage to Czerny: Studies in Virtuoso Technique*. Sometimes we can remember things, other times we can't; some things are repeatable, other things aren't; sometimes people come back, other times they are lost forever; sometimes we can hear ethereal music, other times we can't. Such is the nature of life.

By focusing on the things that are not always present, or not always accessible, or retrievable, or audible, but that we nevertheless know exist, by reminding us that there is a distant sound, Jonke touches on the most meaningful aspects of human existence.

JEAN M. SNOOK, 2010

1 *Spiegel Online*. 4 Jan 2009.

2 A title of my choice, because I did not want to perpetuate the infelicitous English name given to Czerny's piano exercises whose original German name Jonke used as the title of his book. The piano score is called *School of Velocity* in English, which to me conjures up the image of a velodrome. Besides, these less than lyrical piano exercises are of only peripheral significance in the second part of Jonke's book. The entire book, though, can easily be understood as studies in the virtuoso use of language.

3 *Der ferne Klang* is also the title of Austrian composer Franz Schreker's best-known opera, first performed in 1912, but the opera is not referred to directly or indirectly in Jonke's novel of the same title. Jonke's "distant sound" is open to many interpretations. Toward the end of the novel it is the sound of nature self-destructing, the strange sound of the wind blowing through corn fields devastated by insects.

4 That was the first of eighteen prizes and scholarships for literature he would win over the next thirty years, as he was a prolific writer of both prose and drama, and a major player on the European literary scene.

5 *Laudatio* for Jean Snook, Austrian Cultural Forum Translation Prize Award Ceremony, New York, December 1, 2009.

6 Machlis, Joseph. *The Enjoyment of Music: An Introduction to Perceptive Listening*. 4th edition. New York: W. W. Norton, 1977. p. 568.

7 Naqvi. *Laudatio* for Jean Snook.

THE DISTANT
SOUND

since then I've been moving more and more slowly
running down until the speed limit
is irrelevant

yes YOU had already touched me
so powerfully lightly tenderly
that I broke down shocked
by your affection

in that summer
when YOU went away
and it was so cold
that the gardens caught cold

the tulips coughed at me
the trees and bushes were constantly sneezing
the grass gave out a milky phlegm
the meadows had gotten hay fever

then finally after so many years
YOU suddenly came back
even if for so short a time
then we at once happily
took up with each other
as if until then
only a few weeks had passed
in those few minutes that were gone almost before they had begun

and also in the days counting down
as our euphoria petrified
we implored each other to try always
to meet again
NOW I AM ALWAYS HERE
past hours seem to me like decades
waiting in vain since then
I've gotten older by fractions of seconds
in this century that will soon have been lost so simply
shortened written off disappeared
I usually don't believe anymore and can't
keep trying to feel my way through except possibly probably
to go on playing billiards with a sort of blind man's cane

Just now, all the chimneys of the apartment building up ahead suddenly started to play stirring music. At first, deep blasts from their blowers came puffing out of the chimney hoods, breaking randomly from the flues, sometimes spitting, sometimes erupting like belches. Astonishingly soon, though, they had all joined together to begin a disciplined, darkly trumpeted fanfare. It was organized like a perfect funeral march, sounding almost in unison, just as if all the bass tuba players and contrabassoonists of our city and the surrounding countryside had hidden in the attic of a single building, perhaps for a secret meeting of some exceptionally mysterious contrabassoonists' society. Their extraordinary music kept blowing out of the attic and across the plain for a very long time.

But then, when you got closer to the building, it gradually seemed to you more and more clearly to be a sea-going vessel, floating around on the shimmering horizon that had flowed away, melted by the summer. Its fog horns were greeting you from a great distance, sounding a friendly welcome for your long-awaited return to yourself.

The opened windows were fluttering like flags, waving freely through the landscape, as if the walls of the building had grown sails.

The gates are opening and shutting like fans, and when their edges hit against the walls, the crumbled mortar dust forms a veil that flutters through the alley to gently envelop the next head it encounters, namely yours. And you notice, distortedly mirrored in the trembling panes of glass all around, that this completely muddied light here, dimly glittering up and down, is streaming sadly away, being blown past, forced through the streets of the city by the wind from the plain.

You see, the dilapidated wooden huts over there are really, as we've said, colorfully painted rowboats that have broken loose and are rocking through the overgrown gardens, sometimes lifted up by the waves in the tall grasses, soon tilting down again, some of them even tipping over. The sky, against whose edge you lean your tired shoulders from time to time, is now as familiarly unfamiliar to you as the most familiar home, in which nonetheless almost everything comes again and again to seem different to you, stranger and stranger, just as your astonishment at the most unexpected surprise always seems suspiciously familiar.

Somehow I must have jumped out of my skin so completely that I no longer care to think of myself as a person in me.

So I see myself as a sort of subject that I'm observing, as someone walking along beside me, and I'm starting to have thoughts about my new companion, such as he is.

What I think now seems more important to me than if I was to think it directly without taking a detour around myself. Of course it's strange that you can think about yourself the way one thinks about someone else—you think to yourself—because you've never been especially good at thinking about other people.

But you never had thoughts like this about yourself either, and you only became important to yourself again after you thought you had freed yourself from yourself, made yourself a sort of neutral person, at least I think that's what happened.

Or had you really, without noticing it, turned your thoughts away from yourself and toward someone else who has less to do with you than you want to believe?

Why do I have the impression that I suddenly want to concern myself with myself even more than before?

Or is it possible that when I see myself this way it's not me at all, but rather a memory of myself, and that's what I'm busy contemplating?

Does this house still seem like a boat to you?

Yes, I really do feel more and more intensely that this building here, in which I've been living for some time, is like a steamship plowing its way between the suburban roofs, traveling through the hills and out of the city. I just happened to be able to catch it at the last moment before it cast off when I came back on board just now from my daily walk, after successfully navigating my way up the stairs and through the stairwell.

On the top story, you saw yourself appear in the big mirror that covers the space on the wall between the door of your apartment and the door of the apartment across the hall.

Are you sure you really unlocked the door to your own apartment, and not the door repeated beside it by the smoothly polished glass in the mirror?

You enter your room, which offers a scenic view of this late, sinking afternoon. It has flowed in through the open window from the sky.

One shouldn't allow one's own thoughts all-too-regular or all-too-close contact with each other, you say, which is why you're in the habit of being rather formal with yourself, preferring to address yourself with an if I may, sir *rather than a* hey, you. *You are doing your best to force your own thoughts to associate with each other more and more frequently with an* if I may, sir *and not a* hey, you, *either because it appears advantageous at the moment to maintain a respectful distance, or else, an entirely different matter, to give your completely deflated self-esteem a little boost, a little prop. It may be necessary in any case to keep some distance between thought processes and conclusions that are surfacing or have surfaced, and why not make yourself feel a bit more important by showing a little more respect for yourself.*

If more people showed themselves a little more courtesy and conversed with themselves in their own heads with if I may, sirs *instead of always presuming to be on intimate terms with themselves, much or everything would be entirely different, but no, courtesy to one's own person is something that, in our part of the world, remains as unknown today as it was in the past.*

Naturally one should keep all communications on a formal basis, especially with one's own person, but careless lapses still occur too often and the unsuitable hey, you *gets used, a tone to which you thoughtlessly lower yourself time and again for the sake of simplicity, although in your case especially we are dealing with a* You *that bears only a faint resemblance to your own person.*

There is nothing more beautiful than a conversation with yourself in which you consistently address yourself with if I may, sir. *Because when your thoughts address themselves informally with* hey, yous, *that often leads to one taking offense, and often a real hostility develops in your own thought process, both among and between your various ideas, and when your own opinions can't even get along with each other inside the same skull, that naturally causes a state of violent agitation that soon becomes entirely unbearable.*

And what about I, *you then ask yourself, why don't you ever use the word* I *when speaking of yourself?*

Don't bother me with that, you say. I, *what does* I *mean? Can you explain that much to me? No? Well, see.*

One could perhaps at best only say I *to oneself if one's sensations and perceptions, which are, after all, the most useful things one has at one's disposal, were really fully able to sense and perceive everything sensible and perceptible, that is, if they were not dependent on and restricted by some anatomically middle-class body, which because of its amateurish construction* can only *impede their full development.*

And one could only approach such an I, *if at all, very slowly and tentatively, and of course exclusively as,* sir. *I do believe that I might be on the right track, especially with this idea, you think. In any case, I won't be giving it up again. The matter is certainly rewarding, and, let us ask, what do you think about it,* sir?

Nothing?

How very typical of you, sir.

But right now, I'm inclined to think that one should leave no stone unturned. In any case, I have no desire to wind up being subjected to all sorts of hateful reproach someday, namely from myself, for having left the most important thing untried. I really have no desire to find myself continually badgering myself. And if one finds that one can't get one's own words out of one's head, then one should probably separate from oneself, if you know what I mean—or rather, if you, my dear sir, know what I'm getting at.

It's best to go our separate ways, in opposite directions from one another, until, at opposite edges of the horizon, we dwindle to the smallest dots and then disappear completely, until suddenly, some day or night, you find yourself standing on the shore of the sea, having overlooked the fact that it was somehow understood that, without any ado, light as a feather, you would be dissolved by the resounding stillness of the ocean.

You still think of the house as a ship.

You yourself, however, seem like a talented young actor who got burned out at the beginning of his promising stage career. His first and at the same time last role, was to portray someone of your name, but he wasn't up to the task, because the absence of useable scripts made it impossible for him to rehearse the part; even to yourself, and not just to others, you are the worst actor imaginable for the development of your personality:

Have you then gotten yourself lost so deliberately, so continually stood in your own way, that you've got stuck at the beginning of your journey? Did this journey consist of never leaving the place you had long since reached, where you've always been, and that you had already tried countless times to enter once and for all? Were you supposed to settle down there, to stay on at this point in your life, enveloped by the motionless, immovable stream of air?

You see veils of air flare up indistinctly over the distant forest, and trembling cracks and tears appear in the hazy sky. You see the wind race between the telegraph poles, organizing the flashing light into glistening, bewildered bundles of rays, blowing them together into rolling piles of light, and chasing them across the plain to the horizon, where they smash to pieces or plunge down the other side. A shimmering gray-streaked foehn wafts away over the edge of the forest. The backlit trees seem to be polished black. Flocks of birds bump against the uppermost edge of the forest and are sucked up by the setting sun as it glides past. You see that it's a transparent balloon, heated redhot, so pale-skinned, glaring, and wrinkled that it is almost crumpled by the ever more densely smoking clouds that come rolling in. They are finally dispersed by a storm of light that scatters their last wisps of smoke toward the outskirts of the city and ushers in the twilight.

Thus the approaching evening starts to stream into the building where, heedlessly, inwardly breathing a sigh of relief, you've managed to trap yourself while trying to escape; it comes into the room through the window, pushes toward you like a skin, a slowly darkening colorful fur of light envelops you pleasantly until only your buzzing, concentrating head is still sticking out, the rest of your body is almost switched off or somehow pulled out of its cage of skin; everything that was previously so insurmountable now seems to have smoothed itself out, so you simply wait for what is yet to come.

The shrill ringing of the doorbell interrupts your concentration, making it impossible for you to continue this line of thought. Startled, you leap up in dismay from your armchair and cover the long way through the hall very fast; presumably you want the distinctive clacking rhythm of your steps to announce your annoyance as clearly and loudly as possible, and quite contrary to your usual practice of letting the doorbell keep ringing as you sit relaxed in your room, you open up right away, although you neither want to know who's standing outside nor what requests or demands he might hope to make of you; you aren't expecting anyone or anything today, because no one has made an appointment to see you, and visits without prior appointment, even from those who call themselves your friends, are just not acceptable. You have refused to tolerate that sort of thing and have also known how to dissuade people from coming. The only valid reason for having opened the door immediately, contrary to all the rules and regulations you have quite obsessively constructed for your future survival, is probably to ask whoever is standing outside the apartment door quite frankly, *what do you think you're doing?* While you want to slam the apartment door shut again without waiting for so much as a syllable of a reply, probably apologetic in nature, an uncomfortable feeling of shame rises up in you, because first, for your person to behave in a way that does not conform to your nature seems ridiculous to you, and second, you have just at that moment realized that this atypical mode of address has been directed toward *a three meter high wardrobe* outside your door.

The wardrobe is blocking at least half of your entranceway, no, substantially more. Not wanting to pass up the golden opportunity to express your indignation to a wardrobe, you listen to the trembling echo of your speech as it rolls through the stairwell from floor to floor and resonates from the attic down to the cellar.

You take a closer look at the visitor so solid in front of you: the wardrobe is standing against the wall between your apartment door and the one across from yours, presumably it's only been there a short time, no longer than a few hours, probably just a few minutes.

So where's the mirror? you ask, because until the very recent arrival of the wardrobe there was a mirror on the wall behind where the wardrobe is now standing, the one you had recently appeared in.

Perhaps it's still there behind the wardrobe, covered over by the wardrobe, you think, but surely the mirror would have been taken down before the wardrobe was moved into this position.

But why would it have been necessary to take the mirror down? You continue to think this through. It actually wouldn't be impossible to have the mirror on the wall and the wardrobe standing there at the same time.

Then again, you think, people were probably afraid the mirror would be crushed by the wardrobe, set down so near and robbing it, the mirror, of its view, so they must have taken it down before setting up the wardrobe, and had possibly already long since hung it up somewhere else.

Or had the mirror on this stairwell wall gone blind, and thus been replaced by the wardrobe?

Would the mirror, you think, really have been so endangered by the wardrobe that people would be forced, out of responsibility, to take it down in advance? Or was the wardrobe simply a threadbare excuse to justify the disappearance of the mirror, to assert that this spot had been needed for the wardrobe and that the mirror had therefore needed to be removed?

Or had the wardrobe been set up to conceal the disappearance of the mirror by covering the mirrorless part of the wall with a wardrobe?

Or was it maybe not entirely outside the realm of possibility that the wardrobe would in fact have been endangered by the mirror hanging behind it, because mirrors are so smooth that the wardrobe might have slipped and fallen? Would not a wardrobe of exactly that size, if it brushed even slightly against the mirror's surface, immediately slip, fall over, go clattering down through the stairwell and wind up smashed to bits against the cellar door?

After having been much too quick to scold the wardrobe, you now begin to accept it as your neighbor, even though it's blocking your door: If you wanted to leave your apartment, after going through the apartment door you would also have to go through the wardrobe door, then through the wardrobe, and then break open the back of the wardrobe with a crowbar. Or does it have a back door that can simply be opened? In any case, you start by tapping on its front door from the outside to investigate the hollow sound of its emptiness.

But as you start to study it in earnest to determine its capacity and decide you want to open it, you become aware of a noticeable rustling sound, or is it a cracking, or creaking?

Did a figure in a gray smock step out of the wardrobe that you just opened, or did it spring around the side from behind the wardrobe? In any case, the gray-smocked figure, with a cap pulled far down over its face, has shot up from somewhere quick as lightning and planted itself in front of you. At first you are only aware of a blurred, unexpected movement, the opening of a gray smock, then a hand reaches into a pants pocket, brings out a handkerchief as big as a flag, and you assume that the man is about to blow his nose. After he has put the crumpled handkerchief flag back in his pocket, you see an index finger move along the lower edge of a nose and then wipe itself off on the smock several times.

You hear the man call out to you in a delighted tone of voice, as if this meeting with you, which is taking place after all, which he had been waiting for for so long, for ages, had spared him all kinds of difficulties right at the last moment. How good, oh excellent, to find myself in the fortunate position of having met up with you today after all, you know, I thought you might possibly not even be at home, but how nice, just think, how nice for me to find you now still here and able to meet with me, just think, at first I was forced to admit that you might be momentarily absent, but how splendid now to find myself standing opposite your person, and how fortunate that I can still reach you. Didn't you hear anything at all just now? No? Or could it be that nothing was perceptible to you because you were so preoccupied with your priceless thoughts? Perhaps some circumstance prevented you from opening the door for so long, and you only now managed to get to it! I haven't disturbed you, have I? I hope very very much that I haven't come at a time when you were engrossed in an activity that would be impossible to continue after such an interruption, because that would be very much at odds with my intentions, but how splendid of you now to have pulled yourself together at last and to have allowed yourself to come over and see how I'm getting along!

So it was you, you hear yourself interrupt the man, who rang my doorbell just now!

No, the man replied, I don't remember having rung your doorbell at all, but rather having knocked on your door very cautiously, gently, and if I could just ask of you now—unfortunately I have only the shortest amount of time for the very people I like the most—either to let me in as quickly as possible, into the safe seclusion of your admirably arranged private premises, or else to have a word with me outside here in the stairwell, whichever you like. For you, you should know, I am also prepared to go anywhere else you might prefer, it's all the same to me where we, where you want to go spend the few seconds of time required to most graciously give me your very valued answer to some of my questions. It will provide me with indispensable, comprehensive information that will be of far-reaching significance for me in my next activities.

You're sure you didn't ring my doorbell just now? you ask him again, you know, I happen to think I definitely heard you ringing it.

Admittedly, he answers, I wanted to ring your doorbell, and left nothing untried in the attempt, but unfortunately I didn't get very far with that undertaking because, as you can and should see for yourself with a quick glance in that direction, your doorbell, you see, has fallen off, crumbled to pieces, probably got crushed, smashed, when an unbelievably heavy object fell on it or was thrown at it; what a pity, continued the man, because he otherwise always carries on him such practical things as door handles and doorbells and keeps them handy, but today of all days he doesn't have them along, you know, otherwise I would have been able to assist you right away by installing a new bell on your apartment door, what bad luck, other than a screwdriver I have nothing with me today, but I would still beseech you to answer several questions for me. For you, I promise, they will be of the utmost irrelevance!

Amazingly, you invite the man into your room, but explain to him immediately that you won't be able to give him any answers; you won't be able to get any information from me, you hear yourself explaining, because I simply don't know anything!

You don't have to know anything, the man replies.

I don't know anything about this apartment building here, you go on to explain, I don't know anything about the people here, and I don't want to know anything about any of it or them, because absolutely nothing here is of interest to me; I am a complete stranger in this neighborhood and want to remain as much a stranger as possible here, because my strangeness and indifference to this neighborhood, to this building, and also to all the people here, like the strangeness and indifference of these people, this building and this neighborhood to me, are in accordance with an intellectual discipline that I see myself forced to impose upon myself at least temporarily. If this indifference should be put at risk, you hear yourself explain, I will move out immediately! So, because absolutely nothing here is of interest to me, your meeting with me will hardly be of use to you.

But you really *can* be of use to me, replies the man, because all I really want to know from you is just this:

You see the man take out a pile of different colored leaflets, and he asks your permission to lay them out on the table or the floor.

Now I beseech you, he says, to look at all these leaflets that are spread out before you.

Admittedly, you catch yourself looking at the leaflets, but you almost succeed in *not* reading the words that are printed on them, which, as far as you can't help but see, consist of short and precisely written requests that you go to a certain place, perhaps one of the biggest buildings in the city, but go there somehow, or in general, or regularly, and look around or walk around and not go to any great effort or the like.

Then the stranger asks, can you remember, since you've lived here, ever having encountered one or the other or even several of these leaflets at the same time, have you ever come across anything like this before?

I can neither say, you reply, whether I have ever previously come across one or more of these leaflets, or whether I have never yet or only just now for the first time seen one or more of these leaflets, because even now, while your leaflets are still lying visibly before me, I have at the same time long since forgotten them, so I can follow you neither here nor there and I therefore ask that I soon be relieved of your leaflets again and left to myself.

But surely you will know, says the stranger, whether or not in recent times one or more of the leaflets was or were put through your *mail slot* into your apartment, and on that point I would have to categorize your answer as of the utmost urgency for us all.

It's completely pointless, you reply, unfortunately this question too is futile, *because my door doesn't have a mail slot*, look, please, see for yourself, on my instructions a new apartment door was just recently installed that was *specially made without a mail slot*, yes exactly, I felt it necessary to have a specifically *mail slotless* apartment door installed here. No one can simply stick something through the door because I must insist on being able to decide what should reach me, or what should ideally be kept away! In the meantime I do have some pity for the lamentable fate of your leaflets that make such attempts to reach me but are not able to, but you see, that too is one of the temporary disciplinary measures I have imposed on myself, that I must not allow myself to receive any mail; that I also don't *want* to receive this sort of mail is another matter; my capacity as a recipient of mail can be suspended for a while: I have therefore arranged for the time being to have all mail addressed to me sent automatically to a small village on the island of GREENLAND; I have informed the post office here of my move to that tiny village in Greenland and have requested that all my mail without exception be immediately forwarded to me there, and the people in the post office are very conscientious about carrying out my Greenland instructions. To be sure, I have long since forgotten the name of that Greenland fishing village, which is now the only place people think I can be reached, and in a very certain sense I *am* reachable there, where I, of course, have never been in my life and also never will be; so I deliberately chose a multisyllabic, complicated, unusually long place name on the map that is very difficult to remember, and naturally I could ask at the post office any time, or have someone else ask for me, what the name of the place is where I can be reached at present; but why? I'll do nothing of the kind! Because I myself have no news at all to forward to myself in Greenland, I don't see the slightest reason to write a letter to myself in the frozen Arctic wasteland, you know, and the only thing I know for sure about this place with the address where I can supposedly be reached are the two words *poste restante*, nothing more, Greenland poste restante; so I would also have been and would continue to be unreachable for myself if I had to rely on that, and so you can assume that these leaflets, too, which you or your superiors have sent to me with certainly the most laudable intent I'm sure are at best sitting poste restante in some fishing village in Greenland where they were forwarded to me for my worthy attention and now lie waiting for me in some postal box, so I cordially invite you to do your research on the leaflets you have sent me *there*! You won't find me going there, but do report back to me please when you return, how and if you tracked down or did not track down your leaflets there in a neglected, dilapidated fishing harbor postal box that stinks of cod-liver oil! But don't dare to bring my mail from there back to me! It is to remain safely in Greenland, you know, and presumably the employees of the Greenland post office will already be having difficulties storing my mounting pile of letters that is piling up as high as an iceberg, they'll have problems with storage space when filing the countless letters addressed to me, but that's a problem for which I do not feel myself responsible in any way!

You have really misunderstood me, replies the man, because we haven't used the services of the post office in the past or present to send these leaflets, instead we've engaged some of our own personnel to do so, and my task in this context is to investigate as precisely as possible, to check how *thoroughly* or *carelessly* or how *frequently* or *seldom* or how *properly* the leaflet distribution has been carried out, or perhaps also if it *hasn't* been done *at all*, I am, there is no doubt about it, *the supervisor*, not for you, but rather for our personnel who are involved, the *leaflet supervisor*, and the reason I have contacted you is that you are the last person in the district assigned to me who remains to be asked. Since our firm is interested in distributing the leaflets as thoroughly and completely as we are able to do, if possible to the entire population of the country, since the leaflets are the expression of a personal conversation our firm wishes to have with each individual citizen, we usually print, that is unavoidable, considerably more leaflets than can be distributed in multiple copies throughout the entire population. It goes without saying that a majority of the leaflets, after having been extensively read by the populace, are not kept and go on to play such a significant role in the paper recycling business that it's hard to imagine what it would be like without them. Especially over the course of the past year, the production of leaflets by our firm has increased to the point that we began to ask where so many leaflets could still be distributed, since when we compared the number of leaflets to the number of citizens of our country, given the widest possible distribution, we found that each person must be receiving twenty or thirty leaflets, that is, if all leaflets were delivered. Nevertheless, everything seemed to indicate that the number of leaflets produced to date was still not adequate, many of our leaflet distributors could never get enough leaflets, and the leaflets they did distribute went so quickly and in such a short time that we were at a loss as to whether to praise such a bold leaflet distribution initiative, blessed as it was with that kind of speed, or whether indeed we ought to have our doubts about such an insatiable ambition for more and more leaflets to distribute, you know, until one day my very own personal enquiries exposed the fact that more than 90% of all our leaflets, without taking the otherwise customary previously mentioned detour by way of our customers, were being taken by the most efficient leaflet distributors right from our firm, still hot off the presses, without wasting any time, *directly to the paper recycling plant.* Consequently, our firm's leaflet production turns out for the most part to be a supply industry directly preparing *new paper for the recycling plant*, with the leaflet distribution employees acting as intermediaries, actually as salespersons, whose friends in the recycling plant receive full payment for the value of the wastepaper, but give only half this amount to our leaflet distributors, keeping the other half for themselves as a private, secondary source of income; and our distributors are happy with their half, because they get mounds of valuable stock delivered most willingly free of charge by our firm to wherever they want, whenever they want, because the transportation of the leaflets from the printer's to the grounds of the paper recycling plant, in fact by our firm's own fleet of vehicles, functions flawlessly, you know. We in the firm are now considering ceasing production of our leaflets entirely, because limiting production to the number of leaflets that can actually be distributed among the population would pose unexpected technical difficulties. I am therefore visiting you today, on behalf of our firm, as part of what is now most likely turning out to be my last responsibility on the subject of leaflet distribution, and will in fact skip ahead to the last of my still-unanswered questions for you: Do you absolutely insist on still being supplied by our firm with leaflets even after to-day? Or would you think yourself capable of coping with the future even without being provided with leaflets by our firm?

Not a leaflet more, you answer, I don't want bits of paper every-where!

He was really very happy that the business with the leaflets would soon be over now, said the stranger, although time and again there would be people, more than you would suspect, who would mourn the leaflets that would soon no longer come flutter-ing into the building, and I fear, he explained in conclusion, that many will soon long for the times when the leaflets fluttered in through their doors, sometimes wistfully eyeing the mail slot at the entrance and wishing for nothing more than to see a leaflet come fluttering through the crack, but there won't be any leaflets again soon, I can tell you that much, it will probably be a very, very long time before leaflets may again begin to flit quietly into the hall!

The man says good-bye sadly, but not without letting a glim-mer of hope shine out of his eyes; you think you notice that this stranger, in particular, fears that without the leaflets the quality of his life will in the future no longer be as high as it has been until now.

The house is still a boat.

You go back into your room, the sun has long since set, you want to find your way back through the dusk, to continue watching the darkness as it falls, to abandon yourself again to the evening land-scape that was previously enveloping you with its bundles of light,

light that had been rolled over the plain to the edge of the woods and dashed to pieces there, or had risen up again like smoke in the foehn. At least individually—some of those bundles of light were still hopping through the steppe like burning animals. The horizon can no longer hold back the night, but collapses under the darkness that is tearing at it, that now inundates the entire plain. In the undergrowth, THE FOREST FIRE has begun, now flickering from distant hills, pushing the glowing streets in front of it. Quietly hissing nests of embers quiver and pulsate, flashing around like misplaced signals, decorating the clouds of smoke that circle everywhere.

Slowly it moves closer to the outskirts of the city, it has reached the edge of the steppe and set the bushes there ablaze. Flocks of birds jump with fright and flutter up from their nests. You see them glowing in the night. Flapping their wings, they try to rise up out of the fire that surrounds them, but most of them lose their way in the darkness over the tongues of flame. They sink back, their singed wings folded in exhaustion, and crash, blinded by the fire, into the sea of sparks.

You become aware of neighboring occupants assembling at the gates and at the open windows, arguing about things, gesticulating at each other; from the murmuring voices rising up to you, you distinguish the phrases: caught fire in the forest, a pity about all the wood, it really would have been better to cut it all down beforehand and to use it ourselves as fuel . . .

Now even the river over there seems to have caught fire. You can tell that it has come to a boil and is letting off steam, frightening *countless flocks of butterflies of flame. They are blown upward from the burning bushes and poured into the red flashing rapids.*

Somehow I must have fallen asleep, because I am filled with the silent suspicion that I am now waking up.

Yes, foggy weather prevails in the room when you suspect that you are waking up after much too long a night, after an exceptionally long night.

That's why your hands are so swollen. You try in vain to push the oppressively solidified block of sleep from your forehead, but the dawn still clings all too firmly and stubbornly to your head. At first you don't even try to raise your head, you just want to bend your legs a little in order to turn yourself over somehow, but you don't even succeed in doing that, you're incapable of any movement, as if your bones had been dissolved into your flesh by your blood.

As if your sleeping body had smoked its way into the room, had been absorbed by the room, by the building, had been swallowed down into the cellar of your own apartment. You try to will yourself back into a sort of half-material consistency, as if your body had managed to slip away but not entirely escaped yet.

On the one hand, you're incapable of moving to the window to check on the state of the forest fire on the horizon. When last seen, it had already come threateningly close to the houses at the edge of the city. On the other hand, you see, not far from your bed, in the shadow of night that continues to flow through the farthest corner of the room, but that cannot be, oh yes it is, a second, neighboring bed quite far from your own.

You shouldn't put up with that sort of thing.

In the room where I usually sleep, there has, to the best of my knowledge, always been just one bed, you say to yourself. Where has a second bed suddenly come from? Or did I push the second bed in from the study to the bedroom because the sight of the bed in the study always distracts me too much from my thoughts? Right, I remember, it wasn't so long ago at all that the presence of the sofa in the study had sent me into a fit of rage, because in the course of my more and more demanding, highly intellectual work, I had lain down on it more and more frequently, had fallen asleep, and recently, as a result, I had had to write off yet another day in which I accomplished nothing at all, so I immediately made plans to carry the bed up to the attic as soon as possible, but not into this room here. Only my shyness about bothering one of my acquaintances to ask him to help me with it had caused a delay. It would have been impossible for me to carry the heavy bed up to the attic by myself. And it wasn't so much that I didn't want to embarrass myself by bothering any of my acquaintances about it, but rather that I wanted to avoid the thus occasioned necessity of meeting with these people, and so I had probably absentmindedly pushed the sofa into this room here as a temporary measure; or hadn't I?

The silver-gray dawn is wangling its way in through the window glass, and seems to have crawled over to the second bed. Now you think you see a movement there, or do you? Yes, as if by a hand or a leg or even something slightly roundish like a skull, in any case a movement presumably carried out by some body part, and indeed possibly by a body part that might have nothing whatsoever to do with you, but is possibly from somewhere else entirely. Or have you already removed yourself so far from yourself that any movement in yourself would no longer be noticeable to you as yours, but would only become apparent a few meters away? No, there was some sort of wiping or waving going on at the remote part of the room that probably had nothing to do with you. Now, however, a second such movement becomes perceptible, yes, it's a sort of creeping on the spot that reminds you of a tipped-over tortoise whose wriggling legs try to dig their claws into the clouds floating in the sky above; in any case, you think, exactly as if there were something in that second bed, how should one say, yes, a something, how does one say that best, a something, yes, the prevailing light conditions are somewhat unfavorable, perhaps it's only a shadow, thrown into the room by the last remains of the night stains, or by the scraps of darkness still stuck to the walls, now thrown in beside me like sludge.

But now you also think you hear something, yes, that's going much too far, it's a sort of undeniable squawking, and although it's quiet, it's unmistakably wafting through the air in the room. Maybe it's harmless, the floorboards creaking. That could be attributed to your negligence. You have rather frequently neglected to oil the door and window hinges, and since you have the doors and windows open all the time in a constant draft, which is absolutely necessary for airing out the rooms, the hinges raise their pitch chromatically in concert against each other, sounding something like an operetta company of female heroic basses accompanied by their friends the coloratura sopranos, all shrunk down to about the size of thumbs.

This creaking sound develops into a tortured, threatened wheezing, and now also panting, that suddenly begins to have something terrifyingly human about it, yes, you think, in the bed next to my bed there is quite definitely a person, there is no other explanation for it, and it's a person who is trying desperately to express himself, but his words keep getting choked off, gurgled up, he hasn't brought out a single intelligible remark, at least I haven't been able to understand anything yet.

How does this person come to be in my room? you ask yourself.

I neither remember having ever offered anyone admission, having opened the door, nor ever allowing anyone to stay overnight, either here in this room or in one of the others.

One falls asleep in one's room, alone and undisturbed; one wakes up to find that there is suddenly another person in the room.

Isn't that a ghost story that has long since ceased to be scary because it's so well known?

Isn't everything that you experience, or rather, everything that you *don't* experience, much scarier than all those all too familiar ghost stories? Because you really experience *nothing*, or else you're not letting even the slightest thing happen to you—but it really does seem that things have stopped happening to you.

Have I become incapable of having an experience, you ask yourself, or have the experiences begun to turn away from me? I've become so bored with even the most exciting adventures that could potentially still happen to me that they probably don't want to waste their time on me anymore.

But what is it like, then, when one really does wake up some-day in such a conventional, commonly known ghost story as you have right now in your own room? It's become such a rectangular-shaped ghost story. Suddenly there is another person here, some-one who has come in or broken in behind your back (how does that actually work? possibly with a duplicate key or even a skele-ton key?), without your expressly giving consent, and also without having informed you in advance, and with whom you neither have nor want to have anything to do, yes, then it all seems really very familiar, but one is still deeply shocked by it (above all by the outra-geous simplemindedness of anyone to whom it may have seemed unique, and funny enough to be foisted on you, of all people).

If only one could at least ignore this sort of thing, but one is usually forced to have an even closer look at it.

In any case, as before, there is still the panting in the neigh-boring bed, becoming more and more violent, a wheezing and gurgling in the slightly rainy damp air of my room, which is filled with thick clouds of morning mist, the sound increasingly pathetic, a pleading emphatic accusation. And how am I sup-posed to behave? you ask yourself, unable to take action to im-prove matters.

The door opens, yes, someone now enters the room with fierce determination, no, it's not just one person, it's two more persons, who likewise have forgotten to introduce themselves, at least to you, so that one is increasingly ignored, without them giving it a thought. This time it's a man and a woman. They go right away to the bed next to your bed, and talk only with each other, almost incomprehensibly, in a whisper. While doing so, they start fiddling eagerly with such frames as are presumably hung over and screwed under the bed next to mine. One of the persons is already almost crawling under the neighboring bed, while the other person is stretching up on tiptoes, slightly bent over the bed and the figure lying in it. Then it's possible for both of them to screw and turn at presumably highly complicated pieces of equipment and apparati that presumably need to be operated by people who really know what they're doing. Both figures demonstrate a certain quite elegant proficiency of movement in the course of their performance, which they carry out with conspicuous gallantry and animation. The words and bits of sentences they are exchanging have become more and more distinctly audible. At first you hear only clipped fragments that sound something like *painful tendons weak current reflex statutes rule right-handed person*, then a clear warning about the threat of *comatose depressed breathing*, which is answered with words sounding something like an elevated *threat to transpiration* or *aspiration*, otherwise *brachial* or *brachayal* or rather *endobrachial* and also *endotrachayal* or *endotrachial incubation* or *intubation* or maybe *intuberant intuberation* or some *intuberative tuberasts*, which could have to do with a resultant somehow *antierotic* or maybe *antibiotic pneumonia prophylaxis* or rather the *pneumoporocellax* or simply the world-famous *pneumoprophylaxis,* or also lead to something like a slightly forced *liguric* or *diuric*, a typical *tracheophonic trachyotonist* or maybe *tracheotonic*, whereupon the language of the two people temporarily changes, significantly simplified, to emphasize the *irrigations of the stomach* that are necessary right away now, or the more exact description of how to warm up hot water bottles, and also the mention of a somehow *pretuberast* or better *prepederast gasping breathing* or secondary or tertiary *schnapps breathing,* depending on whether *exo-* or *endobrachial catheters* or rather *endotracheal catheters* are inserted, which however will have to be carefully differentiated from certain primitive *long-lasting catheters* that are only required for measuring the *quantities of urine* that routinely overflow the pot. Otherwise, it's still important to pay the strictest attention to keeping the uppermost airways free on the stratospheric ceiling with a slightly *porous* or *comatose therapeutic bronchopneumic* and *pneumatic* self-closing *door metabolism trim.* That can be done by changing position at least every three hours, followed, for safety's sake, by *sarcophagal intubation,* or rather just entirely *anal* or else *orotrachealtuberous hypotonsionic* or rather *hippopotamic* or rather *botanic hypothermic,* in case of doubt also *oral,* available in the *mortgage pharmacy,* and in case that is still not enough, in supposed *diuresis* it should immediately be followed by a *Mannitol intravenous infusion* of *glycose electroanalytically* or *electrolytically* by hindering *return absorption* as quickly as possible, you know, because now at last one would finally be able to speak at length about the mucous secretions that so fundamentally control everything, by which, indeed, one's entire existence is continually controlled, or maybe not?

So it is, it is.

In retrospect, pressure paralyses of the peripheral bundles of nerve fibers can only be prevented by carefully, most expertly, placing the person in the correct position, along with the insertion of fatty eye ointments. But that, of course, only after gradually inducing evacuation of the bowels and, of course, continually measuring all temperatures, blood pressures, moistness, water-levels and, naturally, air pressures. Also, in general, the constant observation of the entire body weight, as we know, look here, built in on the lower edge of the bed, of course specifically for that purpose, its own scales with a clearly readable range of weights, at the lower left foot of the bed here, so that for even the most exact determination of weight, to the gram, it is no longer necessary to lift this person out of bed even temporarily, which of course would have been unavoidable if the scales had not been built into the bed, you do understand.

Yes, one does understand.

The two don't seem to notice at all that you are in the room too, but act entirely as if there were only your neighbor, to whose existence you have just with difficulty resigned yourself.

Of course you try right away, objecting strenuously, to make yourself noticed, but it doesn't work, they don't notice the slightest thing, don't take any notice at all. So you ask yourself if maybe they can't notice anything about you, or if they don't want to. They now start to talk about a dangerous flickering in the room, and they take down a bottle that had hung over the neighbor's head, and hang up another; somehow you feel an indefinable shyness toward these people, or is it perhaps that you're trying to prevent yourself from feeling revulsion? But then at last, loudly and firmly, you suddenly know how to get their attention, of course entirely courteously, but while making it unmistakably clear that you are no longer prepared to let them simply pass over you as they have until now:

Tell me, my dear sir and madam, might I ask you a few questions? Yes? I am lying here in my room, please note, my room, you know, I am sleeping, sleeping, please note, entirely alone and undisturbed, you understand, and I wake up, then wake up suddenly, wake up suddenly no longer alone, but rather with a neighbor, with this, I believe, gentleman here, or is it a lady instead, I don't know. You will certainly be able to give me clarifying information about this very soon, won't you? And then, additionally, the two of you appear, turn up here too, you who are just what I've been missing in my collection, as it were. And might I hereby ask you yet again—and you would be able to find my questions in this matter much more understandable if you had the opportunity just once to find yourselves in such a situation, or in a similar situation—therefore, first, to tell me, who is that here beside me, how does that thing beside me come in here without my knowledge, second, and third, just incidentally, how do the two of you simply get in here, why and from where has a key to the apartment been made accessible to you, who has perpetrated this outrageous impertinence, fourth, without asking me in advance, fifth, where did my sudden neighbor get such a key, or was he brought in here by the two of you, so that in this regard it is not up to him to justify it, but up to you, and that apart from making any sort of enquiry of me in advance, and finally and at last sixth or, respectively, seventh, what are the two of you doing here, what are you looking for here, or what have you lost? I am asking, you must understand, for you to itemize your response in the greatest detail, you understand, because I am naturally extraordinarily interested in what is in the process of happening, of taking place here, without my knowledge, let alone a previously obtained consent on my part. And if you should not very soon have seen yourselves obliged on your part to make every effort to comply with my request, I will unfortunately have to reserve for myself the right to initiate legal proceedings against you!

At last they turn toward you, if only very briefly, only to turn away from you again immediately with the observation on the part of the man that of course all the people inside here are to a certain extent not entirely normal, but one shouldn't let oneself get worked up because of that, because if one let them have what they wanted, then one could close down right away. He is speaking of a chaotic standstill that would set in immediately afterwards, and the fact that the people here are the way they are is after all not so entirely incomprehensible, that's mainly the reason why they are here. And then he recommends that his female partner do some very specific thing, whereupon she makes her way to your bed to do something with a piece of equipment nearby above you, after which she pulls some hose-like ropes you had not even noticed until now from your arms and, as you think, also from your legs. Right away you feel freer, obviously the things had you tied to the mattress, whereupon you are given a piece of good advice, namely to be patient, just be patient for a while, because things will soon be all right again. And they speak again in closing about an extraordinary piece of luck you apparently had, and that you, of all people, are said to have had once again, and also just barely once again, because if something hadn't happened at such a propitious last moment, then a very certain thing that one is not going to mention more specifically would now be, well, how to say it, different, probably just quite different. No, now you don't under-stand anything and want to ask for a more detailed explanation, you are someone who is very thirsty for knowledge, capable of learning more, and no one should think you could be left in an all-too-confusing light; whereupon they see themselves obliged to turn away from you with even more disdain, with similar sound-ing observations such as: senselessly having only oneself to blame, one does not have the slightest right, subsequently to make irritat-ing complaints to others, and where one would get with that, one would in any case have to see what could be done.

With even more determination than the two had entered the room, they now leave the room, really rustling out all the more forcefully through the door that now falls shut behind them.

A machine mounted on the wall above or beside the neighbor-ing bed emits a rhythmic hiss that seems to you now to be the pulse of the morning breaking through the frosted glass window, entering with such ruthless, violent energy that the rectangular solid block of air, now gliding apart at the seams, could soon split into a pile of pieces glittering in every color of the rainbow.

Your neighbor has gotten very quiet, has given up his wailing, wheezing, and coughing, you only now and then still hear a con-tented-sounding snoring slip from his mouth.

You make up your mind to ask him later what his name is.

Two ladies cloaked in gray come flitting over, they dance back and forth with leaping motions, somehow wiping the floor wet. Afterwards, they jump up and down behind a shuffling piece of equipment that is automatically rolling around in front of them, brushing the floor dry. They understand how to do a thorough cleaning; you find that sort of thing commendable. Maybe one of the two of them also put this plate for you on the small box beside your bed, on which there might be several slices of bread and a cube of butter wrapped in silver paper, and this glass too, or is it a cup, with a steaming hot brown drink, the smell of which makes you shudder. So it has come to this, someone comes up with the eccentric idea of offering you a drink that emits such a stink.

Icy-cold, the summer heat breaks in again, drawing a blotchy map of this morning on the wall diagonally across from the window. You see a floodplain run through by rivulets of swampy light, blown across by a constant desert wind.

Soon an entire assembly appears. That's all I need! It's probably a delegation from the management to offer condolences, presumably right away, or it simply turns up with general greetings to convey the best wishes and many greetings of the top management. However, it doesn't entirely go off without a hitch, because hardly has one of the members, all of whom are dressed in festive white, turned to you just for a moment, with a courteous fleetingly considerate look, when one of the other members has already tugged at his sleeve, demanding that he pay attention to a certain point, invisible to you, that is hovering in the air of the room. Or another member of the team has pulled him to a slate on the railing at the foot of the bed, a slate that you now also notice for the first time, but which must apparently have always been hanging there. Now it is temporarily taken off for a longer period of time, is passed through many hands. Obviously records of a certain nature are noted down on it, and their assessment causes head-nodding and head-shaking comments. Presumably, right across the assembly, they are of different, opposing views about the QUALITY of an artistic or rather amateurish, it all depends, description drawn or painted on this slate, I think, of a head, yes, maybe of your head, yes, very likely it is a picture, a portrait of your person that the one finds too fleeting, the other too exaggeratedly clear, either completely off the mark, or an all too exact likeness. But above all, all in all, it seems to be considerably more interesting than you yourself, since they limit themselves to dealing exclusively with it, without even noticing you on the side, let alone speaking to you or even indicating that they want to make the attempt, which is partially understandable after all, because as is well known the so-called realistic portrayal of a person or thing has very often turned out to be much more true to life, and also more exact than the person or thing itself ever could be, which after all had only served as the basis for its respective realistic portrayal.

With everyone's agreement, the image on the slate is hung back on the bed railing again. In this case, you have found it more sensible to restrain your need to ask for information, because the very thought of speaking in front of such a large assembly is rather unpleasant to you and requires at least a certain appropriate preparation. You at present are not prepared, because how were you supposed to know that you would suddenly be surprised by a staff of such size. Now, without further ado, they leave the room again, rustling away with their festive long white coats billowing out behind them. They do seem a little disappointed, though, by the silence shown them on your part.

Instead, you now try at last to communicate with your neighbor, but he so insistently suffocates all attempts to address him, nips them in the bud, is interested only in ignoring them, that you soon give up again.

So now everything remains unexplained, all attempts exhausted.

In any case, not much more can happen.

Put to bed like this, you will certainly continue to be well taken care of.

It's not really worth the effort to still keep your eyes open.

So you doze through the hours, or even days and nights, you can no longer tell the difference.

These days cram the noisy, violent summer light from outside mercilessly into the room, flooding it fully, causing the walls, already bent outwards, to almost burst. You long for the cooling silence of the twilit evenings, but when it comes, it is immediately sucked up by the lamps in this room, and beginning to glow, it is crushed to a helpless piece of wastepaper darkness. Perhaps because of that, you dream constantly during the day of the darkness of night. Breathed in by the room like hard coal dust, it blazes fiercely as it burns itself out. And during the night, you dream of nothing other than that painfully glimmering midsummer light during the day, although it ravages your field of vision until it turns into charcoal. Day and night melt away from you in equally blazing brightness. You are trembling in the heat of your deadening insomnia, tried and tested in the smelting furnace. Quite unconsciously awake, you just manage to get through it with a completely unbridled, uncontrolled patience. Like bridging an icily boiling, solidified, but evaporating river, a river that flows far away into the blue skies, skies bored through by hail. The river flows through a hidden firmament's forgotten canals of sunlight, and then courses farther upward in the air, through the trembling flashing nodes of weather crossroads. Traveling on between the shores of the atmosphere, it flows down the dreary deforested avenues of the long since disused, now completely dusty rain streets. Entering the cloud tracks of the eternally frustrated administrative districts of thunder storms, it finds them drained and silent. The river flows on, through the outhouse of the mausoleum for a vanished foehn. It flows through the countless sinkholes of the ruins of the horizon, now scattered into the air. And it pours into the approach paths of our vastly superior wind rose that is stretched out through the entire ether, high over land, like a continuously vibrating invisible tent,

just like, tried and tested in the blast furnace, the gigantic fiery wings of your all-encompassing, numbing insomnia. You trickle away in it, like this river, standing in frozen flames, buried deep in the sky that has turned to steppe. And you flee through the hidden sunlight canals of a forgotten firmament,

so that, right at the last moment, after such a temporarily final ending, you can begin anew again . . . !

Had you ever before been awakened like that, even if only in a dream?

> *so lifelessly dreaming or so dreamlessly living?*
> *or so animatedly dreamed to pieces*
> *or so dreamily lived to bits?*

Listen! you hear a female voice whisper to you.

You feel a pleasantly cool hand on your forehead, and it almost seems to you as if someone were unwrapping your head. It had been all stuck together by the room wrapped around it and by the entire building, including the roof truss. Listen, you should at least attempt to stand up! The cool hand has drawn back, and with a movement as if it were waving at you, it pushes a very dark streaked curtain from your eyes.

You should try to stand up, so that you won't entirely forget how to walk, she says.

Where and when have you seen this face before, you ask yourself, right after the last dusty flaking strip of air has loosened from your eyelids and fluttered to the floor. There has never been a time when you have forgotten this woman's face, even though you quite certainly are meeting her now for the first time!

How much that one has never encountered has nevertheless always been very familiar!

How the ceiling now starts to clear up and the window opens on the room's horizon!

How much of what one suddenly finds every now and then has one always been looking for, like nothing else, without ever knowing about it!

And if one never finds it, as is almost always the case, then there is a perpetual search, about which one has not the slightest inkling, but which nevertheless controls one continuously!

Yes, the face of this woman who has come up to you now for the first time has always been present for you.

Quite concealed, unclear, but more present than everything that is superficially apparent.

Like an insoluble puzzle that has never concerned you, but now suddenly appears in the exact form of the only possible solution, and it liberates you by answering everything so mysteriously.

And so how much is always present and nonetheless never comes up to the surface of the pond, paved as it is with glittering fish stomachs? There are things that, from the very beginning, remain drowned in the deepest ground water of the long-since dried-out drained fountain lakes of this district here, lakes that have dazzlingly simulated your countenance out into the universe.

It would be beneficial, she says, now and then, on such beautiful days as today, to go for a walk in the park that surrounds the building, and you should really try it sometime, she would go, if you wanted, with you, could find some time right now. Later on, though, she would continue to be obliged to perform other stipulated tasks, and didn't you perhaps want to make the attempt now to get out of the room into the corridor into the park just for a little while . . .

You get up, dizziness makes your first steps wobbly, but you're being held, supported by a hand, and to submit to its instructions represents one of the opposites of humiliation.

So now, at last, something that was forgotten for such a long time occurs to you again, although you never knew anything about it.

Maybe she had just very briefly, temporarily, slipped your mind? And now she is surfacing again, indeed for the first time, as you have often experienced.

Like a burning question that has never bothered you, but suddenly arises in the exact form of the only possible answer, and it liberates you by solving everything so mysteriously: that you love it, have always loved it, yes, you have always sought this face, of that you are so dizzily certain, and even if you had never met her, this affection would have continued to exist deeply buried within you.

So, you ask, is that woman, whom I have never met until now, really supposed to be the only one I have ever loved?

I will never be able to forget your face, you say to her in thought, no, you correct yourself right away, because I have never forgotten you, although we are meeting today for the first time!

Intentionally, you exaggerate the weakness of your limbs, displaying a lingering persistence in this pleasantly harmless instability. This causes an ongoing strengthening of her so solicitous support of your body, and an even more intensive contact with her as you walk out through the doors together. You strongly suspect, however, that you never entered through those doors. In any case, you go out now into an unfamiliarly familiar, strangely walled big garden or park that is scorched by the midsummer sun.

And it seems as if this affection for HER, which you will henceforth regard as inevitable, has just now opened up in you like a completely new sensory organ that was hidden for such a long time. Its inevitable boundlessness comes over you with such unavoidably concentrated intensity because it has risen up out of the most deep-set clarity of the most original oblivion. You have become so happy about this unique, suddenly experienced meeting with HER that you can now describe quite painlessly and clearly, without a trace of any bitterness, the misfortune of all the other meetings that you never experienced, that always remained denied and refused to you. Their continual movement out of the otherwise lifelong forgetting into the present time of your memory would basically show up your existence as a long concealment from you of all the rules to be followed in the most essential encounters, encounters that were withheld from you by order of the offices for burying catacombs. A merrily moving mausoleum business, hidden from you, has supplied your esteemed person with the currently crucial refusals. All of them together, though, are easily offset by a single glance at the complete beauty of the curved shoreline of the silhouette of HER face. Its shady bays accompany your burning eyes through the surf of the backlighting, agreeably protecting you, cooling you, and dimming the light:

I have always remembered you, even though we are seeing each other now for the first time, you think again in her direction. Can a few traces of your thoughts perhaps become audible to her, as word voyages impressed in the afternoon light, in the narrow corridor of air between her and you?

Quite apart from that, though, you now find that the right time has come for you to resume asking the still-arising questions, questions you had given up asking yourself: Do you know, perhaps, where I am and why I am here and how I could have come to be here? It was all so peculiarly real to you, no matter how unbelievable it seemed, and not only that, yes, but also rather crazy, you were nonetheless asking her, and her in particular, not to think you were quite so stupid as you must necessarily have appeared at that moment.

I can assure you, she replies, that even the most unbelievable things you are now thinking about yourself will soon come to seem entirely understandable; but hasn't anyone from the staff come to talk these matters over with you yet? They will need to make closer inquiries and go into more detail about other aspects of your life.

No, but instead of that they had at least understood how to react to you with what seemed like the most audible silence you had been in a position to imagine in a long time, and had also obligingly approached your helplessness with the most observant ignorance; she was the first person here (*in the entire world*, you half add) who had now finally come to you (from so great a distance, you think, always moving toward each other, until some day, maybe soon, we will surprise ourselves, less than a tenth of a millimeter apart, and you wish for that more than for anything else); and if you hadn't come past a short while ago, they would probably have gone on even longer with such slipshod attempts, so busily idle, thoughtlessly clever, and carefully negligent, but finally you did turn up in this midsummer, gracious lady, which will soon have scorched everything else under the sun!

What suggestion could she make to you, you then ask, to bring about a small perceptible improvement in your presently so unsettled life?

She will make sure you get to talk with someone right away, she answers, if at all possible with one of the people in charge of everything here, and this will inevitably contribute helpfully to the clarification of your current situation.

You walk a short distance along an avenue filled with the smell of dry, rustling leaves. From their branches, woven far into the firmament above, faded shadow leaves float down upon our heads, and sometimes also get caught in our hair. She leads you into the corridor of a building, you are walking with her through what in marble seems to you the central stone auditory canal of the building. At the end of this tunnel, she asks you to wait outside for just a short while in front of an upholstered leather door that, in comparison to what you have already seen of the building, is very elegantly designed. She then disappears into the room, only to come back out into view again right away, inviting you to come in. Then she mentions a First or Firstviolin (of a quartet, or is he the concertmaster?), who, however, as she adds in a calming voice, is quite content plainly and simply to be addressed as "Doctor." She explains that, as it were, in closing, and then pushes you in through the doorframe.

Far back in the room, a rather elderly gentleman is sitting hidden behind a not very neatly stacked mountain of paper. It rises up from the surface of his desk with slightly dusty, diversely branching ravines and hollows between the thin cardboard file cases.

So this gentleman, as you recall from HER words beforehand, wants to be addressed as "Doctor," and you immediately resolve to make as few mistakes as possible in this regard.

He has had a computer built into his signet ring! Yes, a small calculator has been sunk into its onyx or cornelian, which is probably why he's always poking around at his ring finger like a lunatic, using the point of a pen that is presumably also suitable for drawing or writing or, failing that, then at least for pinning butterflies or other small animals. And so the doctor pokes around incessantly in the signet with its coat of arms on his finger, pokes with the needle-thin point of the pen, presumably at the numbers that are visible to him on the gemmed surface of his jewel that so impresses him. And exactly at the moment when it is poked, it emits a barely audible very high bleeping sound that you can now distinguish. Strangely enough, it happens to him, especially in the course of his slower mathematical movements, that he sometimes misses the surface of his ring with his needle-pointed pen and either pokes into the air, or inadvertently scratches his ring finger skin next to the setting of the stone, or even pokes into his ring finger bone. Naturally, when that happens, the doctor's ring quite unexpectedly does *not* bleep, instead, the doctor looks up for a moment and his face darkens for a few seconds, twitching with a trace of pain, only to turn back again immediately afterwards and continue on determinedly with the calculation at hand, letting his eyes dive down again into the gem. But at the same time he does use one of these mathematically unnecessary moments of interruption to at least temporarily prove to be visibly able to turn toward your person and to show himself prepared to condescend to you.

What do you want? you hear him ask.

Well, you answer, certain things, this and that.

Well, well, and to what are you referring? he asks then, without looking up.

Well, you answer, you're probably referring to yourself more than anything else.

Well, well, what concerns you, he goes on to ask, looking at you now with suspicious benevolence, and where and when did it start to concern you?

You repeat your basic question, so simply complicated lately.

They were unfortunately forced, he answers, to admit you here in this locked institution, as you might often enough have been able to avail yourself of the opportunity to have noticed, just remarked in passing, until your physical and emotional condition would clearly be seen to have improved and been able to be stabilized, in order to protect you first and foremost from yourself, so that a very certain incident would not repeat itself; then he speaks of very particular causes that would have to be found out, the structured make-up of your personality, you know, only then could they, also from a legal standpoint, assume the responsibility for releasing you again, and in due time you yourself would have the opportunity to be able to contribute a great deal to that, which would shorten the length of the procedure considerably to your advantage, but to date, unfortunately, you had contributed next to nothing, well, well, regrettable, and such a pity!

What does he mean, what does he want, what incident is he referring to, what causes? you want to know the exact details at last, you think you have a right to know, one thinks one has gone to bed peacefully at home, and then one wakes up here, how does that sort of thing happen, no more beating about the bush, you want them to tell you outright!

Surely you aren't maintaining that you no longer remember what happened to you? the doctor replies, keeping himself to the point, for your benefit, hoping to take some of the weight off your shoulders, summoning up the necessary simplicity of expression with a certain amount of difficulty, it's true, a little worried the other inmates might accuse him of playing favorites, but nevertheless, on this occasion he will make an effort to confide in you, well, well, do you really not remember a thing, is that really your story? not even the slightest detail? But just try to remember! Not even the merest hint of a suspicion? no matter how vague?

What is it then, you ask, just what are you talking about?

What then, yes, what indeed! he answers. Well, what do you think? SUICIDE! A willful attempt at suicide! You tried to kill yourself! By your own hand! If I am not mistaken, with barbiturates or some sort of hypnotic, I don't know exactly, but you must remember which drugs you were recently able to obtain in such large quantities!

He must be confusing you with someone else, you think, you must be mistaken, doctor, you say, and you are probably confusing me with someone who was supposed to come to you after me or instead of me to talk with you about this, and who probably did attempt to kill himself, but you didn't, and as far as you are concerned, you add, some other information must be known . . .

No, no other information, no confusion, because he didn't make a habit of confusing suicide with anything else, they pumped your stomach, there's no other reason for that, they went to great trouble to prevent you from going to sleep permanently, they would hardly want to waste their time with such a strenuous pumping out of your stomach for nothing, and they didn't want you to make them go through this a second time; you, yes, you, of course others have done it too, but this time it was you who tried to kill yourself! You can't simply have forgotten something like that, can't have let it disappear without a trace!

You want to reply immediately, but quite frankly there are things that make your mouth cease functioning, even when your breath hasn't exactly been taken away.

At first you start to talk indignantly about yourself in comparison to other people, to whom one could tell nothing at all or everything, but you weren't either of those sorts, one could tell you a lot, but couldn't expect you to be so gullible as to believe everything, certainly not this, which in your eyes is nothing but a malicious imputation that is hopefully based on a regrettable, though not entirely forgivable misunderstanding, and you are not going to simply let such slanderous character assassination rest, but rather if need be you will have to reserve the right to initiate legal proceedings against it, etc., but you soon calm down and ask to be excused for your outburst in order to gain time to think about the most puzzling of all the insinuations ever made about you, and thus to be able to examine more closely your situation, which has only just now been made clear to you.

So although you had probably already suspected this sort of thing—but up until this point in your life had denied that it was possible—you have now, after going to bed one night, awakened one morning nowhere else but in the loony bin, where it seems they intend to keep you even against your will. Something must have happened on that evening, in that night, about which you have not the slightest clue, not to mention not even the smallest trace of a memory. But what? In any case, you think they are going much too far when they think themselves justified in accusing you right away of an obvious attempted suicide.

My present existence, you think, is an incorrect imputation. Only your present existence?

Do understand my agitation, Doctor, you say, the fact that I cannot remember anything—and therefore contest everything—of course means nothing, because wherever one goes, one can always be mistaken about the place one came from, in relation to the place one has just arrived at. Think about it, you too, although or just because you are the director of these premises, can make mistakes, and didn't someone entirely different kill himself, and you are taking me for him, even though I have next to nothing at all to do with him? In any case, as before, I believe that I have not in the slightest killed myself, I wouldn't know why, or wherefore, but I am far from wanting to accuse you, Doctor, of not telling the truth, no, no, far be it from me to call you a liar, so someone will probably, yes, someone must have tried to kill himself, Doctor, because how else would you arrive at the absurd assertion that I tried to kill myself, and it's probably a misunderstanding, a mix-up caused quite innocently but by no means by you, Doctor, but rather presumably by no one at all, and right out of the blue, I am unjustly affected by it, because I not only consider it completely impossible, but also entirely out of the question that, to the best of my knowledge, I would even have one such thought in that direction, because I would be incapable of even laying one of my two little fingers on myself or of turning one against me, not so much because I would be too cowardly, but because something like that would cause many complications for me, and, indeed, would be very uncomfortable, Doctor, and it would have unsettled me too greatly to take on something like that! Think about it, Doctor, just organizing such intentions, so elaborately complicated, as you must know quite well from secondhand experience! Who am I to tell you much about it? Just the endlessly complicated, unavoidable preparations that are involved with such intentions, think about it,

Doctor, you would have to, let's assume, buy a rope and, carefully considering the intended event, you would not only have to convince yourself hundreds of times that the rope was strong enough, but you would also have to learn how to properly tie a respectable knot, then the tests of the rope's strength, as in the rope-climbing courses at the mountain climbers' club, quite apart from the exertion required when the club hikes in the alpines, because how else do you think you would be able to properly test the strength of the rope, and often, Doctor, when you want to give yourself, and not, as is usual, someone else, plenty of rope to hang yourself, it can happen that you take so long to learn how to properly handle the rope intended for yourself and also to tie a proper knot or knob that so much time has already elapsed that your own thread of life comes to an end long before you can realize any of your plans, because some other unknown person has given you plenty of rope to hang yourself, before the knot could come undone that you haven't even finished tying for yourself, Doctor, what I'm trying to indicate is just this, if I wanted to make up my mind to kill myself, I would need substantially more time just for the wearying preparations for a possible suicide on my part than would normally be available to me in my life anyway, because I would become increasingly entangled in the undergrowth of details of, e.g., the necessary studies into testing the materials, because what I plan, I plan thoroughly, usually so thoroughly that the planning of the event makes the event itself superfluous or that the planning time extends beyond the end of the time of such an event, so that the event itself, because of its careful planning, does not take place at all; so quite apart from the fact that I have enough other and better things to do, I would have far too little time to kill myself, and would already in advance of that event have died a very natural death, before I had thoroughly worked out the preparations even in the initial phases of my planning, but that's not doing it properly, Doctor, and we shouldn't do things by halves, should we, you are definitely of the same opinion about that as I am, or aren't you, because you wouldn't do things by halves either, or would you try to kill yourself under such difficult conditions? definitely not, Doctor, am I right? therefore, the gossip you are now spreading about me is, in my opinion, if you really want to know, Doctor, an action that has been falsely attributed to me, either unintentionally or maybe even on somebody's instructions—although I wouldn't know on whose—hopefully in error, and let me say again: I do not want to call you a liar, certainly someone will have killed himself at exactly the same time of the crime I am alleged to have committed, someone somewhere in the world quite certainly, that would be a coincidence in itself if at that very time no one at all had happened to try to kill himself, since otherwise someone is always killing himself somewhere, but not I, I can tell you that, Doctor, in the present case the two of us have one thing in common: we are both baffled, something must have been confused, something somewhere has gone wrong, Doctor, but what?

Well, what do you think, the Doctor interjects, why were we forced to pump out your stomach? and you'll hardly be able to deny that, by the way you owe us the greatest thanks, because if we had not been on the spot, you wouldn't be here now!

No, you reply, you are not denying a stomach pumping, perhaps my stomach was pumped, that may be, but what does that imply, and it may just as well have been that I simply felt sick, maybe I ate something bad, didn't pay enough attention to my food, especially not recently, no surprise then if so-called food poisoning that I myself didn't even know about took hold of me, which could not be interpreted as a suicide, maybe I was sick as a dog and couldn't even notice that sort of thing, and without knowing where I was going I strayed to this place, but one doesn't have to try to kill oneself right away just because one feels sick, quite apart from the fact that if I had harbored such an intention and if I had succeeded in completing the necessary planning to carry it out, I can assure you that I would not be standing here before you now, Doctor, because who would have prevented me in such a case from successfully finishing myself off, in order to bring me here, because would my planning not have foreseen how to foil such an intervention? please answer me that, Doctor, since I am puzzled by that, as well as by many other things here, I simply cannot imagine by whom, under what circumstances, when and why I was brought here or otherwise got here, because just as I will deny having tried to kill myself, I will deny having been brought here at all, although I un-contestedly find myself here at present, until you have credibly explained to me all the circumstances associated with this, I'm waiting in suspense for the details, in more suspense than I've felt about anything in a long time.

From memory, answered the doctor, I can't tell you everything right now. He would have to have your medical history brought from the archives, they'd have that now, and when he had your file in front of him he'd be able to tell you everything exactly, then everything would be cleared up in no time, and if you would please just be patient until then, well, well! After that you see and hear him phoning in his request that someone look up certain details in a file with your name on it, such as all the circumstances surrounding an alleged committal, etc., and communicate them to him, but he seems to have gotten impatient already, they aren't complying with his request quickly enough or with enough detail, whereupon he orders them to bring the whole file about you up to him immediately right away on the spot, and something like that can get to be even more of a mess and also the height of . . . The receiver flies back onto the cradle; so, he says, turning to you again, soon you will be able to get information, and maybe, when you are in possession of the facts, more precisely or most precisely, at least as far as the external circumstances of your presence are concerned, which I personally will describe to you straight from the file, maybe some scraps of memory will return to your mind, in pieces, you know, perhaps quite fragmentary or at least provisional, and when you then know more about yourself than you do now, and thus you can at the same time be more completely convinced of yourself, firmly in the saddle as it were and secure, you know, when you are more securely in the saddle, then everything else from then on will be simpler, quicker, will possibly be able to be settled, solved, cleared up immediately, quickly, and we'll see now right away . . .

The door springs open and SHE comes in, at first you see only her dress, billowed out by the wind in the room, rustling from the door to the doctor's desk.

Sometimes, when you have looked out at the river that runs through the countryside, you haven't been able to hear the rustling of the river, only *to see* it in the form of the waves' horizontally striped skin rolling over the river, shaking about, as you now *see* the rustling of her dress through the doctor's office. Then you see, while she looks at you very briefly, a file folder slipping from HER hands onto the doctor's desk, whereupon countless scraps of paper flutter up from the surface of the desk and, changed into bright sulfur butterflies, they flutter out through the office window into the glistening heat of the afternoon; or do most of them, beaten back by the sun's campfire, flutter back in onto the desk to wait there to get their wings properly written on by the doctor? The sun has ignited the air around the city. You notice the blurred outline of its outskirts through the open window. And you see HER rustle out the door again, through which, from the corridor, a smell of disinfectant comes wafting in. With it, the private atmosphere you had until now found very pleasantly refreshing, and which until now had seemed to have made the director's office agreeably darker, is once again associated with the hospital, from which in the interim you had been able very briefly to feel almost removed.

Do you feel better because you finally had the opportunity again to give your opinion to someone who has seemed so important to you and so fully suited to you for such a long time? But are you then convinced of your opinion, even to the extent that the doctor is, and presumably he isn't even half convinced of it, because what could have happened on that evening, in that night, so that a secret had to be made out of it, a secret unknown even to you yourself? You ask yourself time after time what really happened, and now you will soon be able to find out everything from him, you're just waiting with increasing suspense for the information from him that will hopefully be forthcoming right away. Why isn't he saying anything, why is he silent, and instead of turning to you again at last, while still studying your medical history—hadn't he searched around between the sheets of paper right after opening the file, shaking his head in disbelief, leafing through the papers, looking for something specific that he couldn't find, as if your history was missing something that could be taken for granted at the beginning of every other file—he reaches again for the receiver and screams into the mouthpiece to the archives that to the best of his knowledge this sort of sloppiness that he is witnessing today is unprecedented in the entire history of medicine from Hippocrates on, under the protection of the planetary orbits in the zodiac sign of the Aesculapian adder, and should this sort of thing ever happen to him again for a second time in his life or in his practice, he will not hesitate to take measures to have the person responsible for it thrown out of the insane asylum forever.

Yes, well whatever is going on, one hears whimpering coming from the receiver.

So the thing to do is to keep looking, instead of knowing it already and expressing regrets, you hear the doctor roar back, whereupon he starts talking about the incompleteness of a file someone had the nerve to send to him, with the problem starting right on the first page of the file, which wasn't there at all, and then possibly there won't be a trace of the second page either, as he suspects, and what kind of file is that then that doesn't begin with page one, but rather possibly with page two or even page three, and the fact that in this medical history the very first and most important page, the beginning, is simply missing, is one of the most disgraceful scandals he has heard of since the murder of Semmelweis, unfortunately by his own professional predecessors and not as an outside job, because the first page of a file contains the very reason for the file's existence and comprises its justification, and to have the nerve to let a file just begin with the second or third page is something that cannot be allowed to turn into a habit, because otherwise everything will get out of control, and if the first page of the file or, respectively, the entire beginning of the medical history isn't found immediately and sent up to him to go with the rest, there will be consequences. Of course he is talking about dire, unavoidable consequences for the staff; conclusions will have to be drawn, after all. In passing he mentions the name of a wild animal, you don't know whether he intends to send it down into the archives right after the conversation, until then you haven't heard anything about it, but it does seem frightening to you, because the emphasis with which the doctor speaks the name of the unknown animal into the mouthpiece cannot be ignored. So, in conclusion, once again, immediately, the first page—more urgently needed than anything else in the entire world! And one should take careful note: a file without a beginning is always also a file without an end!

The receiver bangs down onto the cradle, and in the minutes following you sit silently across from him. To you, he doesn't even indicate that he has become unsure of things, but rather indicates his firm conviction that the missing file page will be dished up for him, like a dessert. Admittedly, you find his confidence disturbing, his insistence on being absolutely right, so that it almost seems to you that it would turn into the deepest sort of personally embarrassing humiliation for him if you should impertinently succeed in proving, if you possessed the impudence to show that you had possibly *not* tried to kill yourself, as he had so firmly and certainly maintained and simply *prescribed*. But you feel some hope of life again. Things are certainly better than in the past days and nights, during which one would presumably have had no reservations at all about letting you be completely destroyed by neglect, lying on the floor, or in your bed, completely doctored to the point of absolutely no resistance by a so-called medical system that had approached you and your person as a master steam-engine mechanic approaches the repair of a quartz watch.

Of course you don't yet know whether a missing beginning of your file would be advantageous or disadvantageous to you or if your situation would remain unchanged, and you think to yourself that obviously even the paper has gotten impatient now.

After a short knock the door opens and in comes a gentleman who looks as if he could be some sort of head file clerk and who must have given the doctor a secret sign right after coming in, because hardly does the doctor set eyes on him than he gets up like a different person and having gone over to him cordially shakes his hand—after having roared at him just a short time before over the phone—only to disappear with him through the door behind your back out into the corridor, whispering in a most confidential tone, as if to show you quite openly that they are secretly discussing a new strategy to use against you. Do they see themselves so helplessly at the mercy of the arguments you presented that they cannot at the moment give you any verifiable answers in the required written form to your quite definitely clear questions? And does the administration of a psychiatric clinic feel itself so threateningly cornered by a lunatic, of all people, just because they have to come to terms with the fact that the lunatic can irrefutably prove to those who work in the psychiatric clinic that actually all of them rightfully ought to be locked up immediately in their own insane asylum? But doesn't the psychiatric clinic take something like that particularly amiss, coming from such a lunatic as you, from someone they have just given the honorary title of madman? And does the clinic not reinterpret your proofs right away as the last of the proofs of your actual insanity? Because possibly they will now take the line that it's your own fault that how and why you came to be here cannot be explained to you, because if you hadn't tried to kill yourself, the beginning of the file that deals with you would not have disappeared, etc.

The doctor comes back, goes to his desk and unctuously explains to you, as if he were revealing something completely new to you, because he thinks you were overcome by deafness during his previous loud telephone conversation concerning you, or that you at least had the courtesy to voluntarily stop listening: The file in which I would have looked everything up must have been temporarily mislaid; for that reason he also has to postpone the answers to all my questions until a later date; I would like to ask you, he continues, to be patient; soon I will be able to tell you everything quite openly, exactly; to date, enquiries of the personnel in this regard have not yielded any clarification, but rather have produced a contradictory picture, because first, not all of those responsible have been able to be asked, and second, just recently so many people have gone crazy and been admitted that the personnel simply cannot always be expected to know exactly who was admitted by whom and under what circumstances; do you perhaps think you were the only person who went crazy on the day when you were admitted here? Then he goes on to talk of the ways and means to find out, and also of all the ways at his disposal to best go about it, of what he can set in motion, and he asks you to forgive him for the time being, which you agree to on condition that he immediately hands you a piece of paper and a pencil so that he can receive a written declaration from you that you will write for him before he leaves.

But of course, he replies, beaming with joy, while he grants your request immediately, well, well, write, just write, maybe you have suddenly remembered everything, yes, probably you are one of those people who express themselves more easily in writing than by talking, well, well, and to think that that didn't occur to me right away; one has to let people write if they don't talk, and if someone remains silent and doesn't know anything, one assigns him an essay on the pertinent topic! So now that you know how and why you undertook your suicide attempt, my answer has become unnecessary, and we can take what you write as an intermediate replacement for the missing part of the file, can't we ... ?

You have long since started to write something to this effect:

Dear Doctor! You maintain that I attempted by my own hand to do away with myself, and as proof of that you cite, first, your claim that I was admitted here, second, that you or rather your employees pumped my stomach and subsequently gave me medical treatment that you describe as *intensive*, which you say I will not deny because some aspects of it will be indelibly etched in my memory, and third, my momentary presence here, which alone implies that all of this is inevitably and logically in accordance with your esteemed professional opinion; however, I for my part herewith deny both, first, that I at some time in some place ever made even a single decision inclining in that direction, let alone made an attempt that would have had my removal as its aim, not only because next to nothing reminds me in the slightest, even hints at such actions on my part, so that I call such behavior as I am suspected of a malicious defamatory downright slander of me and my person, hopefully erroneous in nature, furthermore since I also deny, second, that what was described to me as an un-avoidable admittance of my person into this clinic here ever took place, not only because I have no memory of such an event, but also because no one, not even in this clinic here, wants to or can convincingly explain to me the mystery of my present (hopefully only temporarily) involuntary way of life with a single piece of credible information that would give conclusive proof of my cur-rent situation; the only thing that I, for myself, do not deny, is the fact that I at present find myself staying here, that alone—I doubt everything else as a matter of principle and am already contesting it on legal grounds—may perhaps suffice as proof for you, but by no means as proof for me of why or how or even *if at all* I was ever admitted or otherwise brought here (the general, temporary, present situation may well suffice for you—quite conveniently by the way—but not for me, as sure proof of a past that can sim-ply be adjusted every which way as required, a past, though, that has usually never happened, but that was quite different); and in conclusion I demand that my release be effected immediately, since under such circumstances no valid reason for the further imprisonment of my person here applies or could possibly be applied. Yours truly.

I respect your opinion in every regard, the doctor answers, after he has studied the document I drew up for him, but unfortunately I cannot comply immediately with your very last request, please be patient! As you see, no one here has anything against you, nor is anyone plotting or scheming behind your back, that must have become clear to you during the conversation we just had, but I simply have neither the ability nor the authority to release you now! Admittedly, we are currently unable to provide you with any objectively verifiable reason on file for your stay here because such written evidence has been misplaced somewhere in the archives, but it will certainly soon be found again, and further, you are just as unable to offer us any credible evidence that you didn't in fact attempt suicide and could thus pose no danger to yourself or others, because what you do to harm yourself could harm others as well, which is why we respectfully request that you respectfully allow us to keep you, purely *pro forma*, under observation at least for a while, otherwise we will unfortunately be forced to resort to such means as would not agree particularly well with you. Besides, you are still, without noticing it yourself or being able to properly assess it, under the influence of the drugs that we have prescribed for you, and we will have to wait for their effects and influence to wear off before you can be released. That may or may not be the reason why you are taking issue with everything at present, with things you don't exactly remember. You could just as well, within the coming hour, suddenly change your mind and start taking issue with everything you do exactly remember, because your own memory is becoming very uncertain to you. Or, as a variation, you could start to vehemently dispute both what you remember exactly, as well as that about which you can't know anything, because both your present memories as well as your loss of memory of everything you never knew have combined into a highly suspicious manner. Naturally, you can just as easily do the opposite, by demonstrating credibly and conclusively both your memory and your forgetfulness of those things you have never known, because then absolutely nothing seems uncertain or suspicious to you anymore, rather, on the contrary, from that point on you are of the firm opinion that absolutely everything is not only possible but is also the case! And in conclusion, then you will perhaps prove things, credibly and conclusively, to which not even the wispiest trace of a memory could lead you, while simultaneously vehemently disputing everything that you would be able to remember exactly, because your own memories will then seem most uncertain to you, whereas at the same time everything about which you have little or no clue at all will quite logically seem most probable to you, which however would have the result that you on the one hand forget everything that is stored in your memory, but on the other hand remember very exactly those things about which you not only up until now but never could have had the faintest clue. Answer me this: Haven't you already remembered the sort of thing that has never happened to you, which you have never encountered?

Yes, yes, you answer, one often remembers having traveled through a country whose border one has never crossed, or one remembers conversations with people one has never met, or one remembers swimming in a lake on whose shores one has never set foot, because it has long since trickled away, and no one can forbid anyone else from remembering having climbed a mountain whose peak one has never touched because it doesn't even form the framework for the foundation of a sunken island, etc.

Then we are in agreement after all, replies the doctor and suggests that you meet again in the evening for a less formal discussion than has been possible up until now, in the park, on the terrace, or even in the salon, and until then he wishes you the very best . . .

As he uttered the closing sentences, you had walked out of the room together with him, and he leaves you standing in the corridor, at the end of which the afternoon light, coming in from outside through a large window, is writing a short description of the landscape. The key words appear diagonally across the corridor wall.

As you approach the window, you see far in the distance, only indistinctly, a moderately high mountain range, with a chain of interlocking hills, behind which the approaching evening is still well hidden.

Then you stand at the window and look out onto the plain below so far that your eyes, which are gliding away out of the building, become immersed behind the edges of the surroundings and go blurry.

Yes, the surface of the plain: how it rises and falls just a little, swinging up and down so slowly as to be barely measurable, like a thorax or diaphragm of the landscape, as if one of the breathing organs of the continent were located deep under the earth's surface in this region.

While walking down the marble steps, you come to a door with the sign *Archives*, and it pops into your mind as a welcome and excellent excuse to ask HER right away, urgently, for a more detailed explanation of what might have happened at the beginning of your story . . .

You find HER busy organizing the files of recently deceased patients, an activity which SHE, as soon as she sees you, immediately declares to be completely unnecessary, and she immediately interrupts her work to continue her walk with you that was too short. Instead of commenting on the strangeness of your file, you start to talk about your difficulties with the doctor, who seems completely crazy to you, by whom you feel not so much locked up in this building as in the abnormality of his thought processes, where you feel he intends to keep you under lock and key. SHE advises you not to simplify things in so complicated a manner by over-estimating the role of yourself in the head of the doctor, whom SHE knows rather as one of those people who, if he were in the position to do so, would certainly, by declaring them crazy, collect a majority of the population, and lock them up here to celebrate the most wonderful funfairs. And he would arrange it so that the few excluded people—who voluntarily remained outside, declaring themselves to be the only normal ones—would have to pay for the fairs as a form of adult education promoting folk therapy.

Of whom does SHE remind you so exactly that you cannot suppress the thought that you have met HER often and have spent a long time with her? You ask yourself that again and again, while not forgetting to view HER with a steadfast look.

Isn't her face exactly the same as a school friend's from more than a decade ago, the one you always wanted to get involved with, but nothing ever came of it? With the slight difference that her slightly crooked lips slanted upward, protruding to the right, whereas HER lips could be compared to the strictly closed ellipse of the shore around a summer pond, and the former girl's nose sloped on a somewhat crooked course to the left, whereas HER nose . . . etc. Back then you had also hardly exchanged a word with her, only just the most necessary remarks, but by silent mutual agreement, every time the opportunity arose, you shared the darkness created by the lowered blinds during didactic lectures with slides and film shows, sitting next to her in the smell of turpentine that rose up from the floor boards, and while doing so, you used to prop up your arm next to her so that it was at the same level as the trembling pear-shaped softness of her growing breasts, and in the close quarters of the school benches you almost or even slightly touched them with the excited nerve ends on the back of your hand, causing her to breathe deeply several times, not with the expression of aversion that such touching might have caused, but rather to increase the intensity of your touch through an associated slight rise and fall of her softest hills of tenderness, which let both of you glide into a dream of mutually felt beautiful silence. All the didactic pictures, motion and still, dispersed. The only expression of your modest reciprocity back then took place in silence, probably because the density of her clouds of speech would otherwise have caused you to flee.

You ask if SHE has a sister.

Whatever makes you ask that? SHE replies, no, not at all; why?

Just a question.

What has made HER come to you, you ask, and if SHE always acts that way to free people from the boredom of being in their rooms.

No, SHE replies, she never acts that way, and that is also not HER duty, it was just that when your file came into HER hands and she saw your name, SHE wanted to check for herself to see if it was really you.

What were you said to be, you ask, and who were you, in HER opinion?

Years ago, SHE answered, I knew you very well, although you couldn't have known me. I was studying at the Conservatory with the best voice teacher in the country. One day, that singing teacher, using a voice training method developed by him for me, suddenly ruined my voice. My vocal chords, which up until then had been bridges that spanned the night, dried out. I had to tear myself away from music and all thought of it. The doctor you just spoke with helped me greatly: since I had to find work that did not require a voice, I took the job he offered me here. Back then,

I regularly attended your concerts in which you introduced your new compositions. I always wanted to ask you to write a few songs for me, but shortly before I got around to it, the professor ruined my voice. So I know you somewhat better than you me.

What a pity, you reply, if you had come to me then with your lost voice, I would have found songs for it. And for so long, then, without knowing it, we have been indefinably close friends with each other. There must have been something in the air; otherwise we might never have met again.

Of course, SHE answers, we don't have a clue about many things that are in the air, and that's why we get surprised, but don't we relate everything else that's in the air to us as well, although it doesn't concern us in the least, and feel left out if we don't get little surprises?

But very often there is nothing at all in the air, you reply, because so often there is no more air at all around us.

Yes, SHE says, back then, with my voice, I began to build a house for myself, to make myself independent of the publicly imposed state of the art, but before I finished building it, it was torn down by a professional; you, too, have gone to great lengths to build up the world of sounds in which you live, as if the present conditions did not prevail at all, but just the conditions of your music. But the entire rest of the world has lost interest in you because you are always moving farther out of it, surrounded by the shadow of your tonal tapestries that are constantly moving around through abandoned areas, protected in a typhoon tent. So it could happen sometime that not only today's world turns its interest away from you, but also that the skin of sound and shadow that surrounds you makes itself independent of you, because it has hardly anything more to do with you and, tired of you, disappears from you, takes off, moves somewhere else or is left behind somewhere by you, without you, neglected, disintegrated, dissolved, blown away under the wounded, cracked desert plain of dawn, yes, it's possible that one day your world of sound and shadow could refuse to accept you, because you are no longer good enough for it; one day you will find yourself standing there worldlessly, entirely without a world, having gotten lost in another world, yes, I worry that this will happen to you.

I would like, you say in response, when I am out of this building again, to be able to meet you again in the city or elsewhere, as often as possible; I would wish very much not to have to get so entirely separated from our mutual forlornness as you describe it. Is that possible, and is that what you wish too?

SHE doesn't exactly know, SHE says in reply to my question, SHE doesn't live in this city, but rather in a certain outlying village, not far from here; every day after work SHE returns by train from the insane asylum at the edge of the city to her village, only to travel back again every morning from the village by train to the city to do her daily work in the insane asylum at the edge of the city. Therefore, SHE tells me, I often, almost daily, spend time in the train station café, either while waiting for the train home in the evening hours or after arriving in the morning, if the train doesn't happen to get stuck as usual in the sticky remains of the morning mist and I still have time before starting work at the edge of the city. If you came to the train station café from time to time in the evenings or early mornings, we could meet each other. But not too often, because if we were together too frequently we would soon start to be of too much help to one another in accelerating each of our respective losses of the world with hopeless heartfelt devotion to each other, lost in each other, we would dissolve. I would be afraid of getting lost even sooner, which is inevitable in any case, just because, in trying to help, I might adapt rather too well to your destructiveness, your despondency, quite aside from the fact that my necessary abandonment of music would be jeopardized by such an arrangement.

I find in myself, you reply, no resistance to losing myself completely in you, to surrendering myself to you with complete abandon; I would be happy to see myself entirely lost in your forlornness, safely at your mercy.

Quite so, SHE replied, and you should check this sentiment against your own words, perhaps you have already gotten much more lost in me than even you now realize; possibly there will soon be nothing left of you at all, so watch out! Then I would admittedly still be with you, but at the same time I would have been completely abandoned by you, because I would then feel nothing more of you, because you would have become so completely worldlessly lost in me that what might still have remained of you would then have been allowed to evaporate; and what would I do then, so entirely alone with you, when on the contrary I'm used to dragging myself along alone *beside* you?

I could try, you reply, to take some world into myself again, also because of the shame that would come over me if I were completely worldlessly helplessly handed over to you, and I wouldn't be able to endure that.

If you succeed, she replies, in tracking down some still available bit of world for you to find! You would have to go on a voyage of discovery again! But it's not as if any Tom, Dick, or Harry like yourself can simply claim one of the remaining free bits of world, as you're saying just now, to please me. It will be more difficult for you than you think, more difficult than ever before, because much of what was until recently still within your reach has in the meantime locked itself away again, and less and less will remain, just barely reachable for you, because you have moved displeasingly far away from a genuine need for the world, farther than ever before; it is possible that you will fall so far from your own view sometime that you can see neither your own form nor the dilapidated recreation room of your respective environment. I would gladly help you find the way back to yourself, if I did not feel myself exposed to the same danger. I fear that everything happening around me is becoming more and more blurry as it flows away from my field of vision.

We should at least, you answer, not fail to make the attempt to approach each other as consciously as possible, as we otherwise seem capable only of being forlorn and nothing else, because would we then not be in a position, as lost in each other as possible, to be able to attain an entirely new, but familiarly different sort of self-awareness that was previously unknown to us? And if we did fail to make the attempt, then we wouldn't be far short of having to drag ourselves heavily through the rough savannahs of the still remaining remnants of time? And doesn't strong mutual inclination consist for the most part of the inexplicably overwhelming need for the utopian tender exchange of two tenderly utopian imaginations? And haven't we in that, of all things, already come so very close to each other?

You've gone deep into the garden with her, where the late afternoon sun has gotten caught behind the brushwood of the carefully interwoven treetops in the defoliated woods.

A breath of wind rolls softly toward the two of you, caressing you, stroking and touching your serious figures that remain motionless and unmoved. It just moves along the ground, never higher up than your knees. Instead, it starts to play with the shadows of your bodies that are cast on the ground, has them flutter up and down, gleaming, silvery, glittering, back and forth, has them swing into each other and sometimes also hint at tenderly touching each other, although your two figures that belong to them remain standing next to each other as previously, unmoved in respectfully rigid longing. Countless withered vines, very closely tied together, have woven across the ground of the plain in differently patterned fields. At the horizon, the vines break through the air, climb upward and bind with the light, like the concave bottom of a huge basket whose ends are hung up on the silted cloudbanks.

Believe it or not: On the ground, in the flickering of the grass, you see that while your two bodies have remained motionless as before, their shadows have made themselves quite independent of you, yes indeed, and at the beginning of a passionate embrace they ardently cross over each other, lie fluttering in the blowing grass, and you allow yourself to draw this to HER attention, adding: Should we allow our own shadows and their play to make fools of us, or can it be that the two of them are a little ahead of us? And as you want to start saying that you want to write for her now the songs she didn't order back then, your face is blocked by her lips.

As you finally begin to embrace, you become more relaxed, and you continue to watch your fluttering shadows that are spurred on by the wind to rapturous passion, blown wildly through the grass. Cast off by your figures, they have made themselves quite independent of you and are driven around the two of you until you are tied together, enveloped by them.

How does it happen, and can it be real, that your fingertips, suddenly wandering along the hem of a cloth fence, hesitantly cross under it, whereupon a soft hill seems to swell up toward them, on which your aroused longing surmounts the peak of a taut puckered hilltop, and a slightly rounded tender point sensitively stretches itself toward the protection of your hollow hand, as if it had been waiting for it for such a long time?

But your fingers continue their excursion over the hill countries of your skin landscapes, now finding safety under the protection of a triangular tent roof, and they wander along over an unkempt meadow of steppe grass or tufts of hair until they reach the shore of a sloping ellipse that one can glide into without difficulty, whereupon it becomes possible for your deepest desires, incredibly easily aroused, to devote themselves increasingly to gaining entrance, and, having entirely escaped from you, to spurt away.

Now the mild breeze has blown your shadows away from you, or had they asked the wind to take them away with it, to be able to embark on a long journey to the next rain crossing the country?

She still isn't sure, or something to that effect, is what SHE says when starting to speak again, and perhaps sometime when we are very far apart from each other we will both have the opportunity to discover something we have in common again. And if that happens, we will probably no longer simply ignore it as now, as if it were still left behind, left over from yesterday. At the present point in time, though, unfortunately, it should understandably be temporarily put to rest, and she continued on with remarks of that sort that you don't entirely understand.

When it then seems that you have nevertheless succeeded at last in expressing your response to HER more personally than previously, in making it more worth considering in the course of an average monologue, which you allow yourself to deduce from HER consenting silence, you wouldn't even have noticed that she was absent from your side if the thus unfilled space in the air beside you had not all too conspicuously obstructed the bend in the path you were about to take.

You then see HER waving back at you briefly from a window far away.

But I will encounter you daily from now on, you say in thought to HER absence, and some day you will tell me exactly how all this here with me must have been.

Are those the shadows of your embrace, previously blown away by the wind, that are thrown back intact at your feet from the bushes?

How does one best behave when one has lost one's shadow but gets two back?

In the meantime, I have found out who you are, says the doctor, when you meet him on the terrace in the early evening. You are a composer, and you won't deny that! Of course not, you reply, why should you, and you qualify that by telling him that you compose next to nothing anymore, although years ago you had once worked your way up in the so-called concert business of this city, from which, however, on your own initiative, you deliberately and intentionally ejected yourself, because that sort of business seems extremely ill-suited for the type of music you have in mind, music that you yourself are not even in a position to write, because the development of the human sense organs has undergone a terribly widespread anatomical stagnation.

So how do you make your living? he asks in the same tone of voice as if he had asked how you make your dying.

My publisher, you reply, of course knows that I'm not composing anything more, and has therefore commissioned me to make the most detailed notes of all my analytical thoughts about both the future of music and the music of the future, by describing how and why I no longer compose anything; he thinks that by writing down all my thoughts about a music that is, at least today, still not able to be composed, I will at some time start composing again of my own accord, without noticing it myself, and someday I will suddenly be in the position to compose that music that has not yet even touched the farthest reaches of the imagination, which is why until then he has commissioned me to write the definitive account of all my thoughts about the world of sound, and thus to write nothing more or less than my theoretical life's work, for whose closing, final completion, however, I intend to need all the time remaining to me until the end of my life.

That all seems imagined now, even as you explain it, with the considerable difference that you foisted it on yourself.

After his great interest in your exact date of birth has been satisfied and you have once again given him an exact description of what happened on the last evening before you woke up here, the doctor, under the pretext of very profound intentions of tracing the development of your personality, starts asking you about your mother, your mother's profession, your relationship to your mother, her position in your life, etc.

That's going much too far; leave my mother out of it, you interrupt him and threaten to break off the conversation immediately if he doesn't do so, my mother is none of your business!

But why then, and perhaps that is of greater significance than you know . . .

I have, you reply, nothing in the slightest to do with my mother, at least not in regard to my current presence here; I do not want my mother to get dragged into this madhouse, there's nothing here that concerns her, and besides: one doesn't bother one's mother for every little thing! Or perhaps you do?

And your father, he then goes on to ask, how was your relationship to your father?

You can leave my father out of it as well, you say, giving the same answer, why are you suddenly interested in my father, he has just as little to do with it. You will have to limit yourself to making do with me alone, I don't talk about my relatives, it's not my style to discuss family matters with strangers from outside our circle.

It's not our custom to do that sort of thing, and both Mother and Father would be very upset if they knew that I was discussing family matters here with a stranger, and a doctor to boot, an educated person! My parents would be wondering what you, Doctor, thought of me for starting to wash the family's laundry in front of you, they would imagine your sheer horror at my disturbing behavior, chatting freely about confidential matters outside the closest family circle, and they would be deeply ashamed. For that reason, you will not be able to tempt me to divulge things to you that are not only none of your business, but that you also would not understand, so it's useless to waste even a word on it, wasted time, quite apart from being an affront to decency, that sort of thing is simply not done!

Well then, let's forget about your relatives, he continues, and talk about you: Which distressing event, or which of several distressing events from your childhood can you tell me about?

To which you reply: In recent times it has unfortunately become common practice to lay the blame for everything on one's childhood. Anyone today who can demonstrate that he had a terrible childhood is immediately congratulated for describing his terrible childhood and is generally praised as an outstanding, many-sided character!

So what sort of dreams did you have in your childhood, nightmares? he goes on to ask.

You're eventually going to have to tell him something, you think to yourself, because the actual reason that you're not telling him anything is that nothing at all is occurring to you, no matter how hard you think, and not so much that you don't want to tell him anything, but gradually you start to feel ashamed about the unimaginativeness of your memory, which is keeping your past compressed, like a transparent sticky skin compresses a dry sausage, and so you simply start to make things up, something like this: You often dreamed you had fallen into the pond and were starting to drown, you screamed for help until someone came over and asked why you were screaming so much, to which you roared back, wasn't it obvious that you were drowning and had already sunk deeper and deeper, to which the response was, however, that was not really possible because the pond had been emptied a few days before, but in spite of that you sank deeper and deeper, and at the bottom of the pond, breathless, you were tied down by a sort of invisible water dust cord and buried alive. And once you dreamed you had gotten lost in the woods, no clearing, no path out of the thicket, you were just astonished at how light it was in the woods until you finally realized that all the trees must have been cut down some time ago, because you hadn't been straying around among trees, but rather among millions of tree stumps, and the entire landscape all around you was an endless pattern of sunlit stumps, from which you could no longer find your way out, and their oval and round surfaces reflected the light of day so strongly that now the future often seems to you to be like a mowed plain dotted with stumps of light that bore through your retina . . .

Even while you're making up these stories, they seem as familiar to you as if you had recently really experienced them or dreamt them. Does everything you make up, or much of it, seem to you to have happened long ago, or to have just occurred, just become possible, whereas what has happened or is happening to you might turn out to be an invention? Suddenly you think that what you are experiencing now is so unbelievable that it can only be imagined, because everything you think up seems right away to be something you have experienced.

By the way, I just made all that up, you say to the doctor, whose face shows that your stories made an impression on him, and you are pleased to have taken him for a ride with them.

That doesn't matter, he replies, smiling, all the better, because now I at least know exactly how you think and, therefore, what happens to you in what manner, and what doesn't.

Coming back to his initial position again, he says: In the night after the last evening you can remember, can you perhaps still remember your dreams in that night, that would be of great importance! Maybe you dreamed you had tried to kill yourself, maybe you dreamed you were waking up here, maybe you are still dreaming?

You reply with another dream question: What happens, Doctor, when someone is dreaming and simultaneously dies, does the person then continue dreaming his respective dream to an end even though death has overtaken him in his sleep, even though he may long since have been dead, or does death also take the dream by surprise and break it off? Perhaps the person has already been dead for a long time, but the dream still has an infinitely long time, ages or an eternity, to come to an end, so that the dream often persists after death for all time, because the fact of the person's dying has removed the limits on when the person would wake up from it? What do you think, Doctor? Or what happens when someone dreams that he is dying and simultaneously really dies, is then the dream of one's own death broken off by the really occurring death, or does the dream of dying then last far beyond the actual death, enduring on past the foreseeable future, and does one then die, as in the dream, in a very dreamlike way, as the continued dreaming runs down on its own? Beyond death, possibly a dreamed, very long, perhaps eternal dying, and is that a dreaming of how people always forget everything very exactly? Doctor, let me keep my dreams! Because I haven't lost all my dreams yet, probably because I haven't even found the most important of them, the really substantial dreams, I'm still looking for them. Also, some of the ones I thought were lost keep coming back to me after a long trip, but in the course of time most of them have ripened into nightmares, from which I often awaken much too late. No, Doctor, I have unfortunately dreamt nothing that concerns me or that would, with regard to my situation, even consider justifying itself to you!

But tell me one thing: Do you want to continue living, or how in general do you want to live?

You bet I do, Doctor, but without you and your annoying appearance. I now wish for myself, you continue, an existence that I would not have to keep on justifying to you. By asking me here time and again about a life I have nothing to do with, you are spoiling my real life, which you ignore. I am constantly being forced to remember myself, so that I am not forgotten, until one day I will really have forgotten everything, and then you will believe everything. It already happens often enough that I no longer know what has to do with me, or to what extent, and what doesn't. So I suspect everything of having a connection to me and lose all ability to act without restraint. But, you say, I would like to make the present, as it is freely felt by me, more complete through me, and I through it. Without your getting involved, Doctor! And I would like to feel that the world around me is a little more dependent on being perceived by me. I would like to feel that my existence doesn't keep swimming away from me and running out and away, as it is now running into you, Doctor. I would like to exist and not be someone who has existed, as is almost how you see me now, Doctor. This afternoon, Doctor, I saw the hot, burning sky, but in doing so I didn't have the feeling I was seeing this sky with my own eyes, but rather that I was being seen and almost burnt by this sky. I felt that the fading afternoon sky had a burning interest in observing me. Under the strict observation of such a sky, Doctor, from which I suffer surprise attacks, I start preferring to hide myself, to creep away, because it is unpleasant for me to feel constantly caught in my own existence. If I were no longer forced to meet you, Doctor, everything would quite abruptly take a turn for the better. I would like, above all, to live in such a way that I am no longer subjected to the outrageous impertinence of your assumptions and unreasonable demands!

Above the distant railway embankment you see a transparent balloon hovering through the continually dissolving, drowned hours of this lost day, sailing to the port of the river. The entire horizon is now locked in under the skin of its sphere, like the flickering light of a Chinese lantern. The blossoms that fall from the bushes this evening have petals that quickly metamorphose into insect wings. Flashing, they hit against the edge of twilight. These fireflies streaming out of the bushes, hovering through the grass, may be the ones who set the fire on the plain!

Or the remaining light that stays behind, sticking like glue. Or is it the air that is smearing something over my eyes, ears and lips? Yes, this age smells quite like dried up, burnt mush, don't you think?

This morning you are quite surprisingly awakened by the man in the next bed, who is still all tangled up in tubes attached to machines, good morning, and how pleased he is to finally make your acquaintance, his name, by the way, is Heger or Hengstler or something like that, he doesn't rightly know anymore, in any case he is a detective, probably a store detective at the moment, previously he was a private detective, as which, ages ago, after years of searching, he succeeded in tracking down a suitable wife for himself. By the way, he goes on, I have found out that you are suffering terribly from not knowing why you tried to kill yourself. He too has tried to kill himself, but he knows exactly why: because of a woman, he hasn't forgotten that, but he has entirely forgotten what the woman is like, he can't recall that at all. Just one thing: she must have looked like no other woman, one of a kind. He retains a fleeting memory of her voice, a splendid voice, so full and pure and somehow velvety, bell-like, metallic, probably a singer. You move in musical circles, do you perhaps know a singer who sings with a full and pure voice, and of course clear as a bell, with a velvety, metallic vibrato? No? Perhaps you can help me to find her again, then I'll help you by instructing my detective agency to find out how and why you tried to kill yourself, that's what you want to find out, isn't it? It's not? Well then, help me by taking me to the opera sometimes, where we're sure to get to hear the lady. What? What's her name, you want to know, you rascal? How should I know that, unfortunately I've also forgotten that, but if you should happen to get out of this building sooner than I do and if you encounter a woman whose singing is pure and clean, velvety and bell-like, a great rarity in these times, I request that you send me a telegraph immediately! In return for that, I've already set my detective agency in motion to find out for you why you are supposed to have tried to kill yourself. Isn't that fair?

In the archives you find out that SHE isn't here today. SHE has HER day off.

By the shore of the artificial pond in the center of the park, you want to sit on one of the benches, but that isn't possible, because some sort of waterfowl, you don't know which type, has not only liberally relieved itself on every surface you could sit on, but is also completely occupied in persisting in that activity, without a pause, with a touchingly eager enthusiasm.

When you then provisionally start to clean the surface of one of the park benches with a piece of newspaper from the recreation room, you are immediately interrupted by a man who, judging by his appearance and his clothing, could be the gardener. He angrily starts to find fault with your foolishness in carelessly fiddling around with a ridiculous piece of newsprint.

Why? you ask. Are these birds perhaps dangerous? You try to imagine the type of threat these colorfully feathered waterfowl could pose to you, is it possible that their barely visible beaks, always submerged in the water because of their constant urge to feed, are actually secret weapons whose power could lead some easygoing person to underestimate them!

Hardly have you given up your efforts to clean the coarsest dirt off the bench and turned away from the park furniture than two of the water birds lift off from the surface of the pond, flutter over to the bench you have just left, alight on the back-rest, dig their claws in, puff out their feathers, as if they wanted to demonstrate to you their older, inherited, established right, and then proceed without delay, as a sort of agenda, to the activity they engage in most often, which demonstrates the sense and purpose of their crouching position on the back-rest of the bench, by right away letting some dark, moist droppings fall down behind them, spraying onto the seat board of the bench that you previously tried to clean, bursting apart there or whizzing through the cracks between the boards to land on the park ground under the bench.

Does nothing occur to you? asks the supposed gardener. Take a close look! What do you think, why do the birds always sit on the back-rests, but never on the seats? Is that not strange? No? But that's the whole thing about it, because they always want to sit higher up than where the excrement they let fall splatters, half a meter higher, do you see? Of course there has to be a serious reason for that sort of exaggeratedly abnormal behavior toward the excretory products characteristic of its own species. At first we tried to keep the benches here and also in the city park useable by frequent, often daily cleanings, but this water bird excrement had eaten its way deeper and deeper and more and more corrosively into the wooden planks of the bench seats, until a chemical analysis of the excrement revealed that the waterfowl feces develop a bafflingly corrosive, most highly saturated acid content as soon as they leave the animals' guts and make their first contact with air. The animals' feet would be corroded, their feathers injured, if they were not able to avoid all contact with their own excrement, for which the construction of the benches with the back-rests offers them an architectonically ideal basis. That is why in future only the back-rests of our park benches will remain, because the bird droppings will soon have corroded the seats . . . You absolutely have to wash your hands! Your skin, while you were fiddling around there with the ridiculous scraps of newspaper, may have come into contact with this stuff, which inevitably causes severe rashes, revolting eczemas, come along . . . !

You accompany him back to a building, going along an avenue whose trees in full bloom not only radiate an intense fragrance, but also hold the twittering of countless songbirds.

Many of them sit or stand for the entire time at their disposal under one of the archways, staring at a very specific single point in the firmament outside the arch. It could be the most important point of their lives because, not having stopped their continual observation of it, and having been captivated, hypnotized by the eye of the horizon, they have perhaps long since been blinded by the burning brightness of this piece of sky.

Others come up to you and report on the progress being made in the building of a bridge across the sky, which is what they're watching. They describe to you a suspension bridge hung high up above the equator, on which right now a train is crossing over the ocean, and in its locomotive the state president is deep in conversation with the stoker about the clear advantages of ovoid coal as opposed to charcoal. Or they explain to you, using all the rules of the art of a wonderful parapsychosophistry, the ground rules of a primarily philatelic irrigation system, by means of which the expansion of the Gobi Desert, which will soon have covered the entire planet, can be slowed somewhat.

Inevitably there are many who have gone crazy because of so-called actual history, who insist on being considered historical figures, and indeed in almost every instance as dictatorial textbook figures, who admittedly are almost all dead already, but even from the textbooks they can still make some people crazy, can tyrannize them quite dictatorially from the history books into subjugating their own identities until they go crazy. Maybe that's why so many insane people want to be represented as tyrants, and why all tyrants are nothing but crazy people who force others to take them seriously, with the insane people feeling most fulfilled as a truncated melancholic tail-end of the remaining carnival rubbish of a world understanding they were forced to learn . . .

But you are only aware of most of them in the night, when they start to beat their heads incessantly against the wall, as if they wanted to shake something unspeakable out of their brains or to crush it within their skulls, something unspeakable but not just to them.

Some of them also incessantly stamp their heels in double-dotted rhythms into the ceiling above you. That sounds like a despairingly tapped complaint whose tears drip slowly through the walls of the building, trickle through the cellar and seep elegiacally into the sewers, from which, having passed unharmed through the purification plants, they get into the city's drinking water.

So the entire night is filled with encoded messages hurled outward from the attic of the building, with news from a world that runs much too bureaucratically to be interpreted as a dream, but is much too disorderly and confusing to be categorized as a bureaucratic reality, so that it sometimes may seem dreamlike again, like a life in which even the dreams proceed and come to an end in strictly bureaucratic ways, an existence full of dream bureaucracies and bureaucratic dreams, organized into nightmarish, bureaucratically organized processions . . .

Every evening flocks of jackdaws fly in from the surrounding countryside and gather in the trees around the building. Their metallically clanking, endlessly gabbled, canonically formed screaming choruses fan the wisps of twilight from the sky into our heads and dirty our hair as they blow it about. They circle the building several times, as if demanding an account of it on their tour of inspection before they sink into the treetops. While they do so, it turns out that no one is in a position to carry on his respective activity, his respective thought, or his respective conversation without pausing, because everyone inadvertently looks up, as if, without noticing it, one was briefly receiving an unknown new directive from somewhere.

Otherwise, the tinny-sounding derision and mockery that flutters down feathered on everything is full of numbing restlessness, quick-witted impatience and merciless pity, a thousandfold giggling and suffocating laughter about those many, endlessly exploding jokes that one can never tell because one will never make them up.

As soon as the first streak of silver is visible in the sky, they rise up out of the trees and with them their air-piercing clouds of tonal hail. They hack up and tear apart the veil of dawn that is spread over the landscape, collecting it under their plumage so that they can strew the scraps of it into the swamps later on . . .

Unfortunately, SHE doesn't appear, not even in the course of the following days. Your questions as to HER whereabouts are answered first with, oh, the clerk has taken a holiday or has been granted a leave of absence. But SHE is also said to have gone away to take a training course. Then again, SHE is ill. Then the talk is of a termination of the employment by HER or by the institute. Then, too, she was summarily dismissed for not showing up to work and having no excuse, as had happened before, etc.

One day they explain to you in the archives, yes, this female patient you're talking about was released several days ago with a clean bill of health. And on it goes, until they don't know anything at all anymore, or don't want to know anything more. They ask, who are you actually talking about, we don't know any such person, and with that they try to persuade you to regard the memory of this person as a product of your imagination. Every time you ask, you're told something different, until you give up asking. Apart from your wounded longing for HER, one of your greatest mistakes of the past days is becoming increasingly clear to you: that you neglected to ask HER while you had the chance for the detailed contents of the beginning of your recent story, because no one else seems to be able or to want to help you with that, they have neither found the beginning of your file, nor has anyone who was on duty the day of your presumed admission attempted to give any sort of verbal account of what happened. That day seems to have never taken place. And no one is taking seriously anymore your ensuing request to be immediately released.

HER disappearance and the disappearance of the pages from your file, and thus of the beginning of your recent history, do they have anything in common? Did SHE make the pages disappear? But why? To help you? Because their contents would inevitably have left you to the mercy of the doctor and the asylum, or you would have been helplessly exposed to merciless blackmail? Or does one just want to continue to keep secret from you as long as possible how you have been wronged, incomprehensibly sloppy work, above all for your own sake, and is that sort of thing also what's going on with the content of the papers? What else may have happened to you without your having been able to take notice of it? What has befallen you or what have you done without your knowledge? What did SHE want to keep from you by likewise trying to relegate that which you have forgotten to that which everyone has forgotten, by causing the papers to disappear? You remember the first discussion in the doctor's office, at the very latest that's when SHE, before SHE brought in the file, on the way up from the archives into the doctor's office, must have caused the papers to disappear, and with them the beginning of your story to which you are now subordinated, without knowing why and to what purpose. But because you finally want clarity about yourself and your current story, you have to find HER, so that you can finally ask HER the crucial questions, probably the most crucial questions of your entire existence. But why hadn't SHE already told you everything here and explained everything to you, warning you even as she enlightened you? SHE will have had HER reasons. Perhaps it would not only be impossible, but also unwise and dangerous, dangerous for you too, for her to tell you everything here. Possibly, after destroying the papers, she is fleeing not only the asylum, but also you, because the content of the beginning of your story would be devastating for you. In every way, or only if you find out about it, or only if others find out about it? Yes, is SHE fleeing above all from you, so that she won't have to inform you at your request of your own destruction?

But because you need to find out about yourself, regardless of whether what you find out is terrible or disappointing, shameful, pleasant or mysterious, and your longing for HER is getting greater and greater, your inclination toward HER therefore coincides with your absolute need to finally find out everything about yourself, the way to the fulfillment of your deepest desires has also become the way to and the search for yourself, so that your entire future existence is once and for all connected with HER and with the search for HER, the two are mutually dependent; you need to find HER as quickly as possible, because your longing for HER and your longing to find out about yourself are inextricably intertwined, indeed they have become identical, and if you don't find HER soon, then you will also in the future remain distant from yourself, as distant as possible, as you already are now. But in order to find HER at last, and thus the answer to the story of who you are, there is no possibility other than to get away from here, to disappear like SHE did, without asking anyone's permission or informing anyone. Yes, with HER disappearance from here SHE probably just wanted to give you a sign to follow HER as quickly as possible. SHE has probably been waiting for you outside for a long time, to be able to give you the answer to several essential questions!

There's a good opportunity now to escape from the confines of the fabricated existence that has at present been foisted upon you, to return to a life where one can't so easily accuse you of something, fool you and make things up about you. It's good that your civilian clothes were cleaned in the asylum dry cleaner's, and the contents of your wallet seem to have remained untouched.

Repair work began on the outer wall some hours ago, which required that extensive scaffolding be erected around the building. It will now be child's play to get out a bathroom window that, although high up, was never barred, across the scaffolding and over the outer asylum wall. You are ever so pleased about the nimble movements of the many gray bricklayers, you laugh at the jokes they tell each other with peals of laughter as they're standing on the scaffolding, either applying the wet mortar to the wall or, aiming at each other, throwing it in each other's face, slinging it at each other. Their jokes are about the many different ways of falling off scaffolding, based on many different ways of being clumsy, and the high point of bricklayer comedy seems to have been reached this afternoon when one of them finally tells the joke about one of them who, while telling a joke about one of them who falls off a scaffold, and roaring with laughter at his own scaffold joke, totally amused, suddenly falls off his own scaffold, and even after he hits the ground hard, of course breaking his neck on the spot, he keeps on roaring with laughter. It can still be heard even after his death, because his dying is unable to close his laughing mouth. And while the bricklayer joke specialist is telling this sort of thing, he knows how to pantomime such funny body movements that it seems he might fall from his scaffold at any moment, but of course he doesn't fall down, because after all that's the whole point of the joke, that he doesn't fall off his scaffold, but climbs down the ladder as usual to signal the end of his work for the day.

Thus, this afternoon passes pleasantly with alternating brightness and cheerfulness, and you have studied the pertinent preparations for flight sufficiently that in the following night, when the head-banging on the walls reaches its peak, it will mask any noises you may make in carrying out your plan, allowing you to escape the attention of the female nurses on night duty, and of the male nurses who stuff people into straightjackets.

For the last time, almost wistfully because of the impending farewell, you look out at the plain from one of the windows in the corridor. Your eyes, gliding forth out of the building, get blurry as they dive far beyond the edges of the surrounding area, indeed so familiarly far as if the landscape opening downwards in front of you were really your navel. Yes, the floor of the plain, swinging up and down ever so slightly and so slowly that the intervals cannot be measured, rises and falls like a rib-cage or diaphragm of the landscape, as if one of the breathing organs of the continent were located deep under the surface of the earth in this region, and then you place your left hand on your diaphragm so that you can compare the rhythm of your breathing with the rhythm of the landscape breathing.

Then everything goes as planned. In the night you go out of the room, across the empty corridor to the bathroom, up to the window there, out into the darkness onto the scaffold full of bricklayer scaffold jokes that have fallen asleep lying there, from there you leap to the outer wall, and finally there is still the jump down until your feet finally hit on the ground of the plain in the darkness, a short roll, then the rustling sound of your steps in the grass. You run to the closest train station you can find on the route through the suburbs, where you just manage to catch the last train to the city center.

You won't go back to your apartment under any circumstances; because that's the first place they would look for you and wait for you after your disappearance is discovered. It will also be best in the coming days to be inconspicuously careful around policemen, railroad and postal officials, as well as the employees of the property security company, one never knows.

In contrast to the difficulty of finding a hotel still open at such a late hour, you easily find a bar at the edge of the city park with its lights still on, the sounds of drunken singing emanating from its windows, and the owner, as soon as she has pushed the last of the inveterate bawling boozers out into the street and has locked the premises, accompanies you up to the second floor of the building into a room that is not very well kept but is comfortable in that it has its own shower, making it unnecessary for you to use the common washroom that is usually for everyone on the floor, which then often, just when you need it, is being used by someone else or is locked, either because in that manner one can give the guest the impression that it is permanently in use by another guest, who is usually imaginary, thereby avoiding the otherwise regularly required cleaning of the shower, simply by preventing it from being used, or it is a way of covering up the perhaps completely filthy and dilapidated state of the sanitary facilities that are hardly ever cleaned because one doesn't have or cannot pay for the personnel. When she leads you into the room, going to great lengths to explain its contents to you in all possible detail and immediately afterwards demanding that you pay the full amount for the rest of the night in advance, you don't hesitate for a second to comply with her wish and open your wallet to pay the sum into her outstretched hand in the hope that she'll then leave you alone, but no, far from leaving you alone she now tries to excuse her behavior, that may seem strange to you, by explaining that one has to understand that sort of thing, because by now collecting the sum for the coming night, she will later have all the less cause to fear that you could suddenly disappear in the middle of the night, possibly without having paid, and that you would leave by the window, it was on the second floor and very easy to do, this sort of thing had already been proven to her often enough through bitter experience, since others had always taken advantage of her obvious trust, which is why recently she always insists in payment up front for the coming night for rooms that are on the second floor, and she does so always, as you should know, without exception, very strictly, because if you now nonetheless disappear on me through the window, that no longer bothers me, you know. Don't you feel, she asks, pocketing the money, now that you have paid, don't you also feel freer than if you had not yet paid? Now you are also much more independent, because now, as far as I'm concerned, you can disappear immediately if you wish, even through the window if need be, she says, and expresses her great pleasure in knowing that she won't have to see you again unnecessarily.

You would have gone to sleep immediately after falling into bed because of the strain of the past few hours, if you weren't hearing noises from the next room through the probably thin wall next to your bed, first of all a deep sighing or sobbing, and then also a sort of panting or a panting groaning, then quivering up and down, then also accompanied by a sort of rattling, probably of a mattress frame bumped up and down by bouncy vibrations. Presumably the bed in the next room was separated from you only by the thin wall, and was obviously standing along the same wall in the next room for all that to be communicated to you so clearly, now also mixed with a more and more passionately shouted lament coming forth in an even rhythm. So, you think to yourself about the now clearly identifiable noises, in the next room no one is being forced to get through the night alone, but rather they can obviously be certain of mutually generous help. Not that you begrudge the people in the next room their audible togetherness, but it is preventing you from getting to sleep, and you remember again how, left alone as you are, you are nevertheless persecuted; but by whom, actually, and to what purpose?

To protect yourself against the continuation of all these thoughts, you start remembering HER again as intensely as your imagination will permit, probably the most unusual woman you have ever met in your life, just a few days ago, and for such a short time, yes, so now you will simply think very hard about HER; tomorrow, when you're rested up, you'll look for her; but now you try to think of HER being beside you, as much as possible, and you're quite surprised at the extent to which it is possible, now you wish for her arms around your shoulders, her body cautiously leaning against yours, and then her lips playing around your face again so surprisingly, encircling it, picking the unspoken words out of your mouth, yes, and that too seems to have succeeded perfectly, and then you're pleasantly surprised at how calm you have suddenly become by putting together this intensive image of HER, your imagination carries you even closer to HER, now entirely intertwined with her in this so open dark safe bottomless cave that your room has meanwhile become, the room's walls have changed into her soft skin gliding over your reclining body, brushing past, while from the next room the steadily accelerating panting breaks through with even more shouting, and you think to yourself, perhaps the sound of HER longing for me is very similar, called out almost exactly like that, yes, and how securely now her vagina could suddenly have bound itself around your erect penis, as firmly as possible, enveloping you happily and gently! Then you think you hear HER voice gliding away above you, gently knocking at your temples from the throat of the room's darkness, or is it the rhythmic panting and moaning from the next room that almost sets the wall vibrating? yes, you think again, perhaps the rhythm of HER longing for me sounds just as euphorically despairing, and you don't want to think of it in any other way. So in your imagination you have already felt your way forward and penetrated deep inside her and after a breathtaking plunge through the center of the planet, breathing deeply, you long to be taken in by HER in an antipodean country, and when then at last the tip of your penis has sprung up so that all of a sudden the entire concentrated intensity of your arnica-bitter affection for HER becomes evident, you find your body has surfaced in an endless open sea set in high mountains, and you don't have even the slightest need to reach its shores. How long you have already dreamed of awakening at last on your return to that city where you have never before set foot. Thus you feel the immediate past to be a future lying far behind you, and what you suspect still lies ahead of you seems to be a future past just coming toward you from a great distance, quite sensibly but crazily in the middle of your imagination so gently dissolved by this intensely experienced unconsciousness that you long to show each other as often as possible and by which, at least for a while afterwards, you have been overcome: alone, yes, unfortunately alone again. Even the lamentation from the next room has been muffled for a long time, swallowed up by the separated darkness, already faded away into only traces of voices, the last sighs breathed away resting wistfully, happily.

You are awakened by a confused many-voiced rustling that hisses wildly through your temples, under your skull, as if all the sparrows from the nearby park had chosen your head as the tree to sleep in tonight and were now rising up out of your hair into the cloudy ceiling of the room.

From the shower there is at first only pungent vapor, then reddish-brown drops of rusty viscous liquid, and finally cloudy whitish warm water misty with chlorine.

When you go out into the corridor, you see, in front of the entrance to the room next door, a bed that was presumably pushed out of the room, and after a fleeting glance at it you think there is something in it, hidden from you under a gray soiled sheet, which surprises you at first, you ask yourself why the bed is outside the room and not in the room, but then you no longer find it disconcerting, no wonder, you say to yourself, after a night like that, in need of repairs, ready to be picked up by the workman, and while you want to go down the stairs in the direction of the lounge, the way is cut off by the landlady coming up toward you.

Just think! she calls out, waving her hands around and clapping them above her head as she steps up to the bed in front of the next room, what happened last night just half a meter away from you, just separated from you by a thin wall, so tragic, right next to you, just think, died this past night next to you, here, look! and when she lifts the sheet for you to see, you look into the ancient face of a dead woman.

Didn't you notice anything at all, asks the landlady, didn't you hear anything, maybe just a little, half a meter away from you, maybe it would still have been possible to help, didn't a single sound penetrate your room the whole night long, was nothing audible, and so, side by side, very close together, one is at the mercy of others' cluelessness, or didn't you hear something suspicious, think carefully!

No, you reply, trying to control the trembling in your voice, nothing, nothing at all, unfortunately you slept very deeply, you were almost unconscious; and in your embarrassment, you try to forget how sincerely and realistically the old woman with the sounds of her death portrayed your longing to you with her dying, and how often may it be that the image of a desire is unknowingly borrowed from the portrayal of demise; no, you say again, nothing, really nothing that you can remember, regrettably you slept more deeply than you had in a long time, you were almost unconscious . . .

Then she asks if you'll be wanting your breakfast soon now, if that's why you're going downstairs, because if you do, she'll let them know in the kitchen, the coffee they have kindly kept for you until now, until far into the morning—a favor, by the way, that they do not intend to do for you every day by any means, and kindly remember this in future—now, as mentioned, she would tell them to warm it up . . .

As you descend slowly through the stairwell, you can hardly separate yourself from snatches of the landlady's talking to herself, as if fragments of her complaint were detaining you on the stairs; died, after she had rented the room almost twenty years, but the anniversary was yet to be celebrated, fate did not grant her this pleasure, after her husband had beaten her out of their apartment over nineteen years ago, had downright beaten her into the inn, up into her room, that she had hardly left at all since then, and in a few days she would have been able to celebrate her twentieth anniversary of living there together with all the others, and she might still have waited those few days, that wasn't nice of her, but stubborn as she always was, presumably that's why her husband beat her out of the house nineteen years ago, she had to die last night, presumably on purpose, out of pure malice toward her, the landlady, who had already bought and prepared everything for the party, to rob them of the evening they had all been looking forward to, and now she just had to wait for the people from pathology to arrive, what was keeping them so long, after all, you can't waste time, not even on this sad morning, and they should have picked her up long since, her up there or her mortal remains, and then she'll be dissected, which is naturally what happens when there's no money for a proper burial, and where would it come from, everyone who might still have been related to her had predeceased her over the past years . . .

Without eating breakfast, you leave by the most direct route, not wanting to spend a second longer than necessary in this environment from which you have already turned away. You leave through the workers' entrance as quickly as you can, out into the noisy city streets, as far away from here as possible . . .

For how long now, when I think of YOU, will the ancient face of the dead woman rise up in my memory?

How sticky the light has become recently, you push your body across the main square with difficulty, soon you will be carrying the shape of your personality in front of you on your own hands.

Sometimes you turn, spin around. Not because you're afraid someone is following you, but because you're observing your shadow. As if it could get caught on a hook in a wall somewhere, get left behind there and no longer be able to follow you, and be torn from your body, so that only a few frayed pieces of gray shadow would drag behind you. Sometimes your steps get so heavy that it seems to be costing you a great effort to drag the weight of your shadow behind you. It is resisting your walking as if it wanted to go in the other direction, or is it a gray sack that has billowed out and become bigger and bigger, waiting for the moment when it can descend over your body from behind?

Some streets are soon so flooded and filled up with this filthy, falteringly flowing light that the only way one could still get out of the city would be with a rubber dinghy on the oil-streaked rivulets of sunbeams, rowing in slow motion along the shore of the edges of the roofs. And such air, at first more and more sluggishly liquefying from the gaseous state, then gradually becoming solid, will make all necessary movements outside the house more difficult from week to week, and more and more frequently it will push more and more bodies of pedestrians aside and press them to the nearest walls, and those who walk all the time will one day, increasingly depressed and determined, have to force their way through the street ravines to reach their destination, or to arrive somewhere else, because one doesn't always have to want to reach one's destination. Then when some day the air or the light or both will finally have become a rigid solid body, you continue your line of thought as you push your way in slow motion through the large group of people on the street by the train station, the plasterwork of the houses will be covered with motionless citizens who got stuck to it. When one day on the square and streets of this city all the living people have become rigid, as is sure to happen, and are incapable of assuming more comfortable positions than those they were in immediately before the finally finished metamorphosis of the daylight into a solid body—it will probably only be the light, you think, in which many will then be immovably encased, as in a very slowly ventilated veiled rectangular solid block glowing like summer, often in the midst of making a movement which they could no longer complete . . . yes, like these strange mannequins in the window displays, past which you have to fight your way forward using your elbows when you get to the part of the street nearest the train station, because the crowd in front of the shop windows is always as big as if live theater were being offered behind them. Yes, because the people pile up, bringing a chair from home or renting one at the respective store so that they can sit down in front of the shop window and look in. There are people who insist on taking a whole day or a least several hours' time for viewing a single shop window, only a few manage an entire row of shop windows per day by changing their position more frequently, carrying their chairs with them across the street to the opposite shop window or making it even easier for themselves by simply pushing their armchairs along, if possible, to the next peepshow performance. So it has become difficult to make your way forward more or less unmolested between the chairs that block the sidewalk because of this presumably just recently established daily sidewalk street theater.

The people love the mannequins' completely motionless pantomime, or their uniformly constant, very precise repetition, perhaps because in the displays they have found the most closely corresponding portrayal of their life in this city. They believe they are deeply moved or personally touched because the mannequins' rigid performance entertainingly glorifies the trend of their time and the course of their lives, and also because they can be absolutely certain that their favorite shop-window actors will neither trick nor deceive them . . .

Since SHE had mentioned to you that she occasionally went into the café in the train station, you go to the main train station, a cathedral-like building that is frequently confused with the cathedral in the Square of the Republic, a huge multiaxial marble nave gleaming white in the sunlight through the dusty avenues, with two not very high but massive towers at the sides, and fastened to their platforms are two mighty, heroic, stone women whose pleated dresses fall straight from their high shoulders to their ankles. Each of them is holding a shiny polished stone trumpet up to her mouth, with which she calls from afar all those travelers continually streaming toward the departure nave, reminding them of the trains' punctually observed departure times, blaring down at them, trumpeting toward them that no delays will be tolerated anymore. That is why the people approaching the main train station walk faster and faster, the closer they get to the main entrance of the station cathedral, finally breaking into a run when they reach the main portal, and running through it they push each other aside, pressing forward to the platforms, having flown there, urgently streaming through with the greatest of haste. The heroic women also call out a stony welcome greeting with their basalt trumpets behind all the people who have arrived and are walking out of the hall into the city through the side portals of the station's marble nave and dispersing into the tangle of narrow streets between the ravines bordered by the buildings, not without warning them never to lose sight of the necessary caution they must take when carrying out all their planned activities in the city.

Should one think of the time of one day as a series of movements of the air as it burns in its respective lighting? If so, then the individual hours, finely ground down to seconds, are sucked away by the chimneys at the crossroads, sucked down into the cellar regions, from where in the evenings they are blown back out again as mist and smoke to spread through the twilight . . .

The station café is full, as it almost always is, because it is one of the most centrally located and popular meeting places in the city. It isn't just reserved for travelers as a pleasant waiting place before or after the departure or arrival of the trains; it is also regularly frequented at certain pre-arranged times by judges, for example, then again by lawyers or public prosecutors and also solicitors, or by so-called artists, actors, doctors, journalists and other people in the newspaper business.

You see nothing of the people inside but the newspapers that they are holding in front of them; it's not people, but newspapers that are sitting here, you think, as you sit down at an empty table, place your order and stare into the smoke-filled air that also smells of coffee.

No, she isn't here, although she could also theoretically be hidden behind one of the newspapers, but the newspapers are so big and thick that a woman would probably prefer to read them spread out on the table in front of her, leafing through them, rather than held bent at a slight angle in front of her face, thus making her invisible behind it.

Maybe she'll still come, perhaps right away, and you keep looking toward the door, as if it would open and shut as often as your eyelids open, and fall shut and spring open again, but you confuse your eyelids all too often with the entrance to the café and soon resolve to give it up.

Now you too would like to read a newspaper, first to distract you somewhat, second to inform you very briefly about a so-called reality, from which it is said that you presumably disappeared for a while, but all the newspapers are being used now and probably will be for some time.

The newspapers are so big and so thick, you then think, that one could almost effortlessly wrap oneself up in them, and you imagine how these people sitting here gradually get up and start wrapping each other up in the sheets of newsprint.

After you had once again looked in vain in the empty newspaper stands, the man at the next table suddenly raises his newspaper, if you want, he says, you can sit somewhat closer to me, then you can read along in my newspaper; after all, a newspaper is really big enough to accommodate not only two but, if absolutely necessary, four to five people at a time behind it.

At first you hesitate, but then follow his repeated, friendly invitation and seat yourself beside him behind the newspaper.

It's heavy, he says then, such a newspaper is unbelievably heavy. You should give it a try.

The newspaper almost falls out of your hand; unbelievably heavy, you reply.

See, here, he then explains, a second handle, the newspaper frame has a second handle, right here; and if you're already reading along in my newspaper, then I will also have to request that you be so kind as to at least hold the second newspaper frame handle; that was the least he could ask of you; and besides, I expect you to adapt to my reading tempo, because I am not prepared, he says with great emphasis, to wait before turning over the page just because you are not yet finished with a column that I have long since read, and if you don't get finished with a certain column or can't finish on time, I really cannot always concern myself about that, you must understand!

It still happens that whenever you want to remember HER, the first thing that comes to mind is the ancient face of the dead woman, then you try just to think back to the sound of HER voice, but then the face of the dead woman is suddenly talking with HER voice, which makes you break off any further attempts to remember again for a while.

What's with you, asks your neighbor, why are you always turning away from the newspaper and looking out around the side of it? quite apart from the alarming fact that you're neglecting to hold your newspaper frame handle in a responsible manner, you're also disturbing him, because your nervousness makes it difficult for him to concentrate on his reading, and do you want to read now or don't you? because otherwise he'll have to ask you to get out from behind his newspaper again.

Excuse me, you answer, but now and then you simply have to look toward the door, because you're expecting someone to arrive here any moment now.

That's no problem, sir, is his reply, he doesn't miss anything, even while he's reading the newspaper, and do you really think that even one of the newspaper readers gathered here could allow himself to miss out on even the most insignificant events around him for even a single second, just because he seems to the outside to be hidden behind the page in this manner, but only from the outside, you know, an external appearance; but here, look, because of course every one of these copies of the paper is equipped with a newspaper window that is not obvious to the outside, but can be opened at eye level in the form of a long, thin, horizontal slit. That makes it possible for the reader hidden behind the newspaper, even while he is reading, never to be put in the embarrassing situation of losing the necessary overview, through such a newspaper window slit, of the entire rest of the surrounding newspaper area. Quite the contrary, a newspaper viewing strip pressed close to the eye sometimes also has the capabilities of weak binoculars, because while one orients oneself in the newspaper, one should by no means lose one's orientation around the newspaper, indeed at any time you can look through the entire thickness of the journal, as in the case of our newspaper here with about thirty sheets of paper, you can unobtrusively open the newspaper window slit through all sixty pages at any time, so that from every part of the newspaper you can keep a watchful eye on your surroundings, look, just look!

Quite right, because across from you now you observe a gentleman spreading a newspaper out in front of him on the table and pouring the glass of water that was brought to him with his coffee onto one half of the newspaper, which he then tears off, removing it from the half that has remained dry, elaborately folding it several times and then wrapping it around his head.

That gentleman over there, your neighbor explains to you, from time to time gets or has severe headaches, you must know, he then uses one half of the newspaper, which he has already read, to make a cold compress for himself. The waitress has already offered several times to bring him his newspaper pre-moistened, but the man insists on moistening his paper himself if need be, and for the obvious reason that he probably cannot bear to wrap a newspaper he has not yet thoroughly read around his head. He always works his way through one half of the paper first, even with the most unbearable headache, often with his face completely contorted with pain, before he finally allows himself to wrap his head with it. That seems to provide him immediately with visible relief, because, as you yourself can now see, his facial expression really brightens up, it's as if someone had suddenly turned on a light behind his forehead in a previously darkened room, isn't it, while he gets down to the business of reading the second half of his newspaper as quickly as possible.

The waitress brings you your coffee and, pointing at you, says to your neighbor, you probably want to wrap him up too. She then explains to you, if that pushy one next to you should behave too outrageously, you should report it to her, so that she can have him reprimanded immediately afterwards; you shouldn't let yourself be irritated, says your neighbor, I'm obviously not very popular here, probably just because I sometimes allow strangers to read along in my newspaper, and they probably find that suspicious.

So, but now, he says then, we want to immerse ourselves at last in this stale excitement, to dedicate ourselves to the daily news, and if you think it's more urgent for you to keep watch for your date through the newspaper window, I will offer, so that you don't miss out on the most important things, to read aloud to you those sections that appeal to me.

RIVER CONTROL COMPLETED, says the first headline you see, and you ask yourself about the meaning of such a river control, because hadn't the river always rolled through the country as good as gold, always observing the prescribed water-level marks drawn on the bridges for it by the Department of Fisheries, and never rising above them? Your neighbor is already reading aloud to you: River Control Completed: Yesterday, at a little celebration, our Lord Mayor was finally able to announce to the public that, after so many years, a work of the century has now been completed. Never again will the river rise above its banks, the Lord Mayor emphasized right at the beginning of his speech. That has been stopped once and for all, never again will it be able to flood valuable *Lebensraum*.

While your neighbor continues reading, related images rise up in your memory. Hadn't it already happened many years ago, you think, that a bankrupt government was just able to save the state finances at the last minute, but only because it hadn't minded stooping to the craziest impudence of the century, by getting rid of the river? It is one of the widest streams on the continent, but divides the city at just those densely populated places where the real-estate prices along its banks are the most expensive in the entire continent. The government really had no inhibitions whatsoever about quite openly selling the river in the city to an international company as the most valuable and most expensive of all properties in the center of the city. The company paid for it immediately. And hadn't people talked back then about a huge sum that had far more digits than the number of teeth in a healthy human head? The company wanted to realize its long-since formulated plan of erecting a central office in the center of this country. And the representatives of the company then came and wanted to start building. And when the dignitaries of the state and the city showed them the property they had acquired, that had been sold off, the main river of the country, had the company representatives then not voiced their criticism about it? What was that then? That was a river, not a building lot. Whereupon the dignitaries of the Building Department presented them with a document confirming that the river, according to the regulations of the Land Registry, was a building lot, otherwise they probably would not have sold it as such. Therefore, the company was entirely in accordance with the regulations, one could convince oneself of that by looking through the documents, indeed, they were in possession of one of the biggest building lots in the center of the city. And hadn't the local authorities, years before the planned sale of the river, redesignated the river as a building lot, based on the opinion of the experts, according to the recommendation of reports from experts at the highest level of government? Whereupon the representatives of the international company first settled in the country to wait and see and to gain influence through personal contacts, until they turned up at court one day with an indictment of the river. They really did dare to sue the river for flowing where it now flows, didn't they, claiming that it did so illegally and unlawfully, right through the company's building lot, which it was constantly flooding, and the company considered the thus described behavior on the part of the river to be a critically dangerous threat to its existence in this country. And didn't the courts, to everyone's amazement, decide in favor of the international company and determine, also by force of law, that the river was flowing illegally and unlawfully through the city, because it was interfering with the international company's right to enjoy its property? Therefore, the river had to vacate immediately, or it would be removed, by force if necessary. Then weren't the responsible agents of the executive branch, namely the River and Water Police, obligated to intervene immediately to arrest the river and take it into custody if it didn't disappear right away of its own accord? But they weren't up to the task of diverting the river into the jail, of locking it into the cisterns there. And didn't the local authorities and the international company then agree that they would jointly undertake a diversion of the river from its course, since that had been proven by the courts to be illegal? And they would make it flow on a more legal course through another part of the city where the building lots were the cheapest in the entire country. And didn't they also, by way of preparation, first erect a bridge in this intended district? So that when the river came, it could be crossed over, and this bridge was put there with such speed overnight that the inhabitants of that district had been quite surprised to see it there one morning. At first they took it for the hostel for the homeless that had been promised to them and their district for decades, but had never materialized. Now it had finally been placed at their disposal, overnight! Immediately, people looking for apartments began to settle on it. They moved in temporarily at first, under the arches of the bridge, using cardboard to divide the space into rooms, and then making it lockable with corrugated iron. And then wasn't a multi-story plywood roof truss, colorfully painted, constructed on the surface of the road and divided up into little bridge bedrooms? And then one day wasn't the announcement surprisingly spread about that the river would be moving into its new home district in the coming days? It would flow there in future for all time. And weren't they ordered to clear the bridge immediately and to get out of the way of the announced planned course of the river bed, right up to the new shores the stream of water would have in the coming days, taking with them all things in their path that might hinder the flood of the stream? And didn't the inhabitants of the district then gather together? Their common activity in the hostel for the homeless had created in them an entirely new feeling of belonging, of mutual solidarity. It had only recently been placed at their disposal, but had also been a common meeting place every evening. And didn't they then decide immediately that they would let neither their huts nor their allotments be flooded by the river? Nor would they let the new, now almost finished hostel for the homeless, that they had fought so hard for and finally obtained after all, be so easily taken away from them. Rather, working together, if necessary using force, they would oppose the river. And wasn't it the first time in the history of the city that native citizens, and moreover a whole district of them, had risen up in determination against the otherwise never-contradicted omnipotence of the City Council, together with its Hydraulic Engineering Department, which was always so thoughtfully moistening everything and was especially well inclined toward the citizens, and incomprehensibly also against the omniscient common sense of the Building Department? The citizens were determined to proceed with no holds barred, without hesitating for even a fraction of a tenth of a second. And hadn't they begun with the construction of barricades that were to block all the river's entranceways into the district? They would not have been afraid to extend the upper limits far up into the sky if necessary, if they had been forced to, into the regions of clouds that had been sleeping there for years, because they had as good as next to nothing more to show that they could lose, and were therefore determined to go to any extreme just to get things started. And hadn't the people understood very well how to prepare themselves for the arrival of the river? It would have sought an entranceway to them in vain, collecting instead at the edge of the district, which was fortified as if for a civil war, and rising up to the tops of their barricades, only to pour back into the center of the city. And if need be they would have found it acceptable to flood the government quarter and to bear the consequences for doing so, the government having retreated quite nobly into the shadow play of the avenues, piqued, always with very reserved, superior airs, ready to stand up to even the most inconceivable catastrophes. But then, wouldn't the initially so vehement defenders of the district, worn down by weeks of going backwards and forwards over the same old ground and getting nowhere, during which they had successfully delayed the river, nevertheless soon have yielded again to City Council, which had remained firm under siege? And wouldn't they have yielded to the corrupt wheeling and dealing from on high, calculated by the heads of the economic section from the upper floors of the National Finance Department to get around them and to force the river on them? And thus, once again, as so often previously, they would have been defeated by the contempt and humiliation that the state had never yet tried to conceal it felt for them, and they would have fallen back into the lethargy of their checkered, neglected, shaded allotment shacks, behind which they cultivated the general absurdity of their latest stinging nettle spinach strains, or they devoted themselves to grafting dandelion onto chicory, obsessively fencing off their dandelion leaf lettuce plantations that were mocked by the entire country. That's what would have happened to them, if these people, normally abandoned by everyone, had not been helped at the last minute by a lawyer for prominent figures who suddenly sympathized with them, who had no reservations whatsoever about going to court in their name and thus in the name of the rebellion and of the inappropriate revolt against public interests as well as of the inexcusable resistance against the majestic pride of the insulted public prosecutors who got in a huff about it. He submitted an application to have the river case retried because he thought he had discovered a loophole in the wording of the sales contract for the river. Or he had discovered some other hole, something related, but never entirely or exactly defined or described. And thus, he believed he could make the judges the offer of two trapdoors, with his invincible argumentation, and he would leave it up to them to choose which one they would fall through. But by whom had he been left even the hint of a chance against these river lawyers? Even during the first river trial, as one then deduced from whispered suspicions, the river lawyers had the full backing of the representatives of the international company of world trade with and without limited liability, inc., whose influence had continually increased throughout the land. But then, on the day of the trial, hadn't the lawyer immediately lit the brilliant fire of his logic? His argumentation was irrefutable: the international company's purchase of the river as a basis and fundament for the erection of buildings gave the company the right at any time to erect their buildings right on the wavy surface of the river, however, it certainly did *not* entitle them, if that arm of the river were diverted, to place their buildings on the *dried out* bed of the river, quite apart from the fact that it would then have to be determined whether such a former river bed was a dedicated building lot at all, even if the river that had been declared a building lot had flown in and over it, which didn't mean anything at all, because a river bed that had been abandoned by the river was actually no longer a proper river bed from the point in time when the river could be proven to have left its bed, and of course there could no longer be any talk of a river, and since a river bed only represented a river bed when it was covered by a river and only formed the river together with the water of the river, there could no longer be any talk of a river bed abandoned by a river, because it no longer had anything in common with the river and would thus have to be defined as newly reclaimed land, whose designation in the Land Register would first have to be determined again from scratch, while however the flowing river that the international company had purchased, still properly designated as a building lot, would have flown somewhere else, and of course even when flowing through a presumably other place as a result of its possible diversion would as previously represent unchanged a firmly established property of the international company and would still be as previously properly designated as a building lot, and of course the international company was then free to erect its buildings on the surface of the river in the new district, in the event that the intended diversion actually took place, but the abandoned former river bed could no longer be the property of the company, because it had expressly acquired the river between the shores and nothing else, but there would be no river there anymore in the given case, consequently any land newly reclaimed in this manner would immediately fall back into the power of disposal of the local authorities and the state, who then would have to decide further on its definition; so the worthy international company had, in its acquired possession of the river, to keep to the surface of the river in every regard, as far as the development of the building lots thus made available was concerned, and in all their intentions they had to take into consideration the respective course of the river between the embankments that separated the development from the neighboring building lots which were already no longer the property of the company, but of the local authorities, and wherever the course of the river went, the company could erect little dog kennels for itself on the surface of the river, e.g., on rowboats or also on sailboats or paddleboats or of course rafts with all imaginable sorts of superstructures, or even barges with long rows of houses placed on them, and if one should attempt to take even the most extreme measures and divert the river into the sky between the shores of two clouds, then the worthy international company would have no other option tomorrow with regard to its planned buildings high up in the air above the city than to somehow tie them or otherwise attach them to the undersurface of the river, so that they wouldn't come crashing down on the roofs of the city, in which case they would be liable for the damages, yes, maybe with balloons or zeppelins, which seemed to be the most convenient types of building machinery in such a case, the international company's center, floating up and down, would then probably be the first to float freely, almost independently, in the air over the city, or rather hang down through the firmament from the waves of the river, to which it was attached, it would, as mentioned, prove to be the first settlement built directly into the atmosphere of the planet . . . and then, immediately after this model display by the lawyer, hadn't these negotiations resulted in conciliation? The international company was aware right away of all the consequences, because it had secretly feared that the state, after the diversion of the river had taken place, would immediately lay its public hands on the dried-out river bed, citing the lawyer's so competently constructed legal model architecture. And so the company offered its settlement by declaring that it would dispense with the diversion of the river.

So river control is what that sort of thing is called these days; what a reasonable expression for whatever even crazier impertinencies may have been committed in the meantime . . .

Your neighbor is still reading the text of the newspaper article aloud to you: The difficulties had only become apparent in the course of the construction work. The internationally sought experts' reports drew attention time after time to the absolute necessity, if this were to be a really effective river control in all regards, for the river to have a roof. The entire surface of the river, indeed the entire river basin, was provided with a reinforced concrete roof several meters thick that stretched from shore to shore. Around and on the reinforced concrete river roof, as many vertical format reinforced concrete rectangles as possible were erected, with the dimensions of traditional high-rises, in order to prevent the river from breaking open the concrete roof, over time, and flooding the land. Incidentally, it has already been proven that these impressively high constructions for keeping down and weighting down the river can also be lived in. So from this day forth, we in our city can always know without fear that the extreme beauty of the river we have at our disposal is beneath us, and some of the most impressive and remarkable buildings from previous centuries still rise up from its waves. No one is going to equal that anytime soon, not anywhere in the world! Quite aside from the fact that it had just been time to tackle the real estate and housing crisis head on, once and for all, when they could no longer allow the river to simply flood the most valuable *Lebensraum*, the working and living space in the center of the city!

So it's called river control now, you think, and so it turned out back then that the small farmers' fight against the unreasonable demands of the municipal authorities had been for nothing. But back then they had wanted the river as little as did all the others, and they had bitterly defended themselves against it. If they had only taken it, then we would perhaps still have had it. Or one might have done the same thing there too, or something similar, because this river, as has been proven for so long and is known to the courts, is flowing contrary to the law. No one wanted to have it, because it was in everyone's way. With the viscous elephant hide of its dark gray-green wavy back, it would always have carried with it on its tides the building lots of the international trading company, wherever it flowed, was supposed to flow or wanted to flow, until they then really condemned it to be doomed to disappear forever from the scene. And they had therefore really cemented it over, banished it down into the endless dungeons of their hinternational lack of co-operation and degraded it to a gigantic underground canal tearing through the bowels of the planet, laden with sewage, and immediately made to disappear, never mentioned, and permanently forgotten for all time by the city's residents of this generation and of many generations to come, only still highly welcome as the essential and indispensable confluence of the water closets for the top management, whose sometimes very considerable flushing at least now and then tries to replace the buried rushing sound of the river.

How do you find this article? asks the man beside you.

You reply that you find it simply unbelievable.

Well that does please him. By the way, he is the local editor of this paper they were just in the process of reading together. Then he wants to know if you have already finished reading about the river control.

No, you reply, and you would probably also in future be inclined to avoid that topic, and then you talk about an almost superhuman, but also tremendously gigantic joke about a stair-way landing that seems to have been put into effect here.

What? and he didn't entirely understand, and you were supposed to explain that in more detail; repeat it, repeat right away what you just said!

Quiet! come sounds from behind the other newspapers, we want to have quiet again, how can anyone read a newspaper with such noise?

One of them suddenly gets up, puts his newspaper down on the table and comes over to the two of you.

Don't let yourself be bothered by him any longer! he says, be on your guard, he can get very unpleasant, and I think he's already getting unpleasant! Don't you want to come over to my table for the time being? I cordially invite you. Besides, I can show you something in my newspaper that might be extraordinarily interesting for you: there's an article about cracks in the air, about the atmosphere, which is developing alarming cracks and could possibly break apart or burst any day now, but maybe you'd like to come along and see for yourself?

You want to get up and accept his invitation, but you are physically prevented by the local editor who grabs you by the shirt and pulls you back.

Excuse me, he says, please excuse the previous slight flare-up on my part! But I didn't mean it that way. Besides which, that's no reason at all to simply go away without saying good-bye.

The other newspaper reader, after seeing himself incapable of enforcing his invitation, goes back to his table and behind his newspaper.

Incidentally, the person sitting over there, the local editor then explains, pointing people out, is the world politics editor of our paper, he reads nothing but his world politics page; the person you see sitting over there is the culture editor reading his culture page; over there the sports editor, and now guess what he is probably reading. All of us sit here every day in the café before starting work, closely re-reading our newspaper to see what we wrote yesterday for today, so that today when we are writing for tomorrow's newspaper we don't use exactly the same idiomatic expressions and turns of phrases as we did yesterday and the day before the day before yesterday. We may reuse those expressions that we used the day before yesterday for variety. And these other people here that are not visible to you, I of course mean these other young ladies and gentlemen behind the rest of the newspapers, they are our helpers, trainees and assistants. They read all this for practice, as often and as long and as exactly as possible again and again, as often as they can, so that they finally learn to write the way we do, because after all, they're the people who will be replacing us someday.

All at once, all of them suddenly got up very quickly at almost the same time, putting down their newspapers on the tables, whereupon one could observe a number of ladies and gentlemen hurrying toward the café door and leaving, not without first having put their newspapers neatly back in the newspaper stand. Your neighbor, the local editor, has gotten up too and quickly takes his leave from you, explaining that one has to arrive for work on time, great weight is placed on that. After all, one expects there will be a newspaper tomorrow. Besides, we'll never see each other again anyway, good day!

For a long time now, you think nothing and feel freed of having to be ready to be spoken to from the side at any moment.

Unexpectedly, the face of the dead woman at the inn surfaces in your memory, but you know you were just trying to think of HER again, which is why the old woman's face instead of HER face has automatically sprung to mind, and how long is this going to go on? and your existence, that just so recently seemed capable of having significance, threatens to become quite overpoweringly unimportant again, everything threatens to become so very insignificantly slight and so single-mindedly devoid of purpose that you don't even feel the need to intentionally *refuse* to explain it all to yourself.

Something unbelievably fat is approaching from outside the frosted glass of the café entrance.

It's Kalkbrenner who comes steaming in. Has he become even fatter since the last time? Yes, to the bursting point.

You give him a friendly greeting, and he too is pleased to see you again.

Have you gotten even fatter recently? you ask.

Yes, he answers, and in his present condition he has to guard against being compressed too much.

You're going on a trip? he asks; oh no, you answer, or maybe I am, I don't know yet.

And what is the cause of such indecision, he goes on to ask.

Whereas in the institution you were continually forced to somehow communicate everything to the doctor, which seemed to you to be a useless and bothersome duty, you are now suddenly relieved to have become capable of feeling the need to communicate your feelings without having to find the news of your person as pointless as usual, so you tell Kalkbrenner your story, giving him a rough idea of what has happened to you recently. Suddenly your own sentences sound as important to you as if Kalkbrenner were someone who could make a decisive contribution to solving your problem and could help you, not just could, but would have to, as if he had just come past for this very purpose, and he really does begin right away to occupy himself intensively in thought with the questions of your present existence, a woman, he says, well, well, and you're looking for a woman, and something of that nature is of course always extraordinarily complicated in all weathers, regardless . . .

But are you quite certain of one thing? he asks, are you quite sure that you fled from the institution on your own initiative? Could you not have been tricked into doing so?

No, no, of course not. How could that be?

Don't you think you could in some way have been urged to flee?

No, no, not at all, because you owe the fact that you're outside again to a thoroughly creative flight plan that you thought out for yourself, and how did he mean what he said?

I don't want to disturb you unnecessarily, but, especially because this woman is involved, I have a sneaking suspicion of a very certain nature, regarding this woman, who in my opinion is neither sick nor on holiday nor has she somehow otherwise disappeared, no, not that at all, but something entirely different . . .

Well, what then?

I simply think, the poet answers, and I don't know why nothing can persuade me to rule this out, that this woman, as one can easily deduce from what you say, must presumably have or have had a relationship with the doctor that was kept hidden and secret from you, and then, because your budding relationship could hardly have remained hidden from him, because you had threateningly gotten in his way, he simply, to prevent any further encounter between you and her, forbade any further contact with her and almost forced you to flee.

How logical this conclusion seems, and to think that you never thought of it! These all too suspicious coincidences! The open window high up, had it not originally been barred like all the others? Or not? The fact that they gave you back your clothes was customary, but the amount of money in your wallet seems much too great to you, because otherwise you usually have only the bare minimum with you when you leave the house, often next to nothing, and so it's obvious that someone may have snuck a large amount of money into your wallet in order to tempt you to flee, money that didn't belong to you! How underhandedly mean such methods are! Then the constant evasion of your questions, and the noticeably unfriendly and unwilling conduct and behavior toward you, for no other purpose and reason than to show you out the door of the institution! So possibly, while you had recklessly fled from the insane asylum in good faith, it was in reality a malicious intrigue that had encouraged you to leave, yes, quite right, presumably you had been driven out of the insane asylum against your will, although you would gladly have remained there for some time! Yes! You would gladly have remained there for a longer period of time, but you had been thrown out of the insane asylum, even though you had been in dire need of recuperation!

What should I do now? you ask Kalkbrenner. Wouldn't it be best if I simply went back and reappeared there, just like that, here I am again, now let's see?

I don't think that's very advisable, replies the poet, because if you turn up there again, whether to look for the woman or to lodge a complaint, you cannot prove to them that you were illegally locked out.

You continue to ask Kalkbrenner for advice, what about my lawyer, if I turn up with my lawyer, that's probably the best solution, then no one can touch me, because he would be well informed about the situation from our explanation and would be able to insist on all my rights most effectively, in my name, against them!

What would you want with a lawyer there, Kalkbrenner replies, he would of course be apprised of the situation, but he wouldn't be able to prove anything, and what exactly would he be expected to accomplish? The legal release of your person from the insane asylum, which you have in any case already escaped?

Yes, Kalkbrenner is right, what would you do with your lawyer. You could at most give him the task of forcing your readmittance on the basis of your having departed illegally . . .

So you underestimated the doctor and were outwitted and deceived by him!

What should I do now? you ask again.

Exactly what you already wanted to do, he answered, look for this woman and simply ask her everything. You can ride with me right now. I'm going to the neighboring city together with some theater people. We've rented an entire train car. I don't think the director will have anything against it, rather the contrary. So you don't even need to buy a ticket, because you belong to our group. The village where your girlfriend lives is obviously between here and the neighboring city. You can get out there.

In the meantime, many colorfully dressed figures had come in, easily identifiable as so-called artists because of their affected behavior, and you somehow know not a few of them from before, you benevolently exchange friendly greetings, and when Kalkbrenner puts the question to them whether you can ride along in the rented train car, all of them nod at you right away in a very friendly fashion, and you are immediately taken up into their midst, they are pleased to be able to take you along on the trip, and they indicate to you in all sorts of ways that you should just behave as if you had always been one of them, they were making, they explain, a so-called side-trip to the neighboring city, where they were scheduled to give a performance the same evening, and for that reason they had rented themselves a train car, so that they could continue with any still necessary preparations while en route, perhaps a few last rehearsals to put the very last finishing touches on their performance, undisturbed by other travelers in the train gawking at them, and how nice now to be able to be certain of your company as a companion in the coming hours, at last we see each other again after so many long years, we meet much too seldom and thus are always losing sight of each other, and why is that, why don't we systematically remain in regular contact to keep up with each other's experiences, at least from time to time, and Director Comelli will also find the fact that you are traveling with us, above all in this manner, exceptionally welcome, you are in any case heartily invited to come with them, unfortunately only half the way, as they hear, and as Comelli is now coming into the café and they convey to him the happy news of the extraordinary honor of your presence on their trip and ask him about it pro forma, to make his position as director of the company noticeable even to him, he immediately expresses his general agreement with great joy, walking toward you, and no, and what should he have against it, on the contrary he equates your accompanying them on their trip with an unparalleled artistic experience, and come, and please come now, all of you, he reminds them of their general departure, the train is at the platform, waiting to depart, one has to regard it now as high time to board and should hurry accordingly, and now they are all getting up for their departure, not without paying, they grab their luggage, they have obviously packed their complete theater equipment, the painted theater walls folded together to fit in the cardboard boxes, possibly also an entire peepshow distributed among the backpacks, which they would later know how to unfold and fit together as their own theater curtain, putting it into operation just as practically as everything else, the director helps where he can, now propping up a backpack that doesn't want to climb up the back assigned to it with one hand, now taking a bag with his other hand to pass it along, or picking up a second one to show that he intends to carry it to the train himself, which of course none of the people will let him do, but in this manner he not only gets his ensemble to hurry as necessary, but also lifts their mood to cheerfulness that hurries on quickly ahead of them, transforming even the most arduous task into the greatest pleasure, and even the heaviest piece of luggage they are dragging into a ball that they happily throw ahead of them. He is the last one to leave the café, behind his people, not without waving to the waitress that they will perhaps see each other again soon, not without kindly pushing his assembly of artists ahead of him for a while like a herd, but then taking the lead to show them not only the right way but also the shortest way through the complicated train station corridors, not without occasionally dropping back along the sides to take some of the slower artists in the middle of the group by his swinging hands to encourage them to move more quickly.

When they finally reach the platform, the entire train really is standing ready. The reserved train car is at the front of the train right behind the locomotive, where the train controller with his red cap is already looking at his watch, waiting to raise his green signal disc as a sign the train is free to depart. How sharply he looks just at you, looks after you into the darkness of the train car that you enter, so that you think you can still feel his gaze sticking to the back of your head for a long time. Hopefully it won't be too long before we depart, you think, surely just a few more minutes that you have to survive unscathed, if fearful, experiencing every second of the coming waiting period like a heavy sack, comparable to the theater equipment that is still being passed in and thrown in through the window, one piece after another, very laboriously and slowly.

Comelli is standing at the open window with another man who might be the impresario. This other man now receives a piece of paper of an official railway nature from a conductor who has turned up on the platform outside. He reads it through, signs it and hands it on without comment to the director, who has struck up a conversation with the conductor through the window, and he for his part immediately takes a pen from his jacket to sign the paper blindly and hand it back out the window to the railway official or conductor, with whom he nevertheless continues the conversation without interruption. The conductor may now have considered the conversation to be ended and have stepped back from the train car toward the center of the platform, because Comelli now raises his hand in a farewell greeting, while the impresario, with the expression of most visible disdain, does not waste a gesture on this man and has already turned away from the window and sat down. Now one can see the head of the conductor who has stepped back, there is a brown leather cord dangling around his neck with a whistle affixed to the end of it that any moment now is going to be stuck in the railway official's mouth and will give off a shrill whistle through the vaulted train station in the direction of the controller and the locomotive, whereupon the train will immediately start to set itself in motion, bumping and banging and swaying.

Did you sign it? the impresario asks the director.

Yes, of course I signed it, what else would I do? answers Director Comelli.

So you actually signed it, the impresario responds, it's always the same old thing with you, there's nothing to be done, and you'll probably never learn anything new, will you!

What have I done wrong this time, Master? asks Comelli, it's impossible to please you!

You should by no means have signed it, do you understand! retorts the impresario.

But you signed it too, counters Comelli, I saw it with my own eyes!

No, the impresario contradicts him quite vehemently, that's just it, I didn't sign it!

But if I saw it myself, some of the gentlemen and ladies here are my witnesses, aren't they? the director argues, whereupon some of those standing and sitting around nod their heads to him in agreement.

No, I didn't sign it at all, retorts the impresario even more vehemently, I just acted as if I had signed it, but actually I didn't!

But someone had to sign it, says Comelli in a mollifying tone, trying to get the impresario to calm down again.

That's what you say! the impresario roars back.

The railway official, this station master or whoever else that may have been, would have noticed right away that there was no signature on the paper and would have come back immediately to complain, insisting on the signature, or if necessary he would have had the railway police force us to get off the train, at the very least he could have delayed the train's punctual departure, which is so important for us, explains the director.

That's another one of your intelligent assertions whose opposite you are in no position to prove, in any case, speaking for myself, I did not sign it, just so you have that straight! insists the impresario.

But I clearly saw you fiddling around with your pen on the paper, Comelli says in reply, for his part now getting indignant, you can't fool me, and please prove the opposite to me on the spot!

I certainly did not sign it, continues the impresario stubbornly, I just acted as if I had signed it, I am explaining that to you now for the second time, and I can certainly give you watertight proof of that! Now he pulls his pen out of his jacket and holds it out toward Comelli.

Do you see this pen? he asks.

Yes, of course I can see the pen, and what else would I be seeing . . .

Did I or did I not sign with this pen here, or what did you see? Tell me!

Yes, exactly, you signed the railway paper just now with this pen, quite right, you see how precisely I observed that!

Well, and now I'll show you something right away, replied the impresario, do you perhaps have a pad of paper handy?

Yes, Comelli has one and wants to hand it to the impresario, but he declines with thanks and instead presses his pen into Comelli's hand saying: You write, please, write something here on your pad of paper with my pen! Please!

Well what, well what is one supposed to write, pray tell?

Anything. Whatever you want. Or if you don't want to write something, draw something.

Comelli draws or writes something on the pad of paper with the impresario's pen, but doesn't seem to be entirely satisfied. Press, explains the impresario, you have to press the pen somewhat harder on the paper when you write, so do press, more firmly! Even more firmly, if I may ask! Make an effort!

Now you have tried out my pen on your pad of paper, haven't you, the impresario asks the director after a while, when he has stopped writing, and have you made a real effort to write with this pen?

Yes, of course, a real effort.

And what do you see on the paper? On your pad of paper? What? Well, what?

Nothing. Simply nothing. There is simply nothing to be seen.

Quite right, crows the impresario, beaming, nothing, simply nothing, because nothing more can come from this pen, it's empty. With this pen, as you yourself saw, I signed the railway paper. And what do you think will be visible of my signature on that paper?

Nothing, answers the director with the exhausted sigh of a loser who is visibly conceding defeat, presumably nothing.

Nothing, confirms the impresario triumphantly, quite right, nothing! And for such purposes I always carry this or another such pen with me. So you see, once again, my dear fellow, you still have a lot to learn from me, Director, don't you? So I simply knew how to feign signing the paper or having signed the paper so that everyone thought I had, cunning, isn't it, you're not the only one who thought I had, even the railway official did just now! But you have always signed as usual! Typical! Just typical! Now if something unexpected happens, you alone will be responsible for everything! Have we understood each other? And if something goes wrong, no blame falls on me, because then I won't want to have anything more to do with you and your bunch of bums here! Have we understood each other quite clearly in this matter?

Yes, of course they have understood each other exactly, replies Comelli, giving in resignedly, and he will make sure that nothing happens, and everything will go well as usual as it has before, and it would be ridiculous . . .

Of course you don't entirely understand what the impresario doesn't like about Comelli, how can he find fault with him at all? You don't understand, particularly from the impresario's side, why the two of them lower themselves at all to such petty matters, why they allow themselves such a heated debate, instead of, what to your mind would now be much more important, looking out the window of the moving train, in order to miss as few of the passing scenes as possible. Indeed, since the train has departed, and it has now long since glided out of the station concourse, you feel like a different person, quite happy, relieved, with rightful cause for high hopes and happiness. Not so much because you once again just now finally slipped away from the controller's searching look, that you may only have taken personally because of your present situation, that was only directed at you in your imagination, but rather because you have the liberating and liberated feeling of moving toward a change for the better in your current story, as a result of having found a solution, just as you are riding out of the station concourse, you are also riding out of that story, finally undoubtedly making successful progress in the search for its beginning, in any case being underway at last toward a goal, a rewarding goal, yes, now and then for seconds at a time you are entirely of the opinion that you are on the way toward the very goal of your life, sitting in this train. And how wonderfully everything seems to be working out so easily on its own, almost without any effort on your part, as if naturally of its own accord, yes, you think, there's simply no point in trying to force anything to happen, because after all, everything always comes of its own accord exactly as it should and as it inevitably would have come anyway, and sometimes one just needs to abandon oneself to it properly and then be effortlessly carried forward, and how playfully and conveniently everything has now fallen into place for you! You got on this train here that will lead you to HER and with that to the solution to all the completely mystifying puzzles about yourself. That's how it is, isn't it? In any case there is every reason to believe that is so, which is why you now feel so relieved, relaxed and almost so liberated again after a long time, you are happy for once and full of hope and you understand the impresario and his objections less and less. What fault can be found with this train and this trip, because as is evident to you, everything, as it now is, is undoubtedly fine and dandy, you think, and suddenly you feel yourself rocked so strongly by the rhythm of the train and the locomotive that it seems as if you and you alone were the cause of the forward-driving power of this trip you have begun that will take you to the beginning and thus the source of the recent story you have had to live through, which is now no longer quite so unpleasant as previously . . .

And so it's as if it weren't just your story but the story of everyone traveling here together now in this train car that is still passing through the city, by means of the friendship they have shown you by including you in their group, they are helping to move your story forward, and in doing so they have become so interlinked with it that it has also become their story, almost as if your story were dissolving into the common story of the community, as if you had finally returned from your private story to the whole world, in which your story is linked with the world story, caught up in it, dissolving and almost disappearing in it, and briefly in passing you are also firmly convinced that the existence of this world naturally depends above all on your respective life or must at least be causally linked with it. So you feel as if you were at last released from yourself and had returned to this world, or in any case that you found yourself in this train together with these people on the way into the world . . .

You look out the window of the moving train, and outside you see yourself and your story very far away, clearly, comprehensibly, indistinctly gliding past, whizzing past in the form of the landscape, in which one can very pleasantly, quite exactly, forget oneself . . .

One can be sure of being carefully noted down and entered in the rising and falling lines of the telegraph wires accompanying the trip. One is entered like an unplayable, endless melody on and between the lines of the sheet of music from the air partita that has spanned the city. It sways around in the ropes of the glowing noonday ring stretched high up over the streets. And doesn't the music of every noonday over the city really consist of a collection of endless, impenetrable screams of laughter, whizzing through the air, out of the houses? They have silently washed up, mixed with each other, and are suffocated before they can sound. And they are audible at most as a very quiet but threateningly high humming between the houses, as if millions of invisible, transparent wasps were buzzing over the walls, wasps caught in the atmosphere as in a tightly closed sack that is just being ignited, caught in the turmoil of the streaks of light rolling over the roof-tops, and in the concentrated air wave strudel hazily crossing the railway embankment . . .

The train is still gliding through the suburbs, accompanied on the side by the walls of buildings whose windows open as if to greet you on your way past. And more and more often, in the windows that were opened to say good-bye, one also sees white and colored handkerchiefs waving, being merrily shaken at the opened windows of your train car whizzing past.

You haven't had such a carefree trip in a long time, you think, and take out your handkerchief to wave back. Some people who see this give each other a dig in the ribs and find it ridiculous.

What are you doing there?

I'm waving back.

At whom?

At the people at the windows there, don't you see all the hand-kerchiefs that they're waving at us?

What, handkerchiefs being waved at us, they object, where then, they don't see any handkerchiefs, where are they?

Over there, at the open windows!

Oh, that over there, you mean those dusters that are being shaken out just now?

Yes, dust rags, cloths that get shaken out because these people in the apartments dust their furniture daily at this time and shake the cloths out the window. But go right ahead, if you want to see or interpret dirty dusters and cleaning rags that are being shaken out the windows by the hundreds as colorful handkerchiefs being waved at you and after you in greeting, there can be no objection to that, and if you absolutely want to respond to the shaking out of the dusters by waving your handkerchief, that's your affair, but don't think that anyone is shedding any tears over your departure! No one is crying on your account, no one is waving farewell to you; they're just throwing all the available dirt after you. To think that you don't understand that! Over there now, look, for example, a head with curly hair is being shaken out of that window, and that window there as well, a whole mob, do you see? What a laugh, to mistake them for handkerchiefs!

The train glides through the suburban maze. You're sitting opposite the fat poet, unfortunately not at the window, where two of the presumably oldest members by far have taken their seats, the one white-haired with a monocle shakily fluttering in front of his eye, the other bald, scrawny, and almost toothless, and immediately after the departure, without taking notice of anything or anyone, they begin to play cards, almost indifferently. But when they notice with what rapt attention you are looking at the view, they immediately offer to change places with you and the fat Kalkbrenner, so that you can have the window seats.

Kalkbrenner seems to know the two a little; at least he knows their names. The one is called Karl Rossmann, has been the engineer of the ensemble for ages and has already outlasted many of the current director's predecessors, and of the other, the bald one, he knows only his first name, Giacomo, and that he has been Rossmann's assistant for the same length of time. Both of them are likely being kept on more as living, mobile talismans, because the engineer, who has never been seen doing anything other than playing cards with Giacomo, his assistant, is probably primarily an engineer of the most long-lasting, perennial card games or rather of a single card game, because people say that the two of them now for many years, for exactly how many no one knows, maybe even for decades, have been sitting across from each other over a single game that, as previously, is one and the same, that they either do not want to end or, what is more likely, cannot end at all.

You thank them for kindly giving you the window seat, and they smile at you ever more broadly. Still, they only express themselves through frequent benevolent nods aimed at everyone, often at the most impossible times. Even if the train were to derail right now, Karl Rossmann wouldn't grimace, wouldn't let that stop him from wagging his head at you approvingly, almost as if he were taking a bow. But this is also a form of friendliness that becomes increasingly annoying as time goes on. Because when one of them drops a card on the floor in the course of their card game, and that happens more frequently than necessary, Rossmann bends down to look for the card and pick it up, and in doing so he pinches you in the leg every time, with all his strength.

You start to think about responding with a kick, but are deterred by Rossmann's advanced age. He has kept playing the pranks of his earliest childhood right into his advanced old age, you think then, or maybe he's just started the childish pranks in his old age?

But everything that takes place in this train car, overfilled more with pieces of luggage than with people, pales in comparison to what can be seen outside:

As previously, the insoluble suburban landscape puzzle is gliding past.

Sometimes the train disappears for a while, and you with it, into a black basement corridor under the city, only to surface again soon, driven back up toward the sky through high walled ravines by a shadow waterfall forcefully crashing upward, yes, because the shadows have become fluid in these times, soon they will evaporate again.

Soon we head out of the city, after crossing the last of the city bridges, a bridge that spans the painfully bright, glistening river of the horizon at midday, a river at whose edges flotsam and jetsam washes up from the swamps that hover through the sky. Now the entire sky is probably one big swamp. It stretches along the raging torrents of air to the early afternoon border security enclosures, reaching them soon, because they have moved quite near. Behind the enclosures, all sorts of indigenous waterfowl are swimming overhead, in an irregular, upward branching delta of light. Their wings beat nervously around them, and are soon systematically organized into sparkling sheaves of sunbeams. They, in turn, break through the next hilly fragment of ether located behind them. Then they scatter, as if to prepare a proper path for the train to the next chain of interlinking hills.

Ever more frequently now, the section of track at the embankment is dotted with desert plants, agaves, that have established themselves in the gravel piled up against the rails. Like a huge sort of jellyfish living in the air instead of the water, they have clung to, sucked their way onto the railway gravel. And a lively discussion about them arises in the company.

Agaves, it is said, bloom only once in their lifetime. The stem of the blossom is often over ten, even up to twenty meters high, and in earlier times there are said to have been agaves whose blossom stems must have been so high that one often couldn't see the blossom at all from earth, because the blossom is said to have put its face very proudly in the clouds, to have hidden it.

But once they have blossomed, when the bloom is finished, they slowly, inevitably begin to curl up and die, they slump or roll down limply from the railway embankment, like octopuses of the air whose tentacles have gotten tired and gone to sleep.

Can't such an agave be saved?

No, once it has bloomed, it can't be saved anymore.

Yes, it can be saved, but before it has bloomed. One simply has to prevent its blossom from opening.

Chop off the stem, chop it off before it can bloom, one has to chop off the stem of the blossom as soon as it starts to shoot up into the air and into the firmament as if it wanted to pierce the skin of the atmosphere, chop it off before the umbels of the blossom open!

Chop it off, yes, but the cut absolutely has to be made below the lower third of the huge stem, otherwise it doesn't work.

And why all that, why?

Why? Because then the agave forgets to bloom. Rather, the plant forgets that it had already started to bloom and waits forever to continue blooming some day, and it lives, instead of dying after its otherwise planned blossom would have faded, it continues on, clinging to the gravel along the railway embankment, until it fossilizes.

Look at all these agaves sadly swaying over the rails through the twilight of the railway tracks, with their chopped off thick blossom stem stumps meaninglessly blunted between the tentacles of their thorny extended strips of leaves. The stems have just stubbornly spiraled upwards into the clouds of air over the plants . . . And just to speak briefly, in conclusion, about those gigantic agaves of previous centuries, whose stems were so high that the flower heads of the umbels were usually hidden in the clouds, it is said there were often entire forests of them, just imagine, entire forests full of huge agave flower stalks as thick as the trunks of trees, with their blossoms hidden in the clouds, so that presumably no one was ever able to see them, unless someone climbed up to build himself a hut in the umbels . . .

The train has now also left behind the last of the smokestacks, pressed helplessly against the horizon as if they have died of thirst or hunger, and it's gliding out into the open plain.

You feel as if, on this trip, you have left so much behind at the train station, because at the moment nothing at all is weighing on your mind, and you feel almost weightless. Or is it just the feeling of being underway, underway to somewhere, where what you have left behind no longer has to be laden with any useless significance? Underway to a place where everything that has been, up until now, no longer has anything threatening about it. Because the all-embracing feeling of so-called senselessness is becoming quite significant, because every so-called sense one had been forced to wrap around everything like a cummerbund turned out to be the actual cause of all the pointless, insurmountable problems. Don't the main causes of many agonies lie in those useless, trite, simplifying contexts that arise from self-neglect and contempt, but that you have allowed to successfully affect you?

You lean far out the window, to the place where separated valleys reunite, and looking back at them it seems to you as if your immediate past, about which you know as much as about your future, were just now seeping away in them. But it no longer bothers you as it otherwise does, doesn't make you afraid, and instead of finding it threatening, you find it rather logical, but why, you don't want to be able to explain that to yourself right now, and why should you. Perhaps it is simply the feeling of happiness that comes from constantly traveling, and from the change of location insisted on by that, and the shifts of meaning, so that sometimes a change in location with the accompanying changes in time results in the exchange for a new life. You point in the direction where everything is vanishing. It's not just your direction, but above all one of the points of the compass where everything becomes blurred with the passing of the hours.

Have we even properly said hello to each other today? asks Comelli after a short transitional silence, calling to everyone in our train car. So, how are all of you today?

Yes, yes, quite fine and as usual.

Did you sleep well?

Yes, yes.

And is everyone present, he then asks pro forma, or is someone missing? no? well then, where, for example, is the professor? I don't see him at all.

I mean the concertmaster, he explains in an aside.

Yes, well, where is he? Where are you, where have you been hiding yourself all the while? Oh there, then everything's fine; I thought it would be; and is everything in order? You seem rather crushed today; who has crushed you again? You haven't left your bow at home, have you, the most important thing?

No, it's here.

Where is it, I don't see anything, please show me, get it out for me!

It's there! Packed, packed up in the violin case!

Where?

Up there, see, in the luggage rack as always!

Yes, the violin case, but is the violin really in it?

Yes, what else!

Show me, please show me, yes, quite right, open the violin case, I want to see . . . well finally, so the violin is here too, that's gone well one more time; that's a big relief . . . no, don't shut it again, but leave it as it is, once you have opened the case, you don't have to shut it again right away, because I just got an idea, wait a minute!

At that, Comelli turns to you, his words sounding almost like a command: I ask you, and you can't simply turn down this request, because now that you're with us, traveling with us, then you simply can't take it amiss that I immediately want to seize this excellent, unique opportunity, because we may perhaps never again have such a stroke of luck, to have you with us again, and since we need a happy diversion in the coming hours of our lives, in the form of a musical performance to shorten the trip somewhat, I request most courteously that you, together with my concertmaster, the professor, who may not be unknown to you from earlier times, immediately rehearse and under your direction play and première a piece of music just composed by you at this moment, come here, professor, may I request, so, there we are, gentlemen, and please begin! Go on, go on! Begin! Tell our professor what he should now fiddle on his violin, right away, quickly!

And turning to the concertmaster, Comelli orders him: Go on, go on! Get fiddling! Would you fiddle at last! Why don't I hear anything yet, it's still very quiet here, much too quiet, and would you fiddle at last, Professor, start fiddling what our composer will announce to you right away! Up and at it, Professor!!

Yes, Director, right away, says the professor, tucking his violin under his chin, and turning to you, he says: Please tell me now what I'm supposed to play, so that I can finally begin, please, hurry!

Of course that's more easily said than done, and naturally you have no idea how you should behave now and what would be the best thing to do, well then, you say, my dear Professor, first of all you should simply play one note, a very long stretched out sustained note, please!

What note?

A middle C! Do it!

See, that's extraordinary . . . !

C, not see! Or did I say see? I would like to hear a middle C, no see about it! Do you understand me?

Yes, yes, I understand, C, not *see*! But which note do you want me to perform after the middle C?

Before the ultimate determination of the second note, we first have to decide on the exact length, the time of the first note; because the first note in particular has to have an exactly considered and cleverly planned measured length, above all not too long, just not too long, that's the most important thing, and most musicians repeatedly make the one big mistake of holding on to the first note much too long, because the composers always stipulate that the first note in most of their pieces be held much too long, so that in most pieces of music these days the first note is so long that the second note usually cannot even be foreseen. Most composers get stuck right at the first note and never get any farther, because after the enormous dimension and duration of just the first note, there is usually no time left even for a second note that might possibly follow! Or the performing musicians are so exhausted after playing this never-ending intensive first note of a piece of music that they would no longer be in any shape to play a second note, after such great first notes, one could not with all the will in the world expect either them or the audience to put up with a single second note!

The time has come for someone finally to crusade against this bad practice! I congratulate you!

So the first note, middle C, not too long, but also by no means too short! And one can't be allowed to want to overcome the problem of the first notes being too long by playing the first note so short that nothing at all can be heard of it anymore! So that instead of the first note one gets to hear the second note right away!

Quite right, the professor replies, or even the third or fourth note, indeed, it often happens that a piece has hardly begun when one is already hearing the final chord . . .

Quite right, you say, and most new pieces of music suffer from having their notes played so quickly that hardly has the piece begun than you often can't even properly hear the final chord, usually nothing, nothing at all! And that is too short, you understand, then we wouldn't even need to begin. So, middle C, Professor, what would be the best length for it, what do you say?

At best 20 km, I would think, answers the concertmaster, a round number . . .

Why aren't we hearing anything? Director Comelli now interrupts, you were supposed to be composing something, not discussing, I think, gentlemen, you are taking it too far with your precision! But even precision can lead to slackness, you know, infatuation with detail can make the *Gesamtkunstwerk* impossible, I call that sort of thing precision-slackness. The two of you seem to me to be typical precision-slackness fanatics! So get going, play, he calls out to the concertmaster, play up! no, don't play up, play down! Downplay everything that gets in our way!

Yes sir, Director, right away!

He raises the bow, it approaches the violin tucked under his chin, but the instrument seems to be wrapped in an impenetrable block of air that, although transparent, is solid, because the professor is certainly trying with all his strength to penetrate the airspace above his violin with the tip of the bow, but without success. First the tip of the bow slips, and now the entire block of air together with the violin in the professor's hand starts pushing away, so that the concertmaster's whole body starts turning in a circle, at first very slowly, then faster and faster, in his right hand the raised bow that wants to land on the violin in his left, but can't, because the instrument desperately withdraws from him and flees . . .

I can't go on like this, he says, putting down the bow, it's always the same thing, the same problems ever since I was a child, he explains, the unresolved problems of childhood of course also pursue the grown-up, accompanying him his whole life long until death! He starts telling us about his childhood and youth, the so-called social conditions in his parental home and at school. His violin teacher, from the very first lesson, had to tie him firmly to a coat rack to prevent his left hand with the violin from withdrawing and fleeing from the approaching bow, and so his whole body starts turning, faster and faster, until he is so dizzy he falls down.

Of course I have learned how to play the violin properly, you know, he continues explaining, but a solo career was out of the question, because the soloist has to be able to stand upright and unattached during his public performances, without constantly having to spin around as if he were controlled by an organic carousel mechanism or had to obey an independently active anatomical merry-go-round motor. However, as a concertmaster, you know, I can sit at my work and have at my disposal a chair that I myself constructed specially for my needs in this matter, with seat belts I can put on, I buckle myself in to avert every unnecessary rotation of my upper body, even while sitting, when I'm playing first violin with the orchestra. By the way, I don't seem to be the only one with this problem, because the patented chair I developed is already being used by many other violinists in practically every orchestra in the world, at least in those with a sense of professional pride, in particular though, almost all concertmasters who are taken seriously today play every concert strapped in, and all those violinists in the orchestra who think they don't need to be strapped in are accused quite rightly and with ever more ruthless emphasis of showing a lack of discipline, because it is simply unacceptable for the violinist or violist while playing to give free rein to his associated upper body rotations, of which he is usually inevitably unaware, so that he is constantly looking at the music on the stand behind him and playing that part instead of his own, thereby throwing the conductor off. Your whole life long you want to settle into the performance, to create space for yourself, clinging to the secret hope that at some point all the self-imposed restrictions will dissolve into thin air, and finally all restraints will let go without your falling, but these straps don't tear, they are special straps that bind you firmly to one stretcher after another. Yet if you neglect to strap yourself in, the world will start turning around you faster and faster until it gets dizzy and falls down without your being able to come to its assistance . . .

Calm down, Professor, you calm the breathless musician, let's just try it again, and I'll hold you in place so that such difficulties don't arise anymore!

Do you really think so? he asks hesitantly, still quite dizzy and confused.

Of course, you state more strongly, you stand resolutely behind him and take hold of his shoulders with all your might, you want to give him tangible evidence of your determination to counteract helpfully, preventatively, all possible newly arising urges to turn around.

All right then, he says, but you take responsibility!

Take heart! you say quietly behind his back, directing your voice at the back of his head, and immediately you feel very strong resistance in his shoulder blades. They are already trying to turn to the left, but you believe you're strong enough to nip any new attempt at a turn in the bud. This time he wants to hold the bow at a considerably steeper angle than before, bringing it down diagonally on the violin, very fast, from high up, as if he wanted to pierce the instrument and run it through with the bow like a sword. If only it turns out well this time, you think, and you already fear the worst for the violin, in your mind's eye you already see it slashed open by the bow crashing down from the ceiling of the train car, the bow that now, contrary to all expectations, has penetrated the airspace around the violin and reached the very string it was aiming at, and after the so fortunate soft landing it gradually begins to stroke the string horizontally, more and more evenly, it's astonishing how he did it this time, and what a tone, of course a middle C, as arranged. What a sound, Professor, you say encouragingly, don't give up now, Professor, what a sound, listen, as if brought a long way from a very great distance, brought right in through the train car window, Professor, your bow, look, Professor, your bow is gliding over the entire landscape that is floating past outside the train window, your violin has now turned into the landscape, along with the wires of the high tension strings over the bridge that are stretched through the entire airspace and attached to the horizon, Professor, look, entwined into a curtain bordering the plain. Now you see the steel cable of the transmission line singing across the violin plain, you see the vibration of the transmission string against the landscape that is floating by; there is a full sound through the entire sky, which is stretched tight by the concertmaster's violin right up to the fence along the horizon, the fence that laces in this region very tightly, as if it were supposed to prevent the landscape from falling apart and therefore wraps it up, clearly ties it together and packages it into the transparent sack of its firmament skin, in order to put on entirely new strings over all the hills and vales, but perhaps it is a little too tight after all, and if only it doesn't burst soon from the vibrating and buzzing of the transmission string high tension line over the concertmaster's violin, because now the plain has almost breathlessly shriveled up before your eyes to a chartreuse soap bubble that came arching in through the train window and is now hovering through the train car, its gossamer-thin skin that mirrors the horizon is closing around the fiddle, soon very close to it, and already there is a thin rip in it, glistening, probably scratched into the silvery sky over there by the tip of the bow, and the tear is widening, which in itself is no cause for initial fears, on the contrary, because the tear provides an escape route for the pressure of this noonday sultriness that was weighing so heavily on the area and was almost unbearable, indeed, all the midday steam is obviously departing through the crack above that chain of hills there in the corner of the region, it's being blown out as if through a valve, through which part of the plain can flow away.

There's a generally noticeable feeling of relief all along the line, a real sigh of relief.

The note from the concertmaster's violin has very gently subsided. Everyone feels better than before.

His forehead dripping sweat, the professor puts down the bow and lowers the violin. He packs both of them back in the instrument case right away, where, as he says, he knows they are better kept and protected than anywhere else, which is why he really only ever takes them out as a last resort.

He locks the case, still sighing with relief, puts it back on the luggage rack, and then sits down exhausted.

Thank you, he says, I have you to thank, because if you hadn't held me so firmly, everything would have started to spin around me again until the world around me would have shut like a book that wasn't read to the end, I have you to thank.

People probably always believe, you think, that everything revolves around them, without noticing that it is they themselves who whirl around until they are so dizzy they fall down.

There's no need to thank me, Professor, you reply, it was the obvious thing to do, and by the way, Professor, you played exceptionally well!

Yes, Comelli joins in, and all the others are of the same opinion as he is, you played with exceptional excellence, Professor, as in former times, no, even former times pale in comparison to your playing today. Don't you want to think it over, dear Professor, and contemplate a solo career again? I would strongly advise you to do so and would recommend you everywhere. Do think about it! And in these times no one will take it amiss if you bring an assistant on stage with you for your solo performances, of course he would have to have first-rate training, and he will hold you probably from behind while you play, just as our composer did! On the contrary! Other soloists will imitate you in that, and soon there won't be a violinist in the world who would consider performing without being held from behind by his accompanying assistant! Believe me! And didn't the initial practice run we just had turn out for the best?

By the way, that was an exceptionally beautiful piece that you just composed for us, he turns to you, it impressed me so much because you didn't hold back, you know. An exciting composition has come into being, in which you proceeded extravagantly! Indeed, unrestrained extravagance in the application of the most economical means! That's what I've been preaching for at least twenty years, that the most important thing is to be recklessly extravagant with the most economical means. You succeeded in that in an exemplary fashion. Congratulations! Perhaps we can get together more often in future for collaborative work? It would be a stroke of luck. For us. But perhaps also for you?

After that, Comelli explains the great plans for a future he has been systematically longing for, which he quite prophetically characterizes as not yet exactly estimable, and his eyes begin to shine as he talks enthusiastically and knowingly about a time that will soon be approaching, as if he already had the greatest experience with it; at the same time he describes his utopian ideas as casually as if he were talking about his vivid memory of the vital boredom of a day before yesterday:

To rent a whole train just for us sometime, to set off on a long trip, equipped with proper papers for any country, and at switch points to head off in any direction we want, to travel freely and in a carefree manner through our country, the neighboring countries and all over the entire continent as extensively as necessary, so that some day, completely by surprise, we will find a region, a country, an ideal landscape, where together with my people I will build a huge natural theater. You will now rightly want to ask approximately how such a landscape would have to be constituted, which optical, acoustic or other basic prerequisite qualities for theater would need to be present, but it is unfortunately not possible to answer that question. In my opinion, you simply see such a region, or you are suddenly seen by it, and you know exactly that yes, that's exactly what it is, what you have been seeking for the longest time. You can't picture it, but when you encounter it one day, you recognize it right away. Have you never arrived in an area on your travels where you were suddenly exposed to secretly inexplicable sensations? You imagine that you must have been there several times, but when you search your memory you know it's impossible that you could ever have come into even the remotest contact with this region before; nevertheless, you can't get rid of the suspicion that you have already lived there for at least a quarter of an eternity, a long time ago, you're quite certain you were at home there, in rooms that you are able to draw and to describe exactly, but when? yes, when then? perhaps in the rooms of a long-since cremated, extinguished time? perhaps more than a thousand years ago? who knows, and who should be able to want to know that so exactly? and why not, actually? but it's still as immediate, as tangibly behind you as if it had been at least a week, but no more than a month ago. Perhaps that is also why you are seized by a threateningly strong feeling of unconditionally devoted belonging, combined with a violently straining, irresistibly strong wish for something on the one hand very clearly determined, on the other hand completely beyond any definition and unable to be grasped by the traditional means of understanding. But the very fact that this wish cannot be realized is of an unexpected, peacefully relaxing, overwhelmingly preserved, all-transcending beauty. It is almost fleetingly comprehensible to you when you find it perceptibly enabled in you, comparable to a breaking out of feelings of love, although far and wide no beloved would be present for you to show her such powers of affection, which however does not result in any decrease in this self-fulfilling desire for devotion.

When inevitably you then depart from there again someday, because you have other commitments, one assumes, because you have to go away, you will be seized from that moment on by an almost perpetual urge to travel, or else homesickness, or perhaps both together, compared to which that thing you previously called homesickness, that slightly melancholic ache which used to waft through you, reveals itself as nothing more than a self-imposed, affected bit of posturing. Often, simply for lack of any opportunity to turn back toward our country, it attempts to fill up the space where your feelings reside, the space that is otherwise left empty. Or else you attempt to fill it up for yourself on longer trips with more desiccated, hollowed out, sentimentally affected behavior, like playacting in front of a mirror. Sometimes you absolutely want to imagine that, for you, because of your artificially nervous compulsion to overreach yourself, an acquired self-effacing courtesy requires that you at least at rare intervals permit yourself a familiar hope, a sense of belonging you have at your disposal, a hope that you will soon return to the so-called home region of your choice. Said home region, however, as soon as you have turned up in it, gone back into it, immediately resumes fanning the flames of hatred you have directed at it all your life, which is probably why most of our time at home is spent constantly planning big extensive trips, because everything else is very soon mercilessly ruined for us. But be that as it may, it still happens much too often that one feels obliged to return home now and then, because only there and nowhere else do the travel plans for the future work out in such complete and optimal perfection, because only there, as nowhere else in the entire world, can one look forward with such longing, with such a burning desire, to finally being able to leave again, soon, to embark on a new trip. On that trip, quite surprisingly, one comes across an area as previously described, an area you already recognize from afar as being suitable for you and able to accommodate you, and it will also captivate you instantaneously. And in comparison to it, the home region, with which you have previously been satisfied, seems like a ridiculous and completely frayed, huge washcloth carelessly thrown into the plain and spread out in a somewhat wrinkled condition!

Oh yes, look! No, this way, not that way, I meant this way, at the window! Out the window, I meant to say, please take a good look out the window, quickly! This area here has a striking resemblance to a washcloth, well, what do you say now, it's the spitting image of a somewhat swampy cotton grass frayed washcloth patchwork rug, isn't it? How beautiful it is, if that isn't a lucky coincidence, isn't it, or don't you think so at all? It's your homeland I'm talking about, my dear man, your homeland as a completely slovenly washcloth plain, while our trip at this moment, that is, at exactly the right moment, for purposes of illustration, exactly when I am calling your homeland, you know, your homeland a slovenly washcloth frayed patchwork rug plain, yes, right now, for illustration, a slightly creased, hilly, wavy, rounded plain is being drawn into the train window, and it is covered by a typical, entirely genuine, marshy washcloth workpatch that seems to be upholstered with cotton grass, you see, my dear man, look at it closely so that you don't miss anything, and over there, way way over there, do you see, you already have seen, yes, so, way over there now for variety something has, something definitely, yes, something definitely like marsh marigolds has come onto the scene, or hasn't it?

Yes, Herr Comelli, quite typical marsh marigolds.

Only the sloppy fringes of this landscape will still be preserved for us for a little while, I fear, says Comelli. Or no, it's not so bad at all, not yet, but the fringes, the fringes are somewhere else entirely now, that's not possible, I can't understand it, look, please, look up there now! Yes? Do you see? Don't you see? Now, there, they're hanging down from the sky, the fringes, the sky's completely frayed, and see how far down they're hanging, don't you hear that scraping sound on the roof of our car, almost a clanking? Tell me, where is all this going to lead us! But I just wanted to explain why the landscape that is suitable for a natural theater cannot be described, why we may not be able to describe it! Because if we begin with such academic methods, we will arrive back in no time at our parochial municipal theater operetta mentality, and under the pretext of building a natural theater, we will immediately have changed the suitable landscape into at best a medium-sized spa garden with tasteless fountains, several inevitable little art nouveau public lavatory palaces set up fifty meters apart, and of course, set against an embankment, an open-air theater in the form of a stairway leading upward through a tastefully arranged imitation ancient amphitheater, and we don't want that kind of thing, do we? What we want is to grow with open minds into a landscape-nature that itself approaches us with an open mind, and in it to represent the world as it should be, until at last it comes to be as it should . . . For that purpose we will need the cooperation of all available qualified employees, all will find fulfillment here, and everyone will be within spitting distance of all his unfulfilled dreams.

And just to show you that I'm serious about this project, my dear fellow, I'm going to introduce a man to you, he's sitting over there and not saying much, do you see him, the man over there, good morning, how are you? our future set-designer. Until now, you didn't work for very nice people, did you? you know, this man has spent, we're actually going to have to say sacrificed, his entire life up till now designing his former employer's garden, and he must have turned that garden into a real marvel.

Didn't all the neighbors from near and far gather more and more frequently outside the garden wall to look into your garden, to discuss its beauty in a loud and lively fashion, not only during the day, but also during the night, as they usually stayed there and kept on looking at it, because even in the darkness the impression must have been bewitching?

In fact, this man busied himself not only as a botanist, but also in a limited way as a very artful zoologist, by installing in the trees and shrubs and bushes a huge number of nests of the most diverse sorts of fireflies and glowworms from all over the planet, which is why every evening at dusk the garden began to glow with a shimmering light from millions of luminescent insects floating up whirring flickering in a very certain order predetermined by him, whereas by day all the different kinds of butterfly folk he could find made the air over the garden tremble with their ornamental fluttering. However, when more and more admirers continued coming from near and far, even after the wall had been made higher, the owners found the public gatherings embarrassing and obtrusive and felt threatened, their peace was being disturbed by people from the neighborhood whose compulsion to view the garden was almost as if they had been hypnotized, so that once they had begun, it would have been impossible for them to interrupt their continual viewing of the garden, and sometimes some of them even climbed over the wall into the garden, so that the owners felt physically attacked, and one day they gave their gardener instructions to dig over and destroy the garden again, didn't they, and as a conscientious person you naturally carried out their orders and destroyed your entire life's work.

Whereupon they then dismissed you, didn't they, saying that, as anyone could see and as judged by an industrial tribunal, you had allowed the garden to completely decompose in the shortest time. Fortunately, he met me soon afterwards through the channels of the job office. This man possesses skills that are indispensable for us. We will employ him as a landscape gardener for an entire area, and then everyone in the neighborhood, the country, or even the whole continent should gather around here, the whole world, to view our work: we have never yet been bothered by our audience!

All people will be required to help, everyone would be important, especially you, please think about it, I would do everything for you, I wouldn't even shrink from a production of your unperformable wind-machine opera, the wind itself would play the part of your wind machines, look over there, for example, that mountain range, I would have you knock numerous adjacent horizontal tunnels of varying widths into such a mountain range and then from inside the tunnels drive vertical shafts upward into the plateau, you understand what I'm getting at, I mean a gigantic polyphonic mountain flute complex, a mountain flute choir whose finger holes on the plateau, at least as big as manhole covers, you know, would have to be hydraulically opened or shut from a central machine stand that you would operate, so that when the wind blows through the mountains and thus through the tunnels and shafts, you would decide which notes it would sound as it left these mountains, when it crosses the plain in the direction of the city . . .

But, Director, where do you see mountains here, where?

Over there, don't you see the occasional gray glimmer from the stone ridges?

But those aren't mountains!

Well what else would they be?

No, Director, those aren't mountains, those are holes, yes sir, almost craters, over there, you are quite right, a considerable number of them are bored into the plain like huge bomb craters.

And then why do I see mountains and not holes like you do? Can you perhaps explain that to me in more detail?

Yes, indeed, Director, those are craters and holes, and what you see as mountains are just the inverse or reciprocal reflections of these holes, reflected up from their depths into the glassy air above the plain, see, very gray, almost transparent, but you also see those black or dark bulges of earth at the beginning of those reflection elevations, that's where the holes begin . . . you see!

Oh yes, oh . . . I think, unfortunately you really are quite right . . .

Yes, and what a wind has just come up there, see how it really whistles out of the holes and hisses vertically up out of the craters into the sky! Those are real kilometer-high whirlwinds! Whirlwind pipes from the bottom of the plain to high up where we can't see anything more, you see!

No, no, and no one believes that, rather, it's the opposite, that the wind from the sky bores down into the plain, see, the wind falls from the sky and is mirrored by the plain, reflected back up, which is how it bores these holes and craters into the plain . . .

Since when does a wind blow vertically from above or below? Isn't it common knowledge that wind comes horizontally from the directions north south east west or diagonally and passes over the region, but not from above . . . !

Oh, that may be what you believe, but you have no clue about this world, unfortunately, you know nothing at all about the true hidden workings of nature, don't you see over there now how that breeze is plunging down and striking the earth and being dashed to pieces in the grass down here and spraying apart into the whole world, don't you see the fur flying over that rise where the ball of air just hit in the center . . . ?

But no, that's because it is blown out, flung up out of the holes in the earth, and a wind like that develops the force of the glowing center of the earth when it flees the planet, and I advise you to be careful not to go too close to such holes, not that you would fall in, no, no, nothing like that at all, rather that you would be more likely to fly with it, to be flung out into the universe, but no one would even notice that, not even you, one would establish, and you too would simply establish that you were suddenly gone, had simply disappeared, vanished . . .

Mind you, holes like that whistle really loudly like bass tubas or ships' fog horns, you know, you can hear them from afar, listen now . . .

But those are ships floating up the river, no down the river to the sea, leaving the plain behind, don't you see the smoke rising from their smokestacks against the horizon . . . ?

No, no, that's one of those landscape mouths, out of which it sometimes smokes and steams and breathes, haven't you ever heard of them . . . ?

In any case, the sky here is so churned up and blown full of holes by the many winds, almost ripped to pieces, you said so yourself, Director, frayed, is what you said before . . .

Fissured would be the right word now, fissured like the landscape down below, fissured from the mutually reflected storms and hurricanes. From far away, the sea throws them across the land, through all the broken windows and doors of the horizons, back into the ocean on the other side of the continent . . .

What is our Fräulein Daniele doing now, have you already practiced today, where are you, yes where, I can't find you anywhere, what suitcase have you crept into today, come, just come out!

Now here is something to see, prepare yourself for something, and perhaps it will strengthen your resolve to come with us, when the time has come one of these days, maybe very soon, Comelli says to you while a rope is being stretched at a height of about three-quarters of a meter along the middle of the corridor the complete length of the train car.

There you are at last, Comelli greets a thin girl with flaxen hair, you don't need to be afraid, it's just us here, or do you want to start being coy about it, I'm asking you, what are you waiting for?

She is the most sensitive creature among us, Comelli explains to you, and pay attention now to what she'll have to show you!

In the meantime, Daniele has climbed onto the low rope—obviously she is a tightrope walker—and very relaxed, like every other tightrope walker, she adds to the boredom of the oldest equilibrium act by behaving, while simply walking along the rope in the middle of the train car corridor, as if she were in the gymnasium of a fine arts high school.

Even if she does that in the air over a village square, you think, no one will watch her, unless that gets better . . .

So, and now please pay close attention, says the director then as two people take the rope down, roll it up and put it away, as if that were the end of the practice.

Daniele, having returned to the previous starting point, buries her face in her hands as she concentrates intensely. Comelli calls out through the train car, I request absolute silence, and then everything is very still.

Again now, the tightrope walker climbs onto the rope, except that there is no rope there anymore, it was taken down beforehand, how is she supposed to continue? but she climbs up three-quarters of a meter into the air, first with her left leg and then also with her right leg, she is standing, yes indeed, she is standing three-quarters of a meter up in the air and is starting, exactly as previously on the rope, to move through the train car corridor at that height, as previously on the rope, except that she is doing it without a rope, without greater difficulty or swaying and without hesitating, perhaps just slightly more cautiously than before, it's as if she had an invisible rope under the soles of her feet, but there is obviously no such thing present, because as if to demonstrate that convincingly, several actors reach under her shoes as she is walking along and pinch the air under her heels, no there is really nothing there, just air, like everywhere else. Yes, and unfortunately she has also already very nimbly completed this walk and is now climbing down again, as previously, except now from a rope that is not present, doing so as if it were nevertheless necessary to jump down lightly from the rope, although she could also have left the air diagonally and more comfortably by going down a few steps or over a sloping plane, if she can otherwise walk in the air, but apparently she can only cross through the room at this one place in the air where the rope was previously stretched, or is that just part of her act?

You are probably asking yourself now how she does that, says Comelli then, applauding together with all the others, and you are flabbergasted, yes how does she do it, what do you think? Quite simply and smoothly, she just places herself on the rope that she has made so intensively in her head that for her it really exists. With her thoughts she has drawn it out ahead of her, so that the soles of her feet then glide easily over it and her entire *Gestalt* is carried through the air by her own thoughts, on the rope of her imagination. At present, in order to be capable of such strong concentration and to be able to stretch an unbroken rope of air, she still needs a real rope beforehand and the feeling of walking over that real rope before she is then in a position to walk the same route in nothing but air, which is why her walks until now are still limited to distances the length of the longest available rope that we can stretch for her. But there will come a time when she no longer needs this prior practice run, but will be able to walk through the air of any street on the rope of her imagination, walking away if necessary for days or weeks through the atmosphere over the continent, the country, the countries, on the rope she has stretched ahead of herself in her thoughts, and hopefully she won't ever lose her way in the confusing corridors and tubes of the weather administration . . . Yes, and if you reach out very attentively, you will actually be able to notice a somewhat stretched, slightly rope-like thickening in the air where she passed over it . . .

Stop, Comelli calls out to the two people who were starting to make motions as they had before when they took down the rope and rolled it up, as if they now wanted to take down the air rope as well.

Take hold of that, he says, come, I'm asking you, please take hold right here, so that you see what I mean! Yes, and you reach into the air at that place and there really is something to feel there, the air feels thicker to the touch, almost wound or bound like a tube, the fibers of air form a long drawn out sheaf, but there is nothing to see. Nevertheless, when you let the tube of air glide through your hollow fist as if to wipe it off, you can easily feel the thickening in the air the entire length of the corridor.

Yes, you are right, Comelli, it's quite astonishing!

See, I told you, he says, and now he asks the two at the other end of the train car to take down the air rope and roll it up . . .

But it is as if Daniele has been swallowed by a suitcase again. The director is right, you think, one day she may climb up through the air on the rope ladder of her imagination, all the way to the trembling flashing weather intersections on the shores of the atmosphere. She may walk across cloud tracks through the sky tent, past the crumbling ruins of a mausoleum for an unsuccessful sirocco, and then traverse the whirlwind that bends far away, curved outward above everything, the whirlwind that is continually stretched out through all the ether as an invisibly vibrating net tent, high over all horizons.

All day long a milky hazy sail has been hanging in front of the sun, always moving along with it; probably it is firmly screwed on to it. Unfortunately, it doesn't cast a shadow, quite the opposite, it is able to strew the heat and light down on us as if concentrated by a magnifying glass on this very point on the planet. It offers us no protection from the scorching sun, but perhaps it serves the sun, perhaps the sun planned it just recently, well in advance, as an umbrella against us and the detrimental influences of its satellites.

More and more frequently we see wooden stands on the plain whose sense and purpose we have been trying to figure out for a long time. Sometimes they are only wooden fragments like horizontal bars, but sometimes they are completely developed bedsteads turned toward the sky, carried in each case by four strong stakes or posts jammed into the ground. Well, we think, they are there for the convenience of people going for walks at night who suddenly feel exhausted, so that before they collapse they can simply climb up and lie down on one of them, well, and certain scraps of material or remnants of material seem to support that theory; fastened to the posts, they flutter in the wind and serve as blankets in the night. Nonsense, people reply to that, those are simply horizontal bars on which the province's gymnasts practice for the championships.

What, those are supposed to be horizontal bars, and where then are the gymnasts, where? You see, there's not a single gymnast in sight, because those are frames for beating carpets, nothing else, moth-eaten plush bedside rugs have already been lying on them in those gardens for ages, fluttering in the wind, swinging through the sky, and it's a bit much to call that sort of thing gymnasts!

But ladies and gentlemen, what are you talking about; it is the greatest archaeological treasure in the country, the remains of a people who died out many thousands of years ago. The members of that tribe laid their dead to rest on their wooden stands there under the open sky in consecrated areas that, on pain of immediate death, could only be entered by select privileged people. These consecrated areas spread out further and further, so that one was forced to reallocate more and more areas of the living as consecrated land for the dead, in order to be in the position to continue to show the necessary respect for the memory of the dead. But with the passage of time, when the lands of the dead had taken possession of almost all the remaining land of the living, the privileged people found it necessary to ask the common people to spread out into the neighboring countries, to conquer those countries in war, in order to gain the required new territories for laying the dead to rest. And soon, thanks to the overpowering military effectiveness the common people were able to develop, mainly because the privileged people had convincingly fanned the flames of their fanaticism about death, they had overthrown the entire continent. And to the privileged people, including above all the economists and industrialists who had schemed their way up into that class, who attained an ever more breathtaking precision in the building of stands for the dead that were manufactured in their stands for the dead factories, the area of the entire continent seemed to be required for laying the dead to rest, so that from that time forth, on pain of death, there was no area where anyone could set foot. Whereupon most of the population had to bring themselves to build ships, to embark, which involved the greatest difficulties because the wood that would have been needed for shipbuilding turned out to have already been largely clear-cut for the erection of stands for the dead. That explains the flimsy method of shipbuilding that necessarily followed, as a result of which many people who sailed away to discover new continents capsized and drowned in the storms on the open sea. Only a few of them succeeded in discovering new land, which had become absolutely necessary for the further honorable laying to rest of the dead. Gradually, all the continents that were still unknown at that time had been discovered, on which then the whole development continued as previously, and went on until no one could set foot on any larger area of land. And the very last people who were still searching for new land that didn't exist anymore anywhere, that simply could not exist anymore anywhere, wandered about aimlessly on all the oceans of the planet and died in the storms at sea. Only a very few of them, who had been cast up on those tiny islands that aren't even shown on the most exact sea charts, still remained at the end. But the fact that they had to bury their dead without ceremony in the oceans, instead of laying them to rest in tracts of land that could only be entered by the privileged people, robbed them of all remaining hope. You see, the privileged people had always known how to make the other people believe that they, the privileged people, were hard on the heels of the secret of death. Since we have no authentically valid record of these very last stalwart people, other than the stands you see that remain over there, one can assume that the business with the stands caused them to decline and wither away until they had finally dissolved in the air, or in the roaring of the storms.

Who told you that? How did you get taken in by such nonsense! Horizontal bars, to be used at best for beating carpets! Don't you see? how the people there wash and dry their curtains between the scaffolding, bedside rugs . . .

That's enough talk now of bedside rugs, gymnasts and horizontal bars, frames for beating carpets, and other mystifications! This thing about cleanliness stinks to high heaven. Those are scarecrows, not beanpoles, quite simply scarecrows, what else? And one can even see the people decoratively fastening the different colored cloths and scraps of material, sometimes sailcloth too, to the things made of wooden poles, to the crosswise and lengthwise beams of the scarecrows that are set up here for viewing and for sale, as you see. It is predominantly the world-famous scarecrow dealers who live in this region, every child knows that! Some of them have in the meantime advanced almost to the point of being able to develop the usual traditional scarecrow constructions into figures that more and more closely resemble sailboat masts, yes, some of them have really gotten as far as building a proper sail, at least the rigging, and a very small number of them have already built the requisite boats underneath, or the richer businesspeople among them buy the prefabricated boats in the city and screw their scarecrow sails on top of the finished boats, in which they then depart for the river or avail themselves of the dense inland canal system on the other side of the sky that we cannot see from here. So the lakes, rivers and canals of the plain are increasingly heavily used by scarecrow boats, in which, if one is well informed of the unalterable legal rules of wind tunnel traffic, one can also, as is well known, use a scarecrow that is several meters tall to get down to the shore of the sea through the mouth of the river. To sail through the country with huge scarecrows, often, too, as you see here, through such parts of the plain where it proves necessary to erect scarecrows, then to sail on the river through landscapes whose surface is covered with carefully worked out colorful patterns of the unalterable chains of scarecrow systems . . .

The setting up of scarecrows really does seem to be of vital significance in this region, because in the air, in the low mountains of the sky and its protected valleys of light, you see an unbelievable number of fowl fluttering through the remains of the clouds. You see these constantly feathered vibrations in the air reflected here from the edge of the curved promontory far away over there. One might almost think that these waves of air that come rolling over are feathered with afternoon light. But do you see the huge flock now that is approaching the railroad embankment? Doesn't that look like a ruffled black tubular structure, fleetingly drawn with a thick quill pen on a huge piece of drawing paper pasted onto the ether? Increasingly cuneiform, it is coming toward us, cutting a big slit into the somewhat furry transparent skin of the plain, yes, plowing an ever deeper furrow ahead of it through the skin of the landscape, as if the flock, having just invaded this area, immediately claimed right of ownership of the entire visible region, really taking the skin off it, simple—interesting, isn't it—don't you find it all rather remarkable . . . ?

Oh, please, shut . . . Watch out!

Too late, you should have shut the window in time! Just don't tell me you didn't know what was coming at you, no, at us all, unfortunately, you, oh yes, you, you queer bastard, with your head shrunk by poisoned well water, you son of a lesbian scarecrow, of a hermaphrodite who happened to be straying through the steppe! Have you heard me?

Heard you. Yes sir.

Several individual members of the flock fluttering toward us and passing over the train have mistakenly strayed through the open window and are beating their wings through the entire train car, it's not pleasant, something like this makes people nervous right away because they're always afraid of getting their ears boxed by the powerfully beating wings, and dust whirls up, thick air, so that we can hardly see each other!

Oh yes, and how these beasts stink, do you notice now!

Unfortunately, yes, unfortunately, in comparison, even a pigsty smells like perfume, yes?

Yes, they must be carrion-eaters, you can smell that, although they don't seem much like vultures, they're much fatter and heavier, and probably stupider, because as you see, these carrion birds can't even find their way out of the window, and that can cause serious problems, oh dear! Something has to happen soon, somebody should do something immediately, because it can't keep on like this!

Yes, and something does happen, because the two physically strongest members of the ensemble have already gotten up and are trying to shoo the carrion birds back out the window again, but without success, they simply can't find the way out anymore, whereupon the two men take some pieces of string out of their suitcases and start to capture the wildlife with it. That turns out to be easy in the limited space of the train car, yes, and gradually, one after another, their feet with the dangerous-looking claws are bound, then the wings are somehow bound together, and finally, what else is there to do, they are bound and tied and simply put up in the luggage rack, with the intention of taking the carrion birds out of the train car at the next stop, untying and releasing them. Hopefully the train will stop soon, some are thinking, because the stench of those feathers is almost unbearable. Soon we'll have to vomit, and then, in addition to the stench of the birds, there would be the stench of what several artists have thrown up. The mysterious grandeur of the iconology of their stomach contents would be pasted on the train car walls.

Others are of an entirely different opinion. Why let them out again? How foolish! A godsend! Don't release them! Take them with us! First into the dressing rooms. And after the end of the performance, into the hotel. In the hotel room, we can set up the gas stove and roast them for dinner. A good poultry meal. They're so well-built! There's certainly some meat on them! Or not? The few still tolerable restaurants in the neighboring city are outrageously expensive; we can't afford to go there anymore . . . So we can spare ourselves the search for a place to eat. Before going to sleep, a free poultry dinner, yes, prepare the birds! In the room! The gas stove functions perfectly! And cutlery, we can borrow that from the storeroom! Not the slightest problem . . . !

Of course that idea is rejected with indignation by the majority of the ensemble. Aside from the smell of the fowl, who would want to do the slaughtering?

Right away, if you want, right here and now on the spot!

Just because you want to doesn't mean that you can, without having the blood spray around the hotel room on the walls, beds, carpets, and then you would still have to pluck the birds, that's hard work, no, no, this downy dirt from their feathers would soon be distributed throughout the hotel, and then the roasting, which might take several hours, because this sort of carrion bird, I can assure you, has flesh tougher than hard rubber. And then the danger of fire when the gas stove starts to spit . . .

The plain, undulating past outside is now like a yellow sea with flying fish leaping up from it, as if green grasshoppers wanted to try to save themselves by leaping into the air above the surface of the water, but always fell back again into the wavy, undulating, wilting reedy undergrowth of the endless ocean.

Sometimes galloping riders from better times stand there, ossified by the air into monuments as they rode, impeded by the light in their eyes as they headed toward the sun, gripped by the forests of grass all around that attached to their hooves.

A few mountain ranges wave from a great distance, as if afloat on a mirror, swaying toward you from the far shore of the late afternoon that is streaming away.

One could think the landscape had stood still in the window. If you look out the window now, you have to be careful that your head doesn't get stuck in the plain or your eyes drown while looking at the region.

One could think the plain was traveling with the train at the same tempo, because the picture in the window more and more closely resembles a landscape photograph hung live in the frame.

Maybe the train has simply stopped, look!

Yes, you think so too, the train has stopped, and how briskly the steady wind is driving the light around from hill to hill, and what a healthy, pulsating, changing light the landscape gets from fresh air! In many places, by comparison, the light rots, hangs sluggishly over the ground in permanent calm and gets dull. Here, though, fresh lighting is always blowing toward us, and in a sort of vibrating twilight the afternoon is blown through the village outside.

Isn't that the place I wanted to go to, yes, I have to leave you now, unfortunately, I'm going to get out, good-bye, and many thanks for your pleasant company . . . !

Oh no, please don't do that! The train is moving, don't you feel the clattering floor, and how it's traveling!

What nonsense! It's standing still, the train is standing still, and would you leave this gentleman alone, he can make up his own mind whether he has to get out here or not!

Again you say good-bye, but are held back, oh no, please not that, and the consequences are impossible to imagine. Questioningly, you look at Kalkbrenner, who agrees with you, yes, get out, I think this really is the village where your girlfriend lives!

Oh no, don't get out, please not that!

What nonsense, the train isn't moving, why shouldn't he get out, leave him alone!

So, I'm getting out now. All the best to all of you in future . . .

All right then, if you absolutely must, then do exactly as you want, but getting off a moving train has not yet saved anyone very much time . . . !

Oh yes, I think the man is quite right, it's better if you don't get out, I think, a lot has changed recently, so perhaps it's better if you don't . . . ! Yes, the train, it's moving, it's quite obviously moving again, although the picture of the landscape in the window is motionless as before! But it's moving, one can just feel it, the train is moving! Yes, it's best if you sit down again right away!

Yes, but usually, when one travels by train, it's a big mistake to think the train is really moving.

But of course it's moving, you do feel it, don't you!

No, it's not moving. If you look carefully under the wheels, you can see that it's just the track screwed firmly to the carpet of the landscape that is being pulled away. But you're claiming that the train is moving, don't make me laugh!

Yes, yes, you're right, but this discovery can be dangerous! For example, some time ago a colleague who was traveling with us, an excellent sculptor, looked out the open window at a similar moment and was so fascinated by the plain gliding past that he leaned his upper body and head farther and farther out the window and called out THAT'S IT! YES, THAT IS IT. I'VE BEEN LOOKING FOR THAT FOR THE LONGEST TIME! The sculptor, as befits his profession, was continually on the lookout for THE IDEAL FORM. He had of course never found it anywhere, but had always just about found it. Suddenly, in the midst of the region whizzing past, he thought he had discovered THE FORM, which is why he called out YES, THAT IS IT, YES, THAT'S IT AT LAST! And he stretched his upper body and head farther out the window, so that from here inside the car one could only still see his bottom, with his pants pulled tight around it because of his bent posture. But as one heard him call out once more in the streaming air YES, THAT IS IT, his head was cut off his upper body exactly at the neck by a telegraph pole that was flitting by at that very moment.

The man had obviously neglected to read carefully the sign affixed under the window with the inscription DO NOT LEAN OUT . . .

No, that wasn't it. He had realized that the train had never left the station, but had always just stood still, and that it had always been the landscape moving past us, that the region threw itself past us, leaving us behind it, and he had felt the need to travel on together with the region in which he thought he had found THE IDEAL FORM, he thought he could finally leave the standing train behind him with the help of the area that was gliding past. But unfortunately only his head traveled on with the landscape, the rest of his body stayed behind with us in the standing train, after the landscape outside had torn his head off, you know, so that its remaining supporting structure, although snapped off on top, still dangled for a long time over the window ledge, with his pants still pulled tight across his bottom . . .

Bare trees run past and wave so far in through the window that it seems it's not you moving past them, but them in the landscape leaving you, reaching in through the lowered windows in the vehicle's wall to brush your faces in farewell. The landscape is rolled slowly past, is pushed past, clattering.

But now many of the trees have raised the crippled tips of their chopped-off limb stumps, waving their threatening fists angrily in all directions—but mainly at you.

How pushy! How presumptuous!

As if it was our fault that the next to last government of this plain out there not only tore the clothes off their bodies but also left their underwear in tatters!

How pitiful it is when such a region is so unrelenting in heroic shamelessness!

Yes, yes, that's how it is when a landscape loses its self-control!

Now the train dives through an area where the tube of light is quite stale and decayed, sways into a populated region, first huts, then houses, yes, that is already the neighboring city whose dimly shimmering outskirts one has unfortunately already reached, surprisingly quickly, much too quickly, what a pity, how gladly one would have continued traveling in the train, have remained sitting here, being moved forward.

I can well understand that, says Comelli. One often finds things bearable only because one is continually fleeing from the conditions one left behind, one is moving on, traveling through the country as much as possible, with the sole accompanying illusion that one has found oneself on a lifelong sightseeing tour through a completely foreign land that is none of one's concern, because no one could bear the conditions in his native land without immediately having to emigrate. You know, we traveling artists have perhaps become somewhat strange over the course of time—when we aren't being continually moved through the country, nothing else remains for us but to move ourselves through the country as quickly as possible. Because when the landscape doesn't move around us of its own accord, we have to hurry it on ourselves.

Yes, someone added, because isn't everything that is considered native simply forced on us by a so-called native land, without our first being asked, whereupon we feel legally obligated to have unconditional feelings of home, and with the rope of the country's borders, we strangle the development of the most intimate and essential utopias . . .

The actors prepare to leave the train car and take their suitcases, boxes, and sacks down from the luggage rack.

Delightedly, Comelli remarks to the impresario, who seems to have kept himself somewhere in the background for the entire trip, in an abandoned corner of the train car, that they have arrived right on time after all and can stage without difficulty the performance for which they were engaged, and now he hopes for continuing good collaboration. But the impresario, for his part, does not seem at all delighted by this conciliatory gesture that is offered to him, quite the opposite, he speaks of the appropriate time to terminate his contract, which has just come up right now, he has been thinking of doing so for the longest time, and now is the moment when one can best separate peacefully in mutual harmony.

But why, in God's name? asks Comelli astonished and shaken.

It's too bad, under such prevailing circumstances, to continue on, answers the impresario.

But under what circumstances?

Quite simply, the prevailing ones.

But what prevails?

It seems you still don't notice what is actually going on around you, or where you actually are, replies the impresario dryly, but as has already been said, you assume full responsibility for everything . . . !

Yes indeed, replies the director, and he assumes it gladly, that's just how it is, and if he, the impresario, no longer wants to, then he should forget it, one can get along without him. But nevertheless, sincere thanks once again for the superb organization, of this side-trip as well, he did a first-class job of getting it underway.

The railway embankment glides further into the city, through suburban factory sites crumbling in the twilight, very similar to those of the city we have come from, the early evening bells swallow the silhouettes into their gray veil.

It is a strange city you are diving into; you want nothing to do with it.

One hadn't stopped in any village en route, or had one? You couldn't get out anywhere, or did you overlook the station? So you'll have to take a train back that stops on the way.

Already the train is gliding into the steel cavern of the terminal vault, with its steel roof of transverse arches supporting wire glass surfaces stretching toward each other, filtering the red sunset and immersing the train station in a rusty dome of light.

You say good-bye to Comelli and all the others, thanking them for having let you travel with them free of charge and for their pleasant company.

Until next time then, says Comelli, see you soon, I hope, when we all set off on our new project, you already know you have to come along, you are urgently needed, I insist on your further collaboration, can't do without you, note that!

You watch the artists gradually getting off the train and let them go first. The birds are taken down from the luggage rack and carried out onto the platform. No sooner are they untied than the animals, squawking happily, flutter up into the high vaulted ceiling of the train station, into the highest wire glass domes. They alight on the various steel rods, clinging on with their claws, and soon make their contribution by filling the entire vaulted ceiling of the National Railway with their quavering chirping. Or do they solidify into cast-iron heraldic beasts, as though they have already been crouching up there for ages?

You are still watching the actors as they strap on their luggage, and in spite of their heavy loads, they are almost hopping as they glide away through the lobby into the strange city.

Kalkbrenner has stayed behind.

I'm riding back with you, he explains, if you'll allow me, I can't stand the company of these people any longer, especially the director's voice. His plans turn into chaotic, lovely dreams and have already gotten stuck there. I can't listen to that any longer . . .

So the two of you go to the information booth to make enquiries about when the next train goes back to the capital city of the country.

It's convenient that there are always hot dog stands next to the information booths in train stations. They provide you with the time-saving opportunity to have a stand-up meal while waiting for the person on duty to appear behind the glass wicket.

People say that the absence of someone at the information booth stands in a direct relationship to the difficulties of the hot dog stand leaseholder in earning his livelihood, because in order to survive he has to sell a certain number of wieners per day, otherwise he is ruined and might as well close the stand. The information booth usually tends to be empty when the wiener stand operator has not yet sold enough wieners, and is only occupied again after relatively substantial wiener sales, so that financially the day has been a success, because just the rent for a stand is so high that without selling a certain number of wieners, the wiener stand can't even cover its costs and goes bankrupt. That's why the wiener stand operator may have made a permanent pact with the person or persons on information duty to be temporarily absent for longer periods of time when wiener sales are down than when there is a relatively normal consumption of wieners by the travelers; it may even be that the respective wiener stand operator is sometimes identical to the person on information duty, who then only opens the information booth when he has already sold enough wieners, or when, after the wiener sales adequately cover the costs, he can now and then also alternately find the time to devote himself to answering a few questions that have arisen at the information booth.

The suspicion is almost confirmed, because hardly have we eaten our wieners and each drunk a second glass of beer than the wiener stand starts to close, and already the person on duty at the information booth turns up behind the glass wicket and inquires, as you are half still returning the empty glasses and half already turned toward him, about your particular question.

When does the next train go back?

Go back where?

Back to the capital city, where we just came from.

What? to which city; he doesn't understand what you want.

Surely you are able to tell us the departure time for the next train, or is that too difficult?

Yes, that is indeed difficult, and he is hardly ever asked that sort of question, it's the first time today that he's had a question of that nature.

But that's why he's there, so that he can answer questions about the departure times of trains, or should one restrict oneself to just asking him the time of day?

No, no, he does answer that sort of question and even finds it quite normal, but nevertheless, that was the first time today that he got that question.

Then you have just come on duty, that's why you're hearing this question for the first time today, but in the coming hours you will probably be asked questions like that and similar questions hundreds and thousands of times, and you'll also have to answer them.

No, he doesn't think so at all, otherwise he'd really lose his mind. You want to go back to the capital city on the next train, well, well, but to get there you don't need a train, you just need to leave the train station through the hall over there.

I think, you think, that one has to explain everything to this man in much greater detail, he's slow to catch on; so you explain to him at length how you got here on such and such a train, and that you had actually intended to get out in a village along the way, but unfortunately the train you had taken did not, as you had hoped, make local stops, which was certainly your fault for not having studied the schedule more carefully, and in a word, you now want to travel back . . .

Now I know what's the matter with you, says the railway official behind the wicket. Excuse me for having just now understood what you want, but why didn't you say that right away, and then we wouldn't have had such an unclear discussion. The two of you, as well as all the others who were traveling with you on that train, have fallen victim to a very regrettable technical mishap on the part of the railway: the train in which you were riding had to make a loop out there in the middle of the plain and turn around, because the track in the direction of the neighboring city has been interrupted, is not negotiable, you understand, and that's why the train that departed from the south track here in the main train station or the southeast train station, as it is technically called, made an about-face loop from the south track to the east track and arrived here in the east train station, whose terminal track is laid out at a right angle to the terminal track of the south train station, it came back again, and you thought you had arrived in the train station of the neighboring city! Do you understand that? No? Well, you rode out into the plain from the south train station, turned around there and came back here into the east train station, perhaps you would have preferred to come back into the south train station, but I can't help that! Of course you are entitled, with the same train ticket, which I hope you haven't thrown away yet, to now go through the east wing of the train station into the south wing of the train station and to depart from the south track with the next train traveling in the direction of the neighboring city. But you can't do that until the stretch into the neighboring city is freed up and passable again, which will hopefully be soon, in the course of the coming hours, days, or weeks, and that, without having to buy a new ticket, gentlemen, now there's a suggestion, isn't it? That's a reasonable offer that I hope you intend to accept, don't you? And if you have any more questions about train departures from the south track, please study one of the timetables that are clearly and conspicuously hung up here, and don't bother me anymore in the course of the coming hours! I can understand you, you arrive here and think you have arrived in the neighboring city, maybe you think the train station in the neighboring city looks so confoundedly similar to the east train station here that you confused the two with each other! But in future, be so good as to get your information about the south track at the information booth for the south track, I work for the east track and am sick and tired of the bothersome questions from people about the south track, and if you want to know something about the south track, then please go over to the south track information booth, there someone will really tell you what's what . . . !

So to find out when the south stretch of track into the neighboring city will be passable again, the two of you go out of the east wing into the south wing to the information booth for the south track.

The wicket isn't occupied, but you see a railway official standing at the wiener stand beside it, eating a wiener. So the two of you join him, and each of you orders yet another wiener and yet another beer. Thinking that the railway official just now eating a wiener is the person on duty for the south track, you turn to him and ask how long the stretch of track to the neighboring city will be out of service.

Yes, gentlemen, as happens at least once a month on the south track, the line to the neighboring city has been interrupted, made impassable, because once again a few half-wild crazy inhabitants of the plain have been suffering from lack of wood, in spite of the hot season, and have felled the overhead cable poles along the railway line, together with every last telegraph pole, but not only that; we're already used to that sort of thing; the pole maintenance crews are continually working on the entire stretch of track erecting new poles, our people are excellently equipped, know how to erect new masts even on a relatively long stretch of track in a short time, and have often repaired it again in the course of an afternoon or even, if you will, an hour or a few minutes. But in the present case, these half-wild crazies didn't limit themselves to just felling the masts, we wouldn't even have mentioned such a little thing, no, these wood martens that were at work today must have been particularly wood deficient, because they also undertook the laborious task of unscrewing the wooden ties, to which the rails are attached, pushing them away from the gravel, pulling them out from under the rails and removing them, a heck of a lot of work, but it must have been accomplished at such a speed that not even our fleet of gliders that is continually flying over the stretch noticed anything, they do try to stop the felling of the poles at least a little, even if not entirely. They must have done that in no time at all, working like mad, and to think that they went to all that effort, although that riffraff otherwise shies away from work like no other rabble in the country, if I had my say, I'd know how to eliminate them; first of all, you'd have to capture them together, to clean, clear the plain of them, and then smoke them out. Quarter the unkempt protestors to civilization in barracks and teach these nature fanatics, this riffraff, how to do honest work, you understand! Take strong actions, strong actions right through the plain! As far as repairing the present damage is concerned, that is, replacing the ties, that can take a while, that can definitely take a while, because we weren't at all prepared for something like that.

That sort of thing never happened before, and if we therefore do not have enough replacement ties at our disposal, they'll have to be ordered and manufactured in the railway carpenters' workshop, lathed, that takes time, you know!

There's one thing I don't understand, though, it isn't clear to me, I can't get it into my head: What do they do with so much wood? It's hot outside, no one needs to have the heat on in this hottest of all summers, and to lay in supplies for the winter, that is, to be already thinking of the winter now in the summer, quite frankly, I think these hordes are too dull-witted for that, they don't have brains enough to come up with the idea that they should now make provisions for the cold times that may come, they call something like that reactionary and bourgeois! They just live, as has been proven, from hand to mouth, instead of from summer to winter; so what's behind it, isn't that mysterious? One could almost suspect them of sabotage!

Well now, Kalkbrenner interjects, maybe these people want to build a bridge somewhere or erect a hut, or wouldn't railway wood be suitable for such purposes?

Very suitable! the wood, railway wood is very suitable, railway wood is one of the best woods you could wish for, there's nothing better than railway wood, aside from its enormous calorific value, it is capable of resisting all unpredictable moods of the weather on this continent. Railway wood is extremely suitable for everything, in contrast to these people, who are suitable for nothing; at best, these savages might haul the stolen wood up to the top of a mountain to light a big fire in the heights, but no, not even that, that would fail because they're much too lazy to carry such masses of wood up a molehill, no, these people are stupider than the wood they have stolen! Build a hut? For that, those so-called starry-eyed idealists are much too dense! And a bridge? Never ever! Them and a bridge, unthinkable! Say, do you seriously think those people are capable of building a bridge? asks the railway official, testing us.

Oh yes, you reply, why not, after all, they have to erect some sort of shelter, have a roof over their heads to protect them from the rain, the sun, and to be able to have a place to sleep.

Why shouldn't they build a bridge across a medium-sized river, says Kalkbrenner, something like that can't be all that difficult; they might even be using the stolen railway wood right now to erect a footbridge across an inaccessible ravine smoothed by the air of an abyss, or they're erecting a new log cabin where they can proceed with a school, or an observation tower, which they can perhaps make very easily out of such railway tie wood, a sort of raised hiding place for hunters, you know, so that they can look out better and look into the distance of the plain, so that they can recognize an approaching storm in time from afar, for example, or the approaching foam of the tide of an ocean breaking into the plain . . .

You really believe those people are capable of that? I find that very interesting!

What's so special about it?

You know, gentlemen, I'm all too familiar with this riffraff, have known them for ages, I run into them daily in the context of my work for the National Railway, because unfortunately, often enough, they take a train, without ever having bought a ticket, it goes without saying, but then the railway's facilities are left so filthy that cleaning the vehicles and equipment becomes the most nauseating task; not to mention the damage they have caused and continue to cause, but unfortunately I haven't yet succeeded in calling the pack to account for it and arresting them! As a matter of principle, those people tear down the curtains from the train car windows, and their wives wear them as head scarves! As soon as they enter the compartment, the men, who get on the train with their knives already drawn for that purpose, cut off all the window straps and luggage nets! Of course everything they take is from the first-class compartments; it's not as if they would stoop to equip themselves with objects from the second-class cars! If you walk through one of these people's villages, you will see their wives standing around dressed only with National Railway curtains and National Railway seat covers that they have wrapped around themselves, and all the men wear only National Railway train car window strap belts around their hips! And the very latest thing: screwed onto the rotten wooden walls of their stinking cesspit outhouses you will find the soap mills they have removed from the garniture of our luxury sleeping-car washrooms! Not to mention the ashtrays unscrewed from the armrests, the clothes hooks taken down! Those people cut the luggage nets out of their frames en masse and then use them knotted together as fishing nets in the streams, rivers, and lakes, with which they fish the most magnificent specimens of rainbow trout out of the public bodies of water right under our noses, and of course, it goes without saying, without being able to produce a fishing license! But when I notice that a crank handle or a ceiling lining is missing—a very popular item that can be altered into nightshirts—or that a seat back, armrest or head rest has been torn out, and I want to confront them to make them pay for the damages, they have somehow gotten away, presumably through the window, even when the train is going at top speed, I can't explain it any other way, because I could turn the whole train inside out looking for them, but they're gone, there's nothing more to be seen of them. No, I've had it! I've really had it with that pack! And the two of you take the side of that criminal element with your benevolently supportive view! You egalitarians, you dangerous sympathizers! Well, you just go and pay them a visit, if you're impressed by their behavior! You'll see! Your eyes will pop out of your heads! They would just use their goddamn stolen shreds of National Railway seat-back covers to wave you right out of their villages! You two are making yourselves liable for prosecution for dangerously supporting and failing to prevent a crime, yes, yes, even for incitement to subversively cause severe damage to the National Railway Corporation! Do you know that? Right now I'd like to break a few worn folding-seats off the wall of the train car corridor and hit you soundly over the head with them! Or to clap two garbage containers with folding tables down over your skulls! Or better yet, to box your ears with the torn-off toilet lids from one of the third-class passenger cars that has had a trip through the marshy wasteland with these people! And finally, to wrap the two of you up in one of the circular towels stolen from the automatic dispenser in the National Railway urinal, and to keep rolling it around you until nothing more can be seen of you! To roll you away over the railway embankment! To tie you onto the rusted rails of a disused switching siding! so that you take note once and for all of what I've told you! But I won't do all that. Instead, I will simply walk away from you without a word of farewell. It's best, as a matter of principle, to just walk away from people like you without a word of farewell. Don't you dare to misinterpret any of the movements I may perhaps erroneously make as I walk away from you without a word or a farewell gesture from myself to you! I don't like that sort of misunderstanding at all and in a case like that I will not allow myself to be spoken to. Yes? So, gentlemen, I am extremely sorry to have had to make your acquaintance. I hope we never meet again. Prepare yourselves now for my departure without a word of farewell!

He actually does go away now, slinking very slowly, his head ducked, his hands stiff at his sides, probably not wanting to give the slightest cause for a movement to be misunderstood as a greeting on his part and for us to call back at him: Farewell, you did greet us now after all, farewell. Slowly, almost motionlessly, he moves away, almost as if he were standing still, sneaking away by the millimeter, so that to continue watching his departure without a word of farewell becomes somewhat of a strain, but Kalkbrenner is fascinated by the man, and makes the greatest effort to keep his eyes on him.

Of course we have to disapprove of what the man said just now, he explains, but the behavior he is demonstrating is worthy of our admiration. One can learn a lot from this person, especially now, because his departure without a word of farewell is exemplary, I have never yet been able to watch someone leave a place without a word of farewell with such perfection as this man! It is, Kalkbrenner continues to explain, not at all a disadvantage and also can't hurt if one knows exactly what the proper form is for departing from somewhere without a word of farewell. Should the occasion arise, one can then do so according to the regulations and without a mistake. A technically correct departure without a word of farewell has become a rare value these days. A departure without a word of farewell requires, above all, style, ambition, patience, and immense feeling in the movement of each body part, over which one has to have complete mastery, you understand, everything has to be in exactly the right place! Nothing can remain uncontrolled; rather, everything has to be completely under control. But people today have neither style nor control over their bodies, let alone their feelings, because they don't have any feelings, we won't even mention patience and generosity, it's people without character, a clan—but not related by blood—that neither knows how to leave a place without a word of farewell, nor is it in any position to approach a place! Lifeless riffraff! Part of a successful departure without a word of farewell is, above all, as one can now see, to a certain extent an exemplary posture, but no one even has that anymore today. From such a society as we now have here in this city, that neither departs from anywhere nor approaches anywhere, one can actually only depart without a word of farewell. But no one would even take any notice of that, which is why it remains a matter of complete indifference whether one now departs from these people here in the city without a word of farewell (or even with a word of farewell), or whether one remains among them here in the city without any kind of greeting. And because no notice will be taken even of that, everything that one does has become a matter of indifference, and because it makes no difference what one does, there is nothing more to do here. Therefore, as one always did anyway up until now, the best thing is to just carry on doing nothing.

You see this man here, Kalkbrenner continues, who still persists, unremittingly, as before, in departing from us without a word of farewell, in this stylish manner, with such skill, and does not intend to be finished with his departure for a long time yet! Please take a close look at him, at the exemplary position of his neck, for example! Can you tell me if you have ever before in your life had the good fortune to be able to meet a man who, in the course of a departure without a word of farewell, has been able to display such strong expression as that man there? No? I'm not surprised. The exemplary angle of his bowed head! That is remarkable. Yes sir! Nobody in this city can equal that man's performance, I would have to see it to believe it, you would have to show me a second person here who is as accomplished in the art of distancing himself without a word of farewell with no misunderstandings, you would have to search the entire state for several years to perhaps catch sight of a second person in the country who, in refreshing revival, knows how to depart without a word of farewell so outstandingly well and who can even begin to be a match for this man, can hold a candle to him! And there it is, one should observe this man very carefully for as long as possible; until, you think, he will finally have disappeared, have become an invisible point far back in the nave of the railway station cathedral, where the flocks of birds that have nested in the dome ornately decorate the steel scaffolding firmament with the finely engraved and encoded enigmatic heraldry of their accumulating excrement, and from day to day they paper it further, while imitating the police whistle concerts of the railway police with their hysterical singing that, locked in the hall, whirrs trembling through the twilit clouds of air. Yes, you think, and indeed the imitation is so exact and remarkably genuine that the singing of the songbirds often awkwardly puts the roving rail executives on stand-by duty into a completely useless but unavoidable long-lasting state of alarm. The railway officials searching for the unmistakable incessant trilling of their colleagues' request for back-up suspect that they are being called upon to finally enforce the regulations about the right to remain in the depressing wasteland of the waiting rooms, but time after time they would only be able to arrest the empty unusable rotten benches yawning with dirt. They have no idea that the false alarms are due to the flocks of birds. The blowing of the police whistles, however, makes such an impression on the birds that they are thinking of escaping some day into the far distance. When that happens, absolutely no one will be able to remember the cathedral organ of the sadly weathered railway station anymore. And these birds will then no longer ornately decorate the steel scaffolding firmament of the train station hall with the encoded enigmatic heraldry of their accumulating excrement, always so finely engraved. Instead, they will decorate the very firmament itself, and from day to day they will paper it further . . .

When you indicate to him that you are afraid of going home because people are probably still waiting for you there to bring you back to the asylum, he immediately offers to let you come home with him, says that would please him too, because then he wouldn't need to continue processing a bottle of schnapps by himself that he had already opened some time ago. But before you set out, you invite him into the café near the train station for another few glasses: You want to wait for HER once again, because you want to be there throughout one of the times of the evening that SHE mentioned to you, when SHE promised to come into the café before leaving from the train station to return to HER village for the night.

While on the way home from the train station to Kalkbrenner's place at the edge of town, you see the silhouettes of statues on the edges of the roofs of many buildings, their arms stretching vertically upward into the evening.

Do you see, you say to Kalkbrenner, how the figures up there on the roofs are pointing with such excitement up into the sky with their stone index fingers? Maybe they want to indicate that there'll be rain soon, all of us have wanted it for so long, and finally it has begun a long trip here and will soon bring us pleasant relief, the sky will become clear, and there will be relief from the heat we've been experiencing . . .

Nonsense, he replies, which one of them up there is pointing up into the sky? Who? No one. He doesn't see anyone, in his opinion, the figures up there on top of the roofs are busy, instead, supporting the edges of the domes of air and light over the roofs. The delicate evening sky is threatening to break into the houses, and they're trying to prevent it . . .

Or are they stone roof workers, you then suspect, workers who have ossified, together with their tools, while making improvements, because of their astonishingly slow working tempo, although they still diligently persist, their movements hardly visible. Perhaps one day they'll climb back down to us, when they have finished their work on the roof, in a few years.

Or fall down, Kalkbrenner replies, and shatter on the surface of the street down here, because these statues on the roofs are clearly contravening the relevant safety regulations: They have unlawfully neglected to tie themselves down! And that, although the trade union recently with self-sacrificing obstinacy got the resolution accepted that when working on roofs the workers must be tied on. And they think they're the exception. It would just take one strong gust of wind . . .

Beside the entranceways of tall apartment buildings you see huge arrays of doorbells that lead to the individual apartments, often hundreds of them in one building. The necessarily large number of such doorbell buttons outside the entrance has often led to the construction of a separate stand for the buttons, with horizontally or vertically affixed platforms of doorbells. It always reminds you of the stops on an organ, as you tell Kalkbrenner, and then you speak of a need arising in you that you can barely suppress any longer, to stop at such a building just once and to press all the buttons simultaneously, to use all the stops of the high-rise organ, causing the whole building to resound with a single great scream of bells. All the windows would suddenly be lit up, all the people in the building would leap up, all running at the same time to open their apartment doors, but then they would all find that there was no one outside wanting to be let in. In the stairwells they would all notice at the same time that all the neighbors to the left and right and across the hall and above and below them had opened their apartment doors at the same time as they had, to look for their visitors, also in vain. Did your doorbell ring too? they would then ask each other simultaneously. Yes, our doorbell rang too, they would answer simultaneously. Did no one come to your door either who could have rung the bell? they then ask each other simultaneously. No, there's no one at our door either, they then answer. Only you! How strange! Only you! they then call out to each other simultaneously. Didn't you accidentally ring our bell? they ask, all suspecting each other. No! Why would I have rung your bell? they all answer each other, and adding, why should I ring your bell? What would I want from you! Maybe you wanted to annoy me? Then they all blame each other together at the same time, and again and again they call out to each other: Yes, you probably only wanted to annoy me!

But never yet, you end your tale, have you found the courage to ring all the bells.

Kalkbrenner is obviously impressed, because you've hardly finished your story when he goes immediately to the next big array of doorbell buttons beside the next big entranceway, and right away you see him carefully putting the device into operation with both hands, arms, elbows, so that really not a single button remains unpushed.

But nothing happens.

Not a window lights up. There's no slamming of doors through the stories, no hysterical running through the corridors of the apartment tower. Everything remains unmoved and very quiet. Everything seems to have been in vain, despite Kalkbrenner's most careful efforts.

Maybe the doorbell system is broken, you say. Or the occupants have all ossified in their rooms and, locked in motionlessly, have turned to stone like their stone roofer statues on the edges of the roof.

It's turned off, says Kalkbrenner, naturally, turned off, overnight all the bells are naturally turned off, one doesn't want to be disturbed by night-time troublemakers like us ringing from sheer devilment. I can understand that. At my house, too, the bell always has to be turned off in the night. Sometimes even in the day. My wife can't stand the ringing. A lot of people want to visit me almost every night; I can understand why my wife doesn't want to listen to that anymore.

And he starts to talk about a time when he stood at the window in the nights and looked out, waiting for the shadows of his visitors, who then rang the bell in vain. In times before that, he still made the effort to go downstairs on these occasions to exchange a few words with them, to go on a walk with them through the nearby park, to discuss the problems that had arisen, but although I was as quiet as possible, he says, and moved almost silently, my sensitive wife was disturbed. The creaking of the stairs woke her up. My wife is a remarkably over-sensitive being; she constantly needs to be shown the greatest consideration, that's why I stopped the night-time walks with my visitors. After that, he tells me, he held barely audible conversations with his visitors who were standing under the window, stretching his hands out through the window grille to touch the hands and face of a beloved person outside. But he discontinued that as well, since almost all relationships that were independent of his marriage, he explains—his relationship to his wife was too dear to him—fell victim to a strict process of self-limitation. My wife, he says, describes herself as my anchor, she claims she has to shield me in a good way, and if she weren't at my side, I would probably long since have fallen apart. Nevertheless, she still silently suspects that I am deceiving her with the rest of the people who remain around me, and since I can't cure her of that suspicion, our relationship is sometimes stressful.

My visit, you say to him now, will be a disruption that won't have a good effect on her, maybe it's better if I don't come with you to your place. I could go to a hotel instead, or even go home . . .

No, no, he replies, fortunately she's away . . . My wife regards it as her most beautiful, most fulfilling, indeed overriding task in life to study me down to the last detail. For that reason, for the sake of her studies, she is almost always away. For the sake of her studies she comes back now and then, but just for the shortest time, only to disappear again as soon as possible for the sake of her studies . . .

At his house, you soon start to talk about the day, which has run its course in vain, and the fact that you weren't able to find HER, and consequently have no clarity about yourself and the beginning of your story.

I shouldn't have traveled with you, you say, it would have been better if I had gone away alone, then everything would have turned out entirely differently. Probably being in your company completely obscured my overview of the situation. The director, for example, had only my existence as a musician in mind, and remained completely indifferent to my much more urgent problems.

Your assertion, Kalkbrenner replies, is an insulting presumption. He has suddenly started talking forcefully, excitedly, as you have never heard him before, he is probably completely drunk, and how he swings the liquor bottle through the room!

The search for your girlfriend, he says, with whom you allow yourself to connect the mystery of your own life and its solution, just serves as a pretext for running away, in reality you didn't want to find her at all, instead, you avoided her; not that you didn't long to see HER again as you longed for nothing else, but the fact that she probably knows more about you than can be known to you, as you maintain, although you may simply have had the arrogance to interpret that in her pretty face, causes you to push yourself farther and farther away from her and thus also from yourself. This escape and search or fleeing search that you made for yourself, constructed for yourself, makes her almost as good as inaccessible for both of you. And in the context of your machinations, you have used and misused us and also me, we who you otherwise wouldn't deign to say hello to, as people to help you in your flight, as supernumeraries in your purposeful confession. You immerse yourself in it in order to show an interesting life-justifying purpose for your vegetating. Because the clarity that you allegedly seek would be much too common for you. You could have had it, today, why didn't you get off the train, can you still remember? but how gladly you let yourself be made to feel uncertain, and you sat down again. Yes, you might have obtained it, the clarity and the solution for all the puzzles of your existence, if only you had gotten out. But you were probably too afraid that you would have found her, your girlfriend, and that she would simply have told you that she not only doesn't know the slightest thing about you, but doesn't even want to. You were all too content to let yourself be made to feel uncertain as to whether you should get out at this point of your life, and you simply avoided doing so. But in order not to have to reproach yourself for having escaped yourself once again, you use me and us as a reason for your continuing indecision, as before, about the present hopeless condition of your existence. Who do you actually think you are? You probably think of yourself as the most brilliant of all scholars and philosophers, the sort of person who may exist sometime in the far distant future. Shortly before solving the last still unsolved mystery of this world and the reasons for it, he will delay the last intellectual leap time and again, postponing it farther and farther ahead, not because he is lacking the necessary curiosity, but because he cannot suppress his boundless fear that this entire world might in the end turn out to be a completely ridiculous, erroneous, almost divinely celestial joking cosmedy, a cosmic joke in the form of a really transcendental impertinence, and no one would want to continue living with this knowledge. If I were in your position and didn't know if I had tried to kill myself or not, I would go ahead and shoot myself right now, in front of you!

Here, he screams and opens one of the drawers in his desk. He takes out a Colt 45, black as a raven, and hands it to you.

Here, if you want to! The best way to be sure is to put it into your mouth. And if you really want to be on the safe side, fill it with water first. There is the door to the bathroom!

He empties the bottle of liquor to the last drop, and falls asleep.

The night's huge, violet-colored, glittering dragonfly wings snuggle up close to the roof truss of the building, making the darkness tremble as it breaks in at the window frames and starts to flutter!

You wake up lying on the carpet, Kalkbrenner beside you, snoring loudly. On this morning your head hangs so loosely, falling down from your upper body, and you suspect there is a coal mine in your stomach. The miners are still rescuing the last bits of coal and trying to flee up through the shaft of your gullet ahead of the firedamp, but from the top the owners of the mine force the attacking masses back down your throat again from the larynx. You go on tiptoe into the kitchen, where you take a bottle of liquor out of the fridge, put it to your mouth and try to take a few hefty swigs to counteract the whirling motion of the mine within you. Then Kalkbrenner wakes up too, his face very yellow, his whole body shaking. He pulls back the curtains in the living room. Outside a blue sky gloatingly makes fun of us and the few scattered houses and huts in the surrounding area. Nature, Kalkbrenner says, mocks us time and again, while still tolerating us within it.

Next to the house is a fenced-in area that attracts your attention because there is nothing in it but a lot of small brick stands. On closer inspection, they turn out to be chimneys about one and a half to two meters high rising out of the ground, and in the middle you see a brick chimney-stack about thirty or at most forty meters high. There is no smoke coming out the chimneys or the chimney-stack, and you wonder what purpose the stands serve. You think of the possibility of a building many stories high that is screwed down into the earth, using a large part of the surface of the earth as its roof. Where is the entrance? Outside, a father is going past with his children, and when one of his teenagers asks about the chimneys, he answers, yes, underneath them is hell, and the poor devil had his helpers erect the chimneys over the top, so he doesn't suffocate in the smoke of hellfire, and also so the fire burns properly, and when one of the other children in his care comments, well, but there isn't any smoke coming out of them, he explains, yes, at the moment the heat doesn't happen to be on in hell, probably the devil ran out of coal, and he had to hastily order more from the coal dealer, and when one of the children reflects to the father, yes, but what if the coal dealer doesn't give the devil any coal? the father answers, well, he can't do that, because then the devil will fetch him and let him, the coal dealer, freeze in hell.

Kalkbrenner turns on the tap in the kitchen to drink a glass of water, and the glass almost falls out of his shaking hand. He stares fixedly, captivated, at the powerfully hissing stream of water. Look here, he says, don't you see, here, do you see them? You don't know what he means. But do look here, he asks you to look as he directs your attention once again to the stream of water spraying powerfully into the sink, don't you see them, all the flies, these ants and wasps climbing with difficulty up the stream of water spraying down, and up here in the opening of the tap they creep in and disappear in the gap between the hole in the faucet pipe and the stream of water, I see them time after time, recently bees and bumblebees too, and once, last summer by a fountain, in the brightness of the wide spray of water streaming out of the fountain's water pipe, I even saw hornets and stag beetles laboriously climbing up and disappearing at the top in the entrance hole of the fountain water pipe, their wings glistening in the morning sunlight, here, do you see, the wings of these ants, and bees too, who are climbing up the stream of water, shining faintly like fireflies, and here are glistening ladybugs too, and some who can't make it to the top fall into the sink and disappear in the moss that is growing on the plates at the edge of the drain, light green moss, with frogs in between too, do you see, our water-pipes are full of insects' nests, says Kalkbrenner, the insects produce our drinking water in their nests, they hatch it.

You don't see anything. It occurs to you that he is actually experiencing everything he is talking about. He scratches his whole body, as if he wanted to chase away a mosquito or a wasp, he's probably hallucinating, his shaking is getting worse, the things he cannot help imagining make him feel nauseated and afraid. You begin to get worried about him, try to distract him from his hallucination and start talking about the neighboring piece of land outside the window. He actually surfaces for a brief while from his delirium, even laughs, yes, and so many people have been surprised by that. The puzzle is easily solved, he explains, the firm Hochriegl and Schlumberger has its underground champagne cellar there. Do you understand? In a champagne cellar gases and vapors are produced, some of them toxic, some of them highly explosive, and to make it nevertheless possible to enter the cellar at any time, they erected the chimneys and the chimney-stack, so that the sky, with the help of the chimney-stack, can suck all the vapors out of the cellar, so that there is always fresh air to breathe in the champagne cellar, yes, the sky takes this chimney-stack between its lips like a straw and through it, it slowly sucks the earth hollow. By the way, it's excellent, says Kalkbrenner, that you remind me of it, because today is Sunday and none of the people who work at the champagne cellar are here, so we could fetch ourselves a few bottles of champagne.

The openings of the chimney huts all have bars, no one can get in there, but on the outside wall of the chimney-stack you notice there are iron rungs about fifty centimeters apart, and you try to talk him out of his plan.

You can easily get up the outside, you say to him, up the rungs, but how do you intend to get down inside? you would at least need a rope that you would have to tie properly at the top. With a rope, you could glide down the inside of the chimney pipe, but aside from the fact that you, in your currently weakened state, could be blown down by the wind while climbing up the outside of the chimney-stack, you don't have a rope.

Why are you talking about a rope? he replies, of course you don't know anything about the iron rungs inside the chimney-stack that I can comfortably climb down and climb back up again.

Kalkbrenner has already arrived at the foot of the champagne cellar chimney-stack, and has also gotten past the first iron rungs. You see him slowly and carefully working his way up the thirty or forty meters. As he heads toward the refreshing mouthful he is expecting to enjoy, his climbing of the chimney-stack impresses you as being quite skillful. Do you really think it's the first time I've climbed up here? he calls back down to you. He is already quite familiar with this route. You see that he has already reached the top, you breathe a sigh of relief, now he will climb down the inside, you think, but no, instead of bending down and disappearing carefully into the hole, he stands up straight—if only he doesn't fall—and from up there he views the landscape spreading out below.

What a magnificent view, he calls down, it's never been this clear before, and now he can see very far away, even behind the horizon, and down there is the ocean—that can't be true—the ocean, and the smoke from the smoke-stacks of the ships that are gliding along between the swaying icebergs sleeping in the sun, and now, he calls out, do you hear it too, the foghorns have started a real wind concert, thrilling music that's being conducted from the lighthouse on the shore.

Just go get the champagne, you call back, because you're already very thirsty for it, whereupon he finally lets one foot down into the pipe hole of the chimney-stack as far as the first inner iron rung, then pulls his second foot in after it. You can still make out his upper body, and then he is swallowed by the hole in the chimney-stack. Then you hear him really yelling inside the chimney-stack, he's probably letting out a scream of enthusiasm, you think, or he wants to test the acoustics inside. The thin neck of the wall makes it sound like a muffled pipe, or the foghorn of one of the ocean steamers he previously thought he heard. And the suburb with its scattered formations of huts spreading out into the plain seems to you like a big ship sailing through the waves of sunlight in the plain, and you find yourself under its smoke-stack, which once again emits a muffled thud, probably as he is climbing down he has loosened a stone from the inner wall, causing it to whiz down into the cellar.

You think he's taking too long, and you climb up after him.

Having arrived with effort at the top, you remember his enthusiastic description of the ocean, but no matter how closely you scan the landscape, you don't see an ocean anywhere, just interlocking mountains and hills immersed in glowing, swaying air. Down below, you can see shadowy outlines lying in the oval circle of light on the cellar floor. The worst is to be feared, but you can't make up your mind to climb down after him. Possibly, an iron rung gave way, causing him to fall down. Or has he lost consciousness in the overpowering toxic vapors and gases rising up the chimney-stack pipe? You call down loudly to him, but nothing moves. Or is it that you can't hear anything?

You can't help him without exposing yourself to the same danger, so you climb back down the outside of the chimney-stack. You haven't been seen by anyone, and you disappear unobtrusively from this part of town. You're on the run again. Of course you can't concern yourself about him anymore. Wouldn't it be completely impossible to get help without your being recognized as the person who escaped from the insane asylum? You'd be transported back there immediately. Might Kalkbrenner not just as well have arrived in the cellar safe and sound, have immediately drunk a bottle of champagne and now be lying down there to sleep off his latest intoxication? You talk yourself into believing that.

It really is Sunday. The wind collects the sound of all the church bells from all the surrounding churches in the region and blows it past directly overhead. It lands on the suburban street you traversed while heading downtown, where it is strewn around like tinny-sounding leaves falling from the transparent, branching limbs of the dilapidated, broken-down sky.

Does the city suddenly seem friendlier? The window eyes are shining almost cheerily as they look out from the walls. A trembling, disintegrating shimmer of air flickers through the ravines of the streets and lanes, falling chunks of light sparkle as they hit individual cobblestones and spray into the entranceway of the nearest building, and now it seems that snowflakes are falling merrily through the heat of this hottest of all summers, yes, the ravines between the buildings are being filled up by what seems to be the shimmer of driving snow, a breath of wind blows the flakes whirling along the walls, and sometimes it sweeps them into a calm dead-end street where they fall twirling to the ground and lie there but don't melt right away, as one would have expected, instead, they remain stuck to the asphalt that has been softened by the heat. Soon all the streets you walk along are covered with a layer of fine white summer snowflakes that rolls up and moves along, while new white and gray bits of flakes come whistling down from the roof sills of the city firmament, as if someone were in the process of ripping the sky above the houses into little illegible vapor notes and throwing them away, down into the city below, whereby the format of the horizon scraps flaking down and past has achieved the size of folded business cards, and already people are often being hit over the head by them. But many also remain hanging in the network of wires between the buildings, and sometimes this whole flock of flakes, fluttering helplessly, decorates the clotheslines stretched diagonally from window to window.

The blanket of summer snow covering the streets and squares is already almost knee-high, but that doesn't prevent the hundreds and thousands of passersby from streaming in ever greater numbers out of all the doors and gates and making their way to the center of the city. They are all happy about this winter fairytale in the midsummer daydream, an inspired change from the deadening monotony of the lean times between the Tropics of Cancer and of Capricorn, some of them pick up bigger flakes from the ground or catch them in the air, reaching over their heads as if they could finally catch hold of the sky and pull it down like a headscarf, happiness starts to shine out of the folds of their facial expressions, people wave to each other through the heat of the sudden winter, hopefully exchanged glances of happiness rise up from the depths of their eyes, yes, there is a sigh of relief wafting through even the windows farthest back in the cellars.

It is a paper winter that has closed in on us today, now you see people strewing scraps of paper out of all the windows; some of them are even standing on the rooftops and emptying whole baskets onto the street, paper snowflakes are fluttering out of all the skylights, a winter thick with pieces of paper is dumped onto the pavement, and thicker and thicker squadrons of scraps of paper spin through the entire city, clouding the air so sparklingly with their trembling white that one often can't see a meter ahead. The spiral columns wobble between the walls like silk snakes, form funnels like paper whirlwinds, and are often pushed forward to the gate of City Council, where they are stuffed into the courtyard of the municipal authorities.

What has happened that everyone has made friends with total strangers, that people voluntarily throw hats and scarves at each other? The waving of handkerchiefs is accompanied by cheering calls of otherwise hopelessly uninspired and worn-out slogans of encouragement that suddenly sound as if they had just been invented or formulated for the first time. From which hopeless sleep was this dream saved? You hear talk everywhere of a new day dawning, of a new movement in a new direction that is now being taken, and also of newly set beginnings without end. It's as if, along with the little notepaper-cloud-formations being thrown away, a vanquished, ancient past is being escorted out as well, with a great show of courtesy, and as if, then, the wind had been instructed to sweep through all the piles of paper, the scraps of documents, all of memory's wounded desires, and blow them out of the city.

School is out, the people cheer, and today we're celebrating the beginning of vacation from work; that's why the pupils are ripping up their exercise books and throwing the scraps of paper out the window. And the thick clouds of scraps of paper fluttering from the office windows are from the superfluous files that were collected throughout the year, and are now being torn up and sent fluttering out the window.

And computer rolls, cash register rolls, telex rolls, telegraph rolls, carbon paper rolls and sometimes even worn-out telegram rolls, as well as occasional toilet paper rolls to introduce some variety from time to time. They all wrap themselves around the wiring for the lights and hang down into the valleys of the streets and lanes, ripped to pieces, torn like the flags of dishonored bureaucratatorships, because now at last a new era is beginning, another calendar, a better one, in which everything will prove to be different. One can see how much happiness must have been banished to the bottom of everyone's eyes, must have spent the winter in the shadows of the retina . . .

Yes and no, and that too, but not only, or perhaps just as much, but basically, the general strike, which was planned for a long time, as one can clearly see, has finally begun today, because people are no longer going along with the previous prevailing conditions, rather, they are being abolished immediately, so that they don't get in the way of other conditions; a new beginning has at last been set in motion, which is why people are throwing these millions and millions of leaflets through all the windows and down from the towers and roofs, throwing them around and at each other, in order to write important confidential messages and to make calls about today's general strike so that the entire population will know as quickly and widely as possible. That's why all the leaflets are now fluttering over the heads of the assembly of strikers that is being held here, made up of the entire population, to make known to the assembled crowd on the streets and the Square of the Republic, their hands dipping into the blue air for help, the following resolutions, and to give the order for carrying them out; you see banners and pieces of paper being passed from hand to hand with the words NOT LIKE THAT and NOT LIKE THAT ANYMORE, and you hear people talking about demands that should have been met decades and centuries ago, and you also hear rebellious shouting that people won't put up with this and that for even a tenth of a second longer . . .

Yes, yes, that too, say others, but not only, but rather in addition, among other things, on the other hand, or also, rather hardly to that extent, mainly though, the new government we have waited for so long has just now been installed at last, is already rushing around like mad, right now, and has already begun to work, so that the conditions of the country that were still terrible yesterday are already turning out to be significantly improved today, no one will deny that. In general, today marks the beginning of a new epoch, and people are saying it will be called the age of precious metals. It was opened just now by the president, and the government explained it to the nation on these leaflets sinking down here from the sky, that are hovering over the city, thrown down, you see, by the glider pilots up there that are crossing the entire country to explain everything down to the last detail, to make it more accessible to every last person, and that's why the firmament in all directions is constantly covered by clouds of leaflets. Away over the houses of the city into all the more outlying suburban areas and right through the country, the news of the measures that have just been taken is flying to all the assembled citizens today, as if they lived in the land of milk and honey. Didn't you just hear the entire country express its boundless enthusiasm, and it is still expressing it, listen, because right now it's going to be announced that it has been decreed that we should take suitable measures to enable a more generally understandable future . . .

So let us, all along the line, lurch into motion toward new shores.

From the thousands of faces glistening with hope in the assembly, a surf of happy laughter surges upward and continues on in the air above, a shimmering rises up from the heads in the assembly and forms into a light wave that encompasses the entire square. Blazing on full beam, it climbs over the rooftops, spreads out farther in all directions and scatters out over the outskirts of the city and into the plain as glowing lightning.

Someone taps you on the shoulder from behind; you turn around and see Theater Director Comelli.

How good to meet you here, he says, visibly pleased to see you again so soon, just imagine, everything is going to be entirely different, just think, starting the day after tomorrow, I can hardly believe it myself, and of course you have to come with us, because I simply don't think I can allow myself to do without your collaboration, so we depart the day after tomorrow at such and such a time, much more quickly than any of us would have suspected, isn't it? A good offer from abroad to begin immediately, there, wherever we want, with the construction of the natural theater, and right away at that, and as you know, we need each person, actually everyone, but especially your collaboration is indispensable, and I hope you will believe me, because you too will find fulfillment and be happy! Yesterday evening, it was, the theater porter brought us a message from abroad . . .

Yes, yesterday evening, you say, Herr Comelli, how did you get through that, how did you get to the neighboring city, to your performance there, because while we were thinking that we had traveled there from here, we were on the return trip the whole time; how did you manage to still arrive there on time? Difficult, Herr Comelli, an exceptionally difficult situation, almost catastrophic, wasn't it?

Difficult? Comelli asks, what was difficult about it? I don't entirely understand what you mean now?

But your performance yesterday evening, Herr Director, how did you manage it?

Quite simply, we went to the theater here and did our program as usual. That was quite simple; what did you think was difficult about it?

But the performance was planned for the theater in the neighboring city, not here.

Oh, that's what you mean. Now, to tell the truth, we ourselves actually didn't notice anything at all. We went from the train station here to the theater, where there was supposed to have been a guest performance by the theater troupe from the neighboring city, but it didn't take place because the people from the neighboring theater, on whom we have never been able to rely, didn't show up at all. So, thinking we were performing in the theater in the neighboring city, we simply put on the performance in our own theater, and indeed so outstandingly well, you know, that even the audience didn't notice anything; the spectators, who watched a presentation by their own theater troupe, were uniformly of the opinion that they were seeing a performance by the theater from the neighboring city. After the performance, the people commented very enthusiastically about the substantially higher standard of performance by the neighboring city's theater in comparison to the resident theater here in the capital city which had completely gone to the dogs. But how good it was, and what a stroke of luck, that we were here yesterday evening and not there, because otherwise we would not have been able to answer the message at all promptly accepting the offer, which is the very first condition of a contract. They don't want to lose any time abroad. They know there what's actually important nowadays. That's why the natural theater is urgently necessary there. Please don't miss the train the day after tomorrow, and keep in mind that sometime, possibly every time, there won't be another train for a long time.

Yes, yes, you answer, and when exactly is the departure time?

At such and such a time.

Everywhere now, wiener stands are springing up from the pavement, and they are immediately besieged. A fairground has been set up too, made of colorful boards, full of swaying carousels, and with several bumper cars that slip through a ghost train with a rustling sound. It is almost taken by storm. The smallest family of dwarves in the world climbs up the fronts of the houses at the edges of the square, hopping up until they are in the eavestroughs, jumping over the chimneys, turning somersaults forwards and backwards, and they scold each other, both sides chattering through megaphones across the heads of the people gathered below, calling each other the most cowardly of the most contemptible giants, whereupon the crowd at the fair immediately doubles up with a fit of laughter. It doesn't want to stop and shakes the crowd so much that the walls of the square bend outward.

Yes, so people didn't entirely lose their sense of humor in the course of former times that were so very difficult, you hear the presumably new police commissioner say. He is mixing with the people. He too wants to do everything differently from the way it was done before, and don't look over there, he tells the people, pointing to the National Police Headquarters, completely shrouded in a cloud of paper. Because there, he goes on to explain, they are hurrying to put all the secret police informants' files that were illegally assembled behind the public's backs through all available shredders and even out the windows. Which will be, in fact, as he personally assures them, the first news report of the brand-new, progressive National Police Gazette, namely that such clandestine activities have been discontinued, effective immediately. Yes, even as recently as yesterday, the police had been spying on our citizens left and right, with no keyhole too tiny to peek through—not only spying on our citizens but usually also slandering them, if it had not been able to find legitimate grounds for suspicion. And likewise through the windows there, look, all the files on criminal sentences that were perpetuated illegally beyond the statute of limitations are at last being torn up and sent into the sky, you see, all these small and smaller still scraps of underhanded denouncements, the index cards detailing people's political convictions, all finally shredded to bits, an insidious cloud pouring, steaming out the windows, and immediately afterward, see, metamorphosing into a very dense swarm of butterflies, I think, into a variety of white cabbage butterflies, aren't they, mixed in with several admiral's peacock butterflies that strayed into the swarm. And look, how these countless colorfully marked butterfly families from our offices wobble away trembling out of the city, through the dulled mirror of the stratosphere, far beyond the roofs of huts out there in the high mountains, look, I ask you, and they keep on swaying away into another region that is richer, more hospitable to them, in a word, as densely patterned as possible with heads of cabbage, you know, but which I unfortunately can't see any longer through my binoculars!

Did you see that now? he asks the person standing next to him, as he lowers the general staff binoculars from his face . . .

But the fact that this new detective chief broom that is just starting to sweep is attempting to curry favor is naturally observed by some people with suspicion. For all his big talk about police reform and his boastful assertion that his own officers are busy destroying all illegal files, he not only doesn't know his subordinates very well, he doesn't know them at all, because on a Sunday like this and on their time off they wouldn't take a step in that direction for him, let alone lift a little finger, no, no, those are quite ordinary passersby who are enthusiastically taking action there in the state-maintained private detective agency of the secret police. They evince, as one sees, a zeal that usual state snoopers would not be able to muster, mind you, you know, they aren't entirely ordinary people either, but rather people who under conventional circumstances would probably be called long-haired, unwashed rowdies. They are tearing through all the rooms in police headquarters and flushing out by no means just selected files, but all the written documents, all the harassment by the previous state executive, all of it of a top-secret, malicious nature, because the revolution, yes sir, the long overdue revolution has finally broken out today, it was high time, we couldn't have carried on like that much longer. Please, have a look up at the windows, where the file smoke is finally pouring out. Those are simple but strong comrades, typically bearded, unwashed, anarchic, permanent demonstrators, you know, they got into the police station by just walking past the porter and wishing him a good day. The poor man of course was frightened out of his wits, all alone on a Sunday, was totally flabbergasted, but they simply went in, forcibly invaded the place, if this way of saying it seems more suitable to you, and began at once. From all the rooms, they took all the files, all the papers, administrative files, everything that has even the faintest resemblance to paper, really everything and not just selected things, as this gentleman previously alleged, no half measures! Then they put it all at once through the shredders they've set up by the open windows, crammed it in and drove it through. Everything is properly torn up there and thrown out, so that our beautiful main police station is shrouded in a soft and fluffy cloud, as if the police station were a huge perforated pillow with its feathers and down billowing forth, blown by the wind through the air and soon through the whole country like the seeds from a field of dandelions. So that's how everything is all abuzz up there through all the rooms, because what the feathers are to the pillow, the files are to the official building. But they didn't just go to the police station, these rowdies have also gone into the managers' offices of the National Internal Revenue, and stuff is starting to flutter out from there now too, as if the most unbelievable plucking of all the hens in the republic and all the other poultry in the country were taking place simultaneously, yes, soon this building too will be completely fogged in by a flood of down paper clouds, those unkempt young rascals are doing a good job.

But of course, you're right, because anyone can do that on a Sunday, when the bureaucracy stables are empty, I agree with you when you say it's basically a dirty trick and really cowardly of them too, on Sunday of all days, when no one is sitting in there, the half-wit terrorists should try something like that on a weekday, then they'd see, they'd be flying out the window of the first anteroom in the highest arc before they even had time to say why they were there, because the first office worker who encountered them would have waved those easygoing guys and girls head over heels out of the building again with a broom, but today on Sunday it's very easy, anyone else could have done it too, it's no great feat, but that's the very reason why they're doing it on Sunday, they'll suffer as few losses as possible, and besides, it's not much trouble, today the revolution has finally broken out. Normally you can't even have a Sunday revolution without leaving some signs behind, you can't make an omelet without breaking eggs, but in our revolution today it's not eggshells but scraps of paper and bits of cardboard that are flying through the city air, and if it doesn't suit you, no, no, there can't be any question of something like this suiting anyone, on the contrary, one can probably say clearly that there were certainly many things, no, actually until yesterday nothing was in order, but today everything is so surprisingly different, one isn't used to it, this doesn't happen every day, a special, a very special, yes, presumably an historical event! Look, how gaily the paper snowstorm is already rustling out of the City Council building, out of all the skylights and holes in the cellars, as if people were running through the house with the entire annual production of tissue paper, the roof is completely covered by the cloud, like all the other rooftops too. And now it's the turn of the Courts of Justice, always hovering on their high horses, with all their unfinished trials pushed back and forth on the longest benches that cross the entire state. Then there are the appended accompanying things as well, things raked in and left to go moldy in the underground detention holes. All that is fluttering down now from the swaying scales of justice, restoring equilibrium to the completely overburdened courts, because until yesterday they had determined penalties by weighing your dossier: the thicker and heavier a case file, the more decades got added to a criminal's sentence, but all that's going to be different now. Now no one can be at all suspicious of anyone else anymore, because isn't what's coming out of the courthouse the worst of the cloudbursts of notepaper scraps and hazy clouds and snowstorms of little scraps of typewriter paper? The gathering hurricanes of scraps of carbon copy sheets are breaking out, bursting out of all the slits in the palace walls of the courthouse, until the seams in the walls of the courtrooms burst.

But the insurance buildings aren't spared either, whirling insurance policies are now sweeping over the city, yes, and that is ultimately what everyone has been waiting for, the banks and credit institutes, all in one go, and the crumbling piles of debts stacked up with extortionary rates of interest shoot upwards to the clouds.

The money, what about the money? what's happening with the money, you ask, that is falling into these guys' hands? With such banking schemes, they finance their plans for new schemes and their lavish, chaotic, playboy lifestyles, you can be sure of that, can't you? It's of particular interest to you, you aren't the only one who's been waiting for this, a lot of other people want to get something from it too, that would just suit you, but that's just where you find yourself, typically on the wrong track, at a dead end, because what, yes, what should happen to all the banknotes? nothing at all, simply nothing at all, without regard and without respect for even the highest numbers, shares or certificates of securities, mortgage bonds, loan interest, just as is happening just now, they are like all other paper, see how it is raining down from the manager's floor of the savings bank there, the steamy fog of most carefully filch-shredded bills floats pompously down over the crowd in the square. An astonished murmur runs through the crowd, a whispering, machine-like clamor kept behind their hands, because not very many of them expected something like this, but that's the way it is in a revolution, these rowdies are doing things the right way, working with carefully creative know-how, nothing escapes them, they don't even forget, when first entering a building, to tear down all the notices from the bulletin boards, the plaques with the rules on them, together with the footnotes of the Ten Commandments of unavoidable rules for using the laundry room, because they have once and for all lost all patience with what's written down in black and white, that's over, these bearded anarchists are slaving away like crazy, really working up a sweat. And so much hard work as is being done today on this Sunday has not been done in any one of the buildings mentioned on any one weekday up until now, not by any of the people otherwise employed there, I can tell you that. And do try to understand it from the point of view that it is not only high time, but also very healthy, that for once, everything in such public buildings is dusted, from the farthest cracks to under the most concealed crevices used as hiding-places for folders. The best thing would be to delouse them right away, to get rid of the bugs in the moldy dry rot nests in the holes of the dampest springback binders that otherwise, until today, have never been reached by a cleaning rag, and under the carpets that absorb everything, that people purchased so they could sweep as much as possible under them, but now everything is being swept out into the daylight, isn't something like this very laudable now and then? don't you think so? otherwise everyone would at some point have choked to death on the conspirators' dust covering up legal corruption, with ever thicker feltlike accumulations it would finally have blocked the complex tube system that ran through the official office corridor, if this winter of the bureaucratatorship had not begun today just in time to save everything at the last moment, even if you don't like it at all!

Who is talking quite inappropriately about personally imputed indispositions, you, not I, of course I like it, when seen in the long-term, it's coming at just the right time that everything is changing, fresh winds will finally blow again and entirely new, different and also stronger strings, or high voltage wire connections across the enormous distance, will be put on the now safely-secured state territory landscape, or on the viola dangling under the chin of the new leader, finally, yes, sir! a new order again, a very strict one, you know, will arrive tomorrow, moral norms will be regulated, won't they, everyone will start to feel that at least the last of the old school are about to drop, that will be a pleasure, won't it? that's what you meant? yes, yes, quite, but also entirely different too from what you are thinking now. Say, what kind of work do you do, that would interest me? what? I don't quite understand, you work at the fair, yes? and what do you do there all day long? what?

vacuum cleaner? I don't understand, you run the vacuum cleaner in the ghost train? oh, so it's you, you are the, so to say, ghost-train-conductor, or is it called the ghost-train-ticket-collector? well, well, what an exceptionally pleasant surprise, I've wanted to meet you for a long time, I say, isn't that a surprise . . . ! come on, let's go for a drink.

It's remarkable how many familiar faces are gradually turning up now in the crowd, it seems that everyone and his uncle are assembled at this fair. Isn't that the chief building inspector over there, flanked by Jagusch and Jacksch, and there's Schleifer too, accompanied by Schläfer, how nicely they are getting along now, the two down-and-out virtuosi! and there, why that's the photographer Anton Diabelli running around like crazy, photographing everything he comes across with his Polaroid camera and comparing the finished pictures that he pulls out of the camera with ones he fishes out of his jacket pockets, and isn't that the proctologist disappearing over there? while to his left, no, right, Keldorfer appears, no, you mean Hellberger, the current director of the conservatory, in the company of the funeral director, doesn't he recognize you right away again, your former piano teacher? or is he waving at someone else? no, he means you, how are you, he asks, fine, you call back, everything will be different, he replies, just imagine, everything will be different, the reputation of our conservatory will be saved, because this gentleman here, he points at the master of funerals beside him, is procuring for me, for the attic, the assistance of silent coffin-makers who have already expressed their willingness to clean out the attic of our institute, give my best regards to your brother, he calls in closing before disappearing again in the crowd; and you know these people too, who are just entering the edge of the Square of the Republic and finding their way into the crowd ahead that seems to part for them without opposition, yes, it's the local news editor together with the sports editor and the world politics editor, and with them, that too, must that be, the music critic Pfeifer, who is the only one of them who recognizes you, oh, my admiration, he calls out to you, what a pleasant surprise to meet you again at last after how long actually, surely years, by the way, I have very much admired the stance you have taken in the past years, the fact that you haven't composed a thing, that you have stopped writing, yes, the only correct position, you can say that again, in times like the ones we've been through, to refuse to cooperate was the only true answer to the circumstances, and the fact that you didn't compromise anything, I have always admired that as an excellent political stance, but now everything has finally changed again, hasn't it, now you will hopefully resume composing right away, and I eagerly await the première of new pieces for orchestra by you in the coming philharmonic concerts, you will have to compose them now, opus 6, isn't it, or perhaps even opus 11 already, that would please me greatly, until then I have the honor . . . Beaming with joy he goes on to say, in the name of his colleagues, with whom he is working his way through the Square of the Republic, everything has changed for us at the newspaper too, imagine, everything's new, we're starting again right from the beginning! yes sir, the local news editor takes the words out of his mouth, as he starts to address the surrounding crowd, a new format, as you must know, an entirely new newspaper format, even longer, even wider, even thicker with much more information! He has now climbed up the steps of the town hall and continues his public address. That's why the editorial staff is taking the liberty, on this significant occasion, of inviting the entire population to the fair, and that's why the whole time, both from the building of the newspaper's editorial staff, as well as from the tower of the town hall, as well as from all the other buildings, gliders are throwing an unbelievable amount of newspaper down from the sky into the city, and some of it is torn apart by the wind on the way, some of it flies into the crowd and obscures the sun for most of the afternoon, but he will brighten things up again with the announcement of the new newspaper, the announcement he hereby permits himself to make, promoting it everywhere. It will have a completely new goal and direction, and for that reason all the old newspapers that were still stored in the editorial offices, with pages in the old format, are now being thrown down over the people here from the clock tower, with attached explanatory notes about the new format, the new format of the times from this day forth, with important explanations of the larger format, with a clearer layout than previously, because whereas it used to be that you could cover up only your head and at most a part of your chest by carefully wrapping yourself up in a newspaper, or, in needy times, you had been able, by folding it together, to make a modest hat and now and then a shirt, you would be able, starting tomorrow, with the new newspaper format, to wrap up your entire body without difficulty, and so you will have the best opportunities to make yourself a handily foldable coat out of it, or a raincoat, a cape, if need be even a small tent—weatherproof only in a limited way—that you could take with you on hikes and set up like a bivouac after you had finished reading the newspaper, suitable for one larger person or two smaller persons, for spending the night in the warmth of the latest news, and in this way you could save your money instead of spending it on a hotel room, or if all the hotels were full or all the hostels too far away in the night . . .

Of course newspaper is still fluttering out of all the windows in the firmament, a real newspaper winter that provides slightly fluttering shadows against the scorching sun, many people are now making use of the newspapers that are floating down, folding them together to make hats to protect against the sun's burning rays, the early afternoon hours are already starting to become charred or to glow ominously in various corners, many people, almost all the people, now wear these so-called painter's caps, which otherwise only painters wear, when they are hanging in the scaffolding of the horizon, giving its cornices a fresh coat of paint, yes, this new head-covering seems to have developed into an all-round cap that may not go out of fashion so soon, as a sign of what we all have in common on this lucky day with the oh-so-successful general strike and the new government at the beginning of the holidays and the change in the season on this roiling Sunday, when the people's paper assembly breaks against the cliffs of our walls with a powerful rustling noise, yes, bound very tightly and firmly around the necks of all inhabitants are the looped bonds of community, by which each and every one of them will be strung up later, as the mayor now unambiguously informs the citizens from the window of the second story of the town hall, his posture is erect and he is wearing a brand new suit with a sharp trouser crease and a sash around his waist, which, as he explains, is to symbolize the newly awakened city spirit from this day forth. And soon you start to ask yourself, and probably others are asking themselves the same or a similar question today, what did everyone have against this city that they wanted to write it off? They had no reservations about striking it from the map without having a replacement; people are still happy today in the buildings and feel protected by the walls. How then could all insoluble problems suddenly disappear in an enlightened act of forgetting, in the serenely frantic fair, thrown away into the revolving of the crazy carousel whose dizzy mills had ground everything up, hurled with the bumper cars into the gaping mouth of a ghost train and devoured many times over in it in the intestines of the happiest horror, thrown high and low, drowned with the capsizing swing-boats untied in the domed canopy of Sunday . . . as if now, during the victory for a renewal of existence, everything would move toward complete exhaustion, toward a pleasant collapse? What is it with this city, what is supposed to have changed so suddenly?

Hello, fancy seeing you again, you are interrupted in your thoughts by a good old acquaintance, the most talented pharmacist in the country, who is standing in front of his store and beaming at you. What have you been doing all this time, and why don't you darken my door anymore, I think it's been years. What was wrong that you didn't come anymore at all?

Nothing was wrong, and that's why you never turned up anymore.

Yes, but couldn't you have come anyway? Who was finally able to teach you how to sleep? Come in for a few minutes, he invites you, come in, it's too loud outside to hear ourselves talk . . .

It's a real pity that you haven't been coming around anymore, he says, particularly in recent times so much has changed, everything entirely new, you have no idea about the newly developed remedies, fantastic, I tell you, the best ever, they stimulate while calming, dim while brightening to an arousingly alert sleep, they stimulate unconsciousness, calm while enlivening, dissolve everything into distracted concentration and enable all sorts of complicated efforts while you are sound asleep, everything is changing entirely, you know. Do you need something, my dear fellow? Can you really sleep? or may I give you something? what? the usual, as always? Very good.

And to show you and others, he starts to sample the remedies himself, swallowing tablets and pills one after another to illustrate his claim. They are arranged according to the colors of the wonderful spectral splendor of rainbows that dried out and were put in mothballs years ago . . .

You see Daniele, the flaxen-haired tightrope-walker, standing very high up on the rounded hilltop of the cathedral roof. The Square of the Republic is bursting with human bodies. Before her feet, the rope is stretched from the cathedral diagonally across the Square to the top of the City Council tower. The assembled crowd is looking up at her, eagerly anticipating the imminent performance, their faces stuck horizontally in the air. Comelli is standing beside you. He too is looking up at the tightrope-walker, he has gotten a little impatient, and makes a sign to the girl that she should be starting now. But she indicates by way of signs: no. What no, the director signals back up to her questioningly. Wringing her hands, she replies that they should please remove this annoying rope that is obstructing her air space. Comelli is completely in despair, just imagine, he says, today, for the first time, she wants to do it without using the rope, it's inconceivable, if something goes wrong! But Daniele is now indicating her confidence down to him, he shouldn't be unnecessarily concerned about her, because today, after all, everything has changed, and so now at last she wants everything to be different too. Don't you agree, Comelli then says to one of his people, that she is still simply much too young for that? that comes as such a surprise now, actually like an ambush, entirely unexpected, and I had thought she would wait a few years yet, one can't want to start with such things at such an early age, where would that lead? Imperiously, he signals back to her: rope, first rope! But she doesn't give up at all and answers back, swinging her arms: No, without rope! and with the rope I won't put one foot out into the sky, rope gone, or nothing at all! What's to be done? Comelli asks, at a complete loss, that's certainly not all right with me.

Oh, the poor man, one of the actors explains to you about Comelli, he has never been so worried about his daughter, but he must have known that this would happen someday. What, you reply, she's his daughter, I didn't know that. No, says the other, not his real daughter, only a foster-child he took in.

But then there's something I don't understand, you say, why is he always addressing her as Fräulein Daniele?

Yes, why indeed, we don't know, he's always been exceedingly polite with her, from the very beginning, when they brought her to him as an infant.

Someone else thinks there is little cause for Comelli's fears, look how good she has always been, it's time he let her decide, and why not, what is there against it, Daniele has always done everything so properly and taken perfect care, I think he'll have to give her somewhat more freedom now, to loosen the reins a little, you understand, because it can't go on like this forever, and now and then he'll have to give a little more than before, otherwise she'll really run away someday and take a good-paying job in modeling, where she will model the latest dresses and materials and show them to the entire country, or it's possible she might get a job in a suggestive demimonde fly-by-night cabaret where she no longer models clothes, but rather removes her clothes, up there publicly, and what a pity that would be!

Unfortunately, the director explains, I have no other option but to give in to her. The performance was announced well in advance, we can't simply cancel it now when all the spectators are assembled.

At last he gives two of his people a sign to take down the rope. Daniele, however, makes a little leap in the air for joy on the curved top of the cathedral roof, you see her laugh for the first time, even from this distance you can clearly make out her radiant face high up there.

Now she has put her first foot into the dome of air over the city. Comelli is visibly relieved when her foot really remains in the air at the pre-calculated height as she takes the first step, yes, that is good, and the following second foot also sets down perfectly on the path of air in front of the girl. She moves out over the steep incline of the downward sloping cathedral roof, finds a firm foothold with no cause for complaint, without sinking, yes, everything is off to a very good start now, and, Herr Comelli, just see in what an exemplary manner, far over the ledge of the slate tiled roof, she has started to hover forward now, gliding over the cord of air that she has spun from her imagination, through the space in the blue sky over the full square. And would your daughter's body, Herr Director, not normally have had to slide down the sloped cathedral roof? She is moving across on the imaginary rope, carefully swaying through several quadrangles of air, calmly walking in a straight line over the planned diagonal of the Square of the Republic, albeit somewhat stiffly and without any trace of gracefulness. She is walking farther now, no, she is sauntering forward, tramping over a worm-eaten catwalk that the noonday sun is pushing under her knee-point forward-circling leg slats. No, Herr Director, you don't need to worry anymore about the girl up there, she has long since found her footing, and her vivid imagination would certainly also prove capable of making a safety net and pushing it under herself if an unfavorable crosswind should ever cause her to slip, with her ambitious, slightly awkward, upright way of walking, her absolutely straight, somewhat too-thin figure, Herr Comelli. You see how her long flaxen-blonde hair is blown stiffly downwards at an angle from the back of her head, just as the national flag of the United Kingdoms of the Atmosphere that wrap up our planet is blown downward at just such an angle from the peak of one of the uncounted inaccessible heights. It is often funneled very deeply down to us, unfurled at the edge of the flagstaff, anchored near the stubbornly curved wind-rose shore in a delta of sunbeams, and unfortunately there's still no flaxen-blonde hair, Herr Comelli, is there? Calm down, you're still trembling, but believe me, nothing will go wrong anymore up above us, it's going without a hitch, you see, your daughter of the wind up there, who has become somewhat conceited, knows how to push herself effortlessly farther and farther ahead, through even the trickiest tunnel vault, where the afternoon light crosses. As she performs her evidently timeless, clearly visible walk through the air, no, she's not pushing; it's more as if our industrious star pupil is toddling with great determination, working her way through the academic study of all the unpredictable properties of the omnipresent air pressure. Her university entrance exams have the lines drawn on them by flocks of migratory birds in the classroom halls of the Barometer Conservatory Institute. She has personally pushed exceptionally narrow corridor tunnels ahead of herself. To us, they seem far away, trembling, like faint moonshine in the day, sometimes scaly, somewhat matt, and wrinkled like an iguana lizard, or rather a little like alligator leather. Their skin seems quite thin, and now that things have glimmered down we can see it perfectly clearly and unambiguously. Now she has moved diagonally through the laundry steam fans of a not-at-all-scheduled tail-end of a monsoon trough. It had strayed as far as to go in the window of the town council tower. You see, Herr Comelli, she doesn't have far to go now, soon it will all be over, won't it? and to think that she is doing all that under difficult conditions in the completely wrinkled wizened face of the ether above. It has been incessantly shedding its skin all day long. Now it has almost completely withered and continues curling up and shrinking, and in the process it occasionally throws slightly oily, flashing, crumbling piles of accumulated light dandruff down on the rooftops of the city, into the street valleys, alley gorges, here on the Square of the Republic and thus also on the heads of the assembled relieved crowd, although something like that actually is not good manners. And sometimes Daniele up there is so enveloped in it that we can't see anything more of her at all. But soon she has completely crossed the entire huge fishbone-patterned circus dome of Sunday, yes, her movements are suddenly much freer and more relaxed, also livelier or lighter, in any case happier, more appropriate to the mood among the people on this day. And naturally the crowd is enthusiastic about her, sending ever greater applause up to her, and one of the thunderous waves of ovation almost blew her down from the rope of her imagination at the last moment, down over the rooftops, but there remained only a single anxious hundredth of a second for her to get through, and already she has reached the end of her planned walk for today, her walk through the outward curving transparent bundles of woven light beams arching over the city, and she sits down briefly, leaning against the verdigris-covered weather vane on the top of the city council roof tower.

Many of the citizens assembled in the square have started to discuss the act, its deeper meaning and purpose and also the background significance of the performance, its cause and effect.

Almost all are of the firm opinion that the artist's brilliant performance was an impressive affair of symbolic nature, dominated by an exceptionally illuminating, loftily ambiguous symbolism, it was actually nothing other than a clever depiction of the terrible path of our homeland through the difficult but beautiful past. That's clear, isn't it?

Yes, and they were exceptionally happy that the story had become moving and understandable to all in such a plausible way, weren't they?

Yes, and since however such conditions are gone forever, because after all everything is changing now, it functioned as a very good so-called historical drama, didn't it?

Only a few find some fault with it: somewhat stiff and lifeless, tense and also too long, nothing new, but rather old hat, a slightly worn felt hat.

Yes, quite right, because as you remember, it was over a hundred years ago, wasn't it, that a certain Blondin from Paris did exactly the same stunt, with the slight difference being that the innkeeper, to whom he must have been rude during lunch, may have put something into his soup. In any case, as the man was standing on his rope high up in the air in the early afternoon, already midway over the square, he must have doubled up with a stomach cramp, he almost exploded. In a word, he saw himself forced to take down his pants in the middle of the sky over the gaping crowd, to crouch down and shit on the people, who crammed the square about as much as today, so that the walls of the houses on the edge bent outward. They asked themselves then, of course, what is he up to? what is he doing up there now? what is that supposed to mean?

and he has probably gotten tired, wants to sit down on a passing cloud or duck because a storm is passing by right now above him, or he is catching some sleep and lying down on a wing hovering past that a bird lost in flight; but then suddenly something wet, somehow sticky, liquid, at least not very solid came whizzing down on their heads. At first they weren't quite sure what it was. But very quickly the consistency of the matter was recognized and defined. Of course the people didn't want to be shat on by the artist, not even from one taking a shit in the sky, and they would have lynched him if they had caught him, so the man was forced to flee, first into the cathedral belfry, then he was forced to throw his rope from roof to roof outwards from the city in order to flee into the bushes of the plain that were just barely able to hide him.

Daniele has now stood up from her weather-vane seat and has stepped into the air again around the city hall tower, circling it a few times.

What's with Fräulein Daniele now? Comelli asks with renewed concern, why doesn't she come down now? This is even more dangerous, because before at least she could see the rope to mark her path through the air for a while before she set out, but there's no rope stretched around the tower here for her . . . is her imagination strong enough to cope with something like this?

Daniele seems to want to go back to the tower, but hesitates, or doesn't find a slab of air that she can really step on that would carry her for several very firm steps, in any case she turns away from the tower again and heads out from the city, maybe she simply wants to enjoy to the fullest, at least for a little longer, the new feelings she has just tried and tested for the first time; laughing somewhat helplessly or maybe mischievously, she turns and looks down at Comelli again, raises her hand either in greeting or as a sign that she doesn't know exactly where to go. But already she is farther away and hovering over more distant rooftops outside the square . . .

Possibly, Comelli fears, she can't find her way down anymore, because it's often much easier to go up than to come back down again . . . and he calls after her, as she continues gliding out of the city: Daniele, listen to me, don't lose your way up there in the completely decayed storm buildings of the administrative district offices, my dear, listen, and if you're really having difficulties climbing back down again properly, as I now believe, then you should simply keep on heading out of the city at the same height, where you can easily get into the highest stairwell on the top story of one of the high-rises in the bedroom community at the edge of the city, glide down in its elevator and ride back to us here in the center of the city on the suburban line, the streetcar, subway or the city bus; we will wait for you here, until you are back with us again!

Further on, you notice one of the few bare heads in the crowd that is otherwise wearing and waving newspaper hats, it approaches and keeps coming closer and closer to you on the shore of the square that is awash with newspaper scraps, an unbelievably fat figure, but that's not possible, it's Kalkbrenner, what a relief, so he didn't break his neck after all this morning, he didn't fall down into the champagne cellar! How good! So this doubt too has been dispelled. He's seen you, is working his way forward to you, finally he is there, you fall into each other's arms.

If only you knew how worried I was about you, you say and tell him of your long wait in vain for his return from the depths of the cellar under the smokestack.

Please excuse me, he replies, I myself don't understand how that could have happened to me, but when I first arrived down there, I uncorked and emptied a few baby bottles to start with, and then I must have entirely forgotten you up there, or maybe I had difficulty climbing straight back up the stack again? In any case, I left through the main entrance of the champagne cellar and came directly here to the public festival, which can be heard from far away. While I was on my way, I probably remembered you again, but I thought you would inevitably turn up here anyway, once again, please excuse me! You haven't tried to shoot yourself with the pistol? No. You have quite forgotten that. Very well. Not that I would want to prevent you from shooting yourself, as far as I'm concerned everyone should shoot himself, when and if he wants, but you would have given yourself a terrible fright!

Why?

Give it to me, give me back the Colt, you could indeed have shot yourself, but you would only have remained behind completely terrified, like a little boy, and would have stood there, because the instrument is just a warning-shot version of the original.

And as he takes his Colt back, he shoots at you, to show you that it just goes bang, and he shoots for joy into the air several times, and that can hardly be heard in the general banging of fire-crackers, the popping of champagne bottles being uncorked, the fizzing of the opened beer bottles and beer cans, while the people all around you in the square have started clapping their hands and dancing to the rhythm of the many brass bands set up on the surrounding balconies, all playing different pieces at the same time quite polyphonically, playing to the beat of the wind that is hissing through the tarpaulin folds of the beer tents set up all around, where the beer comes rushing out from the tapped barrels spraying high, and the shattered glasses clink.

Have you already spoken with Comelli today? you ask Kalkbrenner and tell him the good news.

You bet I have, he answers, such news can't remain concealed from me for very long, and the day after tomorrow we're finally off. We've been waiting for that for years. So I'll emigrate with the natural theater, although I can't be as happy anymore today about finally getting away from here as I could still have been yesterday at the same time; how quickly things change, because here things seem to have changed quite suddenly for the better, it would be nice to be able to experience it all personally, but nevertheless I'll emigrate the day after tomorrow with the natural theater and won't come back again for a long time, perhaps never again, and when I think about that today, I get quite melancholic and sad at the thought of leaving now of all times, why didn't we leave yesterday? when we were still so sick of everything that we almost choked on it. Quite secretly, of course, I harbor the plan, hidden even to myself, to remain here after all, because everything has gotten better, different, the certainty at home could be preferable again to the uncertainty abroad, but I am consistent and have made my final decision, because isn't it often so, when you are most determined, before a departure, that you nevertheless do not depart, but rather stay on, that you then often have to wait for many years again, left behind, before you once again make up your mind to go away. That's why you have to go away, when you have really made up your mind, and when nothing more is holding you back from departing than the homesickness that has suddenly returned from afar, from far away, and in spite of it you must go forth, because if you don't leave then, the homesickness that has come flooding back to you from so far away, that had been so foreign, lost to you, will soon, at the very latest after the departure that you have missed or deliberately missed, turn into the wanderlust that has always been so familiar to you, the longing to go away from here will be present in you again immediately, and you will curse the fact that you didn't go away from here, emigrate after all, and you'll stand there as a departed stay-at-homer, left over from overpowering wishes to go home at last to unknown foreign lands, run over, completely distanced from yourself at home . . . And how about you? Surely you're coming along? Are you perhaps hesitating? What is there still to hesitate about? What's holding you back here? What then? Nothing. Perhaps a few unattainable fantasies. It would be good for you to disappear from here, even if everything is different now, but what does that still have to do with you, what difference will this make for you? I think you don't have very much to look for here, even under the changed conditions, but that you have already lost everything. There's nothing for you like getting away! Run for it!

Yes, yes, you reply, but you hadn't quite thought it through to the end yet, but the day after tomorrow you would certainly be at the train station punctually at the departure time, even if only to bid farewell to him and the dear director Comelli and all the others of the theater. I'll probably go with you, you explain, but not everything has ripened to a final decision in me yet, there's still something missing . . .

Kalkbrenner goes on to talk about something that had remained previously unknown, perhaps to all of us, that we had neglected and that must have been unexpectedly brought to mind, he describes his ideas about a necessarily appropriate, reasonable recklessness that had atrophied until now. In the boring excitement here it could only be performed on wallpaper that had already been torn down and gotten filthy dirty.

Do come along! It's possible the opportunity won't come again so soon to get away as cheaply as you'll be able to the day after tomorrow . . .

The people are still dancing merrily in the square, although it often takes considerable effort for them to shake a leg, swinging it up through the almost one-and-a-half-meters-high summer snow cover, the precipitation from the paper snowstorm clouds. Sometimes, wading, they have to push aside and shove away the tide of paper scraps. There is a constant circulating motion of the deposited undulating storm of shredded newspaper, rolled in a mess from the square into the streets and alleys, and pushed back out of the streets and alleys into the square by the people walking there who want to defend themselves against drowning in the clouds of scraps of paper. But soon now, all the remaining paper anywhere, even in the most hidden hiding-places for dust, will have been flushed out and finally blown out of the houses. With Kalkbrenner now, you try to cross a few closely-packed, dense fields of paper dust and fog without losing your orientation in the rustling white clouds of the flood. The two of you wander from shooting-gallery to shooting-gallery, and each of you shoots down a really colorful bouquet of paper flowers before you then take the elevator that rises rapidly to the cathedral tower. You step out onto the observation platform and look down at all the hustle and bustle of the public festival, with the crowds moving spirally and frothing over. Various sexually-hooked-together piles of citizens spin over each other as they roll through the streets and alleys out of the city and back into the city again, pulsating hard in quite clear structural sequences. The built-up bubbles of cumulus clouds of stationary have burst and collapsed and are now flaccid. They now sag in the afternoon sky, which feels quite dry to the touch when you hold out your hand into it from up on the tower. The sunlight's air lips and the pores of its skin feel quite roughened up, quite wrinkly, and cracked open. The hoop skirts make colorful circular patterns on the pavement that are reflected up over your heads toward the top of the tower. No, it is the hats hopping from people's heads, falling on the pavement like rolled balls. Sometimes they also tear the newspaper caps away from each other, willfully rip them up and throw them away, only to help each other make new ones again from hovering newspapers grabbed out of the air. Often, they simply wrap themselves up with the scraps of newspaper and roll each other around. They help each other loosen up in the dance, reaching through their hair, relieving the head sphere support fixtures between their shoulders that were stiff and rigid for years. Besides, it seems to be just a matter of time before the first heads will have snapped and will sink down from the surging bodies into the heaps of paper snow, exhausted in the frenzy of continuing drunkenness. Now the time has come for the two of you to add some decoration to the last dispersing paper cloud mists. You take aim and throw your paper flower bouquets directly down on the first sinking citizen heads that have gotten stuck in the scrap swamp cover. Beside you, the pointed top of the tower is boring through the burning glass above the city . . .

Back down again in the tumult, you can't believe your eyes at first when you look excitedly at a certain point in the tangle of bodies. But yes, you are seeing correctly. Perhaps. Perhaps you are seeing HER, and so SHE has come to the fair too, like everyone else, and what's so unbelievable about that? You go a little closer to make sure. Yes, there's no question about it. From behind, you can make out the gracefulness of HER figure and HER head, you recognize her exactly, a trace from the side in profile, but that can only be HER, there's no other person like that. What good fortune this day now brings to you too, like all the other people. And finally, you think, everything will be entirely different for you too, everything entirely new. You will be able to make a new beginning, now that you have encountered HER after all, after searching so long in anticipation. An entirely new life perhaps. Yes, another existence. So, almost euphoric, you are sure you're right.

You tell Kalkbrenner right away of your discovery and what has come true for you today, almost unimaginably; I think, you say to him, I have finally found my girlfriend, see, look, SHE is walking over there! I see HER very clearly over there now and have to be careful that I don't lose sight of HER again in the milling crowd! See you later, my good man, see you soon then, and take care in the meantime!

Without waiting for his reply, you leave him standing there. You immediately pursue HER, burrowing into the undergrowth of bodies that smell of perspiration and are running with sweat. That is not and never has been entirely easy. You have to give and receive many elbow jabs in the ribs, knee jabs in the stomach too, without having the time at your disposal to lodge complaints. But at last you have finally done it; you are standing behind HER and can now almost catch up to and overtake HER. In a minute, you will be able to gaze again into HER beautiful face, and you'll be able to from now on, for as long as possible, without any haste.

Everything will be different, you think again, and you remember how, whenever you were able to look into her beautiful face for some time, to sink in, getting a little immersed in it, you felt that the world, when it glided through HER face, was filtered very gently by the lines of HER countenance, so that afterwards it was not only more tolerable, but also became beautiful again, as if the environment had been very tenderly bathed by the streets and paths of HER facial features, as if by soft water, and as if the entire surrounding area was capable only of blossoming again and carefully wrapping itself accommodatingly around your shoulders after a voyage through HER eyes. Yes, you go on to think, soon I will only have to bear the world and life in it by looking into and through her face as often as possible, maybe always, and will learn in doing so how one might at last live up to its expectations.

Everything will be fundamentally different, because you will at last be able to get the facts about yourself and the beginning of your story that is slipping away from you more and more. You will learn its causes and the reasons for it, because after all SHE is the only one who still knows something about it, yes, at last you will be able to find out everything about yourself, right down to the last, smallest detail. And when you then finally know everything about yourself from HER account, and have also thrown the last uncertainty about your person behind you, you will also be able to abandon this story, in order to enter into a new one with HER.

Laughing happily about the discovery of HER in person, you step in front of HER and at last look deeply into her eyes, without batting an eyelid.

Something has gone a little differently here than you expected.

The disappointment is not as great at all as if you had had a presentiment of it. Still, you feel a little deceived.

By whom then? By yourself? No, not entirely. And certainly not by HER, how could it be HER fault?

But she is slightly to blame, as if by having had the nerve to make an appearance she had unintentionally made fun of your desires.

It isn't HER, but rather a schoolgirl from a past decade of your life, someone SHE had initially reminded you of very much a few days ago, as you thought, the spitting image of her, but, as you now see, not so much at all, and aside from her slightly crooked upwardly protruding thick lips that had been hit by a rope that broke and snapped back at her, and a nose sloping slightly to the side, there were clearly only a few corresponding, very blurred lines drawn into her face. You had always wanted to have something going on with her back then, but never did have, apart from a silent, unarranged, mutual agreement to sit beside each other in the darkness every time there was a didactic lecture with slides.

No sooner are you standing opposite her now for the first time in almost two decades than the same desires come over your body again in the first few seconds that have been in suspension for years. Astonishingly, you start to tremble with almost exactly the same emotions. They don't so much push aside all the anticipatory thoughts about HER as redirect all the feelings of longing that were not fulfilled in that context to the woman who is actually standing in front of you. You adjust the similarities of the two again, bringing them closer, like a combination of two different reappearing wished-for landscapes that have remained unrealized, and one can say that you are happy to have run across, if not HER, then at least this old school friend.

She, too, seems to be happy that you've turned up, and we don't meet like this nearly often enough, she says, as the two of you go through a gateway into a lounge to combine seeing each other again with a glass of wine. Hardly have you sat down to wait to be served than an older gentleman joins you and asks you not to turn down his fervent request to be allowed to invite each of you for a glass of wine, since it is associated for him with something very important.

Gladly, you reply, but ask him to describe in more detail why it is so important for him.

Everything is different, he answers, and a new life is beginning today for me just now, a new time is really beginning in my life, imagine, for thirty years I suffered from the hiccups non-stop until today, just think, for three decades not a single minute of my life without burps that were often painful, a constant hopping up and down of my stomach in my body, a constant shaking of the diaphragm and constant trembling of the top of the stomach, combined with chronic stiffness of the stomach musculature. Believe me, that is almost worse than if you suffered from a thirty-year fit of laughter about the bad jokes we hear every day around here, it's no laughing matter because you have no time, between the individual stomach hops in the pit of the diaphragm, to smile at even the smallest joke, and associated with that there is also the almost perpetual thirty-year loneliness, because when you are unfortunately forced to bring forth belches all the time, combined with a periodic shout when breathing in after every single punch your stomach gives you from inside, as if it were a boxing-glove locked into the pit of your diaphragm automatically hitting against the surrounding walls, then even the pushiest and most detested relatives stay away, and in your loneliness you often think back on their boring visits with gratitude, and you start to appreciate anybody who is prepared to stay in the same room with you for longer than a minute. There is no cinema, no theater that didn't send me flying out in the highest arc, back at the beginning when I still hoped it could soon subside again, so that back then, thirty years ago, when I often hid under the rows of seats, it became the custom before every performance to search the building for my possible presence and only then to begin, since although I could often hold the noises back for a long time, I was never able to for an entire performance, which then had to be interrupted every time the eternal merciless gymnastics of my guts started up again, because no one could stand the ever-louder, ongoing belching, you know, thirty years of this constant involuntary hopping inside me, as if someone wanted to jump out of me but couldn't find an exit, and I probably don't even need to mention the fact that not even the cleverest of discussions among physicians was able to come up with a solution, with the physicians remaining as clueless as I was. Thirty years of hiccups, and just imagine, today, this very day a few hours ago everything suddenly became very calm in me, and everything seems to have come to an end now and is hopefully over for ever. That's why I have already invited a lot of people today, among them the two of you, people I find very likeable, to have a glass of wine with me, combined with the added request that you make a point of thinking of me now and then and send your wish in my direction that this decades-long hiccupping will never start again, because thirty years is long enough, and that it may never start from the beginning again as it did thirty years ago on a beautiful spring day, he remembered it by the way almost exactly, it could have been one of the most beautiful days of my life, when my stomach suddenly started swishing like a torrent that was buried in me, or to put it more exactly, like a constantly flushing toilet, and then the belching and burping started and didn't stop again until today.

Well, just tell me, your school friend asks him, what it was you ate back then? Was that maybe to blame?

I no longer know. I don't know, maybe black radishes or white ones or carrots, but definitely two soft-boiled quail's eggs.

You should never do that again, she says, otherwise it might possibly start right back up again. You have to be careful about what you eat in future.

And you raise the question what his stomach will do in future, if it has constantly been in the most athletic motion for thirty years, hopping and punching, and now suddenly it's supposed to be so quiet all the time, brought to a standstill forever, and whether that can be healthy for the stomach, and wouldn't it be a good idea now and then to let it at least transitionally hop a little back and forth or up and down, in itself, through itself, to intentionally start it jumping again in order to accustom it slowly to the new standstill . . .

No, no, he replies, because then it wouldn't stop again, I already know it much too well, it has to be left in peace!

After you drink to an end to his thirty-year hiccups, as final an end as is possible, he goes on to describe for a while the difficult days that now lie behind him, the most difficult years of his life, and speaks of many of his desperate, amateurish countermeasures, and in his sentences soda spatters out of glasses, hard bread crusts clatter between his teeth, and sugar cubes rattle in bowls, with him snorting like a horse all the while, after which he says good-bye, because his request has been granted and he doesn't want to stand in the way of your private conversations any longer, he says. He mixes in again with the other patrons at the bar who, intentionally belching, raise their glasses in a toast to him. Now you notice the landlady behind the bar, she suddenly opens the window and throws out an entire laundry basket full of writing pads torn to little bits, the last of which she has just finished crumbling into the basket, calling out that everything is entirely new, for her too everything is entirely new now, and she starts talking loudly about her life until now, which was determined above all by the notepads she has just thrown out the window. She not only very laboriously wrote out the bills, but also did the arithmetic, which took more and more of an effort, but now at last she has at her disposal this brand-new cash register machine in front of her, please take a look, that can not only write but also do the arithmetic for her, so that in future no one will ever be able to pin the blame on her again for her mistakes in arithmetic or writing, or fool her about how much they ate and drank their way through at what price at her establishment, because the automatic cash register never makes a mistake, nothing escapes its eagle eyes hovering around everywhere, and now the time of pads of paper is finally gone out the window.

Now you recognize her again. It's the landlady of the day before yesterday morning and the day before the day before yesterday night with the death of the old woman in the room next to yours.

It would be best if you went immediately to a different inn, but how should you justify that in great detail to your former classmate, and besides, your glasses have just been topped up again . . .

Considering that you haven't seen her in almost two decades, she seems basically very little changed in the pleasant, slightly darkened coolness of the inn, which she immediately starts to fill now by telling you about her recent past, rustling slightly and talking somewhat through her nose, in words tumbling out very nimbly over each other and sentence loops incorrectly knotted together, actually she has always been very happy and has also been married, that is to say, she is of course still married happily to an electrician, but not to one of those common little short-circuit repairmen, but rather to the boss and head of all the electricity pylons that criss-cross the country, that are under his command and have to stand at attention, arranged in rank and file, when he turns up on and underneath them, a difficult and dangerous job that consists roughly of his opening the window of their mutual home every morning at daybreak and climbing out into the dawn on rungs hammered into the fog onto the closest electricity pylon he comes across, and his job is constantly to clean and repair it, which is why for this purpose he always carries with him in his tool case, that is constantly hung around his shoulders, a certain number of diverse fats and cloths and rags and oils and also pinchers and pincers and screwdrivers and screw wrenches, when he once a day crosses the whole state from one border to the opposite on the steel cables of the high-tension power lines, often sliding creepily along the wires and decorative moldings of the sky like a skater on a tightrope, over all the hills, to continue his work in the evening, right after his return from the steel scaffolding of the sky down through the window of their mutual home, as he undertakes the electrical repairs that accumulate daily in such a house, such as replacing blown fuses or lightbulbs, to return then the next morning from the bedroom window into the rest of the night and therefore into his area of responsibility in the precisely marked grid of the atmosphere above the plain that is assigned to him . . . or something like that, you aren't really listening to her.

As you look at her more exactly while she is talking, you think she hasn't changed much, her nose hasn't gotten any more crooked, her lips are slightly larger and therefore the upper lip turns up somewhat more, but that seems to you more an erotic intensification in contrast and comparison to twenty years ago, her breasts are of course much more than twice as large in circumference, but there is still just a trace of the beginnings of an upward-bent pear before the hills taper to an end, below them the first unmistakable signs of a paunch, which is however of no great consequence in terms of her external appearance, she has simply become a real woman, you say to yourself and look beside you at her thighs, which have naturally become considerably fatter over the years, she is pressing them firmly together, which makes them even more fully rounded, and hadn't you always, when you saw a woman's thighs pressed together like that, almost inevitably felt the strangely insatiable desire arise to try to push yourself in between there, somehow pushing in, as into a pair of scissors, for example, that can only or hardly be opened with difficulty . . . ?

If only she didn't talk non-stop, as if there was a sentence-spraying and word-preparation device of anatomical-mechanical construction inside her mouth.

Shall we, you suggest to her in one of her rare pauses, make our way out of here a little into the nearby quiet municipal park? It's been quite exhausting today in the entanglements of the crowd on this glowing white Sunday, hasn't it . . . ?

Slowly roaming through the municipal park with her, along the shore of an artificial pond, you think at first of sitting down with her on one of the benches, surrounded by the complete solitude of the park, that like the buildings seems to have released all its living beings to go to the fair in the Square of the Republic, so that not even the edge or point of a single forlorn park warden's hat could disturb you, but that isn't possible, because a sort of waterfowl that was only recently introduced here has not only already relieved itself astonishingly extensively on all the seating surfaces, but also continues in this activity as previously non-stop, fully occupied, possessed by a touchingly sedulous zeal.

Clean a seat with newspaper, you think, but you have something else in mind for the newly-formatted newspaper you have brought along.

Shall we, you suggest to her, go over there, right to the back of the park, and see if the newspaper editors were lying or telling the truth when they claimed that a small tent could be constructed from one of their newspapers?

Oh yes, she replies, and that would interest her very much, and perhaps right over there at the edge, almost where the plain begins, where the municipal park starts to flow out into it, behind the last of the trees sadly clinging to the soil . . . ?

She has gotten very quiet, astonishingly, and it's hard to believe she is capable of it, or have her speech clouds discharged a little in the meantime . . . ?

But back in the farthest part of the park she starts to cry quietly to herself, whereupon you immediately put your calming arm around her shoulders and ask her if you did something wrong.

No, not you, she answers, still sobbing, but what I told you just now at the inn is from a long time back and no longer true, because her electrician has long since ceased climbing in and out of the window of their mutual home, instead, he is probably climbing through another or several other windows. Now she has almost stopped crying, wipes her tears on your shirt in a familiar manner, and her head is lying in the hollow of your chest wrapped protectively in the palms of your hands. You have started kissing her hair.

Don't be too upset, you say to her, an electrician is always just an electrician, who thinks electricity is the feeling he's been lacking.

Now your lips touch her forehead, then you glide over her cheeks to the shore of her upper lip that a breaking rope had turned upward over two decades ago.

She is happy, she says, to have met you again today at last, because in the long intervening period she has often liked to remember you, time after time, with very serene thoughts . . .

While you kiss her, embracing her tightly, and your one hand gets in under her blouse, the other wanders down toward her private parts under the tent of her dress, you feel almost as if this was happening in the present of nearly twenty years ago, and you glide back into your own memory of that time and see her before you and feel her like a form from that time now leaning against you, you feel your unchanged longings, that have remained unfulfilled for almost twenty years now, rescued to this place, as if they will soon now, in the coming moments (twenty years ago, or perhaps as in the coming minutes twenty years ago), finally be fulfilled, as if it wasn't just worthwhile to wait so long, it was good . . .

Above the park, the afternoon sky, which until now has been pleasantly pulsated by the wind, turns molten in places. It has been made even more brittle by the trembling of the heat and is slowly starting to crumble into small shadow confetti, here and as far as the eye can see. And getting slightly darker, it sinks down over you.

Now you see real cracks and tears forming in the shrinking dome of light.

Or has this afternoon simply started to construct its old silver staircases across the evening into the darkness of night . . . ?

When your fingers have finally reached her source and are climbing over its soft embankment, she suddenly says to you: Pity, my dear, but I unfortunately can't screw you today, not until a few days from now, when we meet again and from then on again and again, as often as we want . . . And she speaks of her joy about a shared future that will be much more beautiful than even this Sunday. And until then the time will go much too slowly for her too.

What is this? No sooner have you pulled your hands out of her blouse and her dress than it seems to you as if in the past minutes everything that you had still seen as a similarity with HER has crumbled away from her countenance, as if your caresses had defoliated her face!

And just now you think you are able to notice how ugly she has gotten in the past decades, not a trace left of the pear-shaped upwards swelling tips of the domes of her breasts, you probably just wished them onto her figure, instead, quite ungainly, they almost fall out of her shirt, as if they could roll away through the grass of the park onto the plain and smack down in the nearest swamp. And how fat she has gotten, but the worst thing now is her face. It's not just that all the similarities with HER that you read into it have fluttered away, but also that as this first similarity progressively disappears, another similarity seems to you ever more insistently to be surfacing on the shore of her face. And ever more alarmingly it gives you a revolting shock, almost as revenge, because breaking through in her features more and more obviously is a similarity, at first very far removed, but gradually, under more intense observation, it becomes inescapable, a similarity with the face of the old woman in the room next to yours who died two days ago. Yes, you think, in a few years she will look almost exactly like that one, and it almost seems now as if the dead woman wanted to communicate something to you through the face of your former classmate, but no, it's nothing temporary, it had always been buried in her face, even back then almost twenty years ago, and the longer you look into her eyes now, the more overcome you are by disgust, not only at her, but also at yourself and your past physical contact, incomprehensible, that all that can just hit you in the eye now for the first time, why didn't you notice it before? Because she hasn't changed one iota, or has she? no, your view of her has changed so very suddenly, must have gotten different! Is she then really as you see her now, or are you just imagining all that, no, you can't see everything differently, because it apparently does not present itself to you differently!

You can't stand it anymore, no one can require that of you any longer, despite the dictates of interpersonal courtesy, that is simply too much, you have to get away from here, you say to her, wait here, I'll be right back, just to step aside for a moment, yes, and you do step aside, but come back, no, you flee, not only from her, but out of the park by a different route and into the city, to disappear back into the fair, to dive quickly, briefly, through a river control of your forgetfulness, and to bury the worst in the tides of those inland waters of memory, may they evaporate as soon as possible . . .

When you get back to the square, it is empty. Full of piled-up paper at least one meter forty high, reaching up to your stomach and almost to your thorax, but empty, deserted by almost all the people. Only a few figures are still folding up their last booths and loading them onto the side of wagons at the edge of the square, where a narrow path remains that can be walked on. The ghost train conductor takes the plug out of his inflated rubber Frankenstein and throws it onto the colorfully painted caravan. It's the last thing, the caravan is packed to the hilt.

At the edge of the square, the first people from the garbage collection service have turned up with their wagons. Dejectedly, they start their first vain attempts to clean the square. Not just the square, the whole city is in such a state, all the streets are blocked, it's as if this city has been turned into a cesspit, a dumping ground so large that it could accommodate the dirt from the whole continent for several decades. The paper that snowed down is piled up in heaps, some of it is completely filthy, and some of it is damp, people must have sprayed water around out of hoses. One can't fend off the depressing impression that a short time ago a large part of the world was assembled here and used this city as an inordinately large open-air toilet. In its pit, you now stand on top of billions of scraps of wiping paper that have fallen off and are hanging down dripping everywhere, like fringes from the hind ends of the earth's population. They must have sat together on one privy hole very high up in the sky. Yes, you get the vague impression that you are in the center of a huge manure heap, from whose humus until recently exotic flowers with colorful blossoms grew and bloomed. They have now shrunk, decayed, and spoiled, wilted and collapsed in the slowly decomposing remains of their leaves that are still stuck to the walls everywhere. They now attract only vermin, swarms of flies build their nests in the paper, and soon the wood wasps will also discover a new paradise. Sometimes an individual foot sticks out of a paper whirlpool, the foot of some drunk who has drowned in the flood of paper. Sometimes there are two legs, and even individually snapped off hands, like rotting tropical plant stalks in a savannah. Now and then you'll see a snoring head with its eye blinds let down and the gate hanging open.

Starting from the edge of the square, the people from the garbage collection service are slowly shoveling the dusty paper sludge onto their flatbed trucks. One can tell by looking at them that they won't finish the job today, nor do they have to.

Why is the party over already? you ask one of them, and where did all the people go.

Don't know exactly, is the answer, but not much room left to move here, everything completely torn to shreds. And so some people withdrew to the various outlying villages where they could stay with friends, or to the neighboring city. And many simply went out into the plain, to the objectors to civilization who had settled in the folds of the hill country. They must have finally become reconciled to their existence there, or something like that. And many simply went to the edge of the city, where the shore of the plain begins, because, as they had heard, they could dance to some sort of music there, or something like that, without having to rely on brass bands. All the players had already completely exhausted their lungs here by panting out through the brass pipes. So as I was saying, simply to the music created by the wind in the corn fields that surround the city, there's supposedly the possibility of dancing there, and do look over there yourself, I can't explain it exactly, I know nothing more than the fleeting glimpse I caught in passing, you know.

Meanwhile, individual piles of paper have been shoved together in a makeshift fashion. Each of them is several meters high. They are distributed in the Square of the Republic like white to dirty gray haystacks, but they are twice the height that haystacks otherwise reach. From these piles, the trash collectors have dug the boozy stranded dancers out of their paper scrap cloud graves and are assembling them around the edge of the square, where they will probably all keep snoring in chorus, lying there until tomorrow morning. And when darkness falls in a few hours, the hissing of their heads will offer the loneliness of the night birds a hissing choral concert, rolled out rumbling through the night. Their snoring, soon feathered as if by shadow birds, rises up through the twilight into the evening, meets in the middle of the square, collides at the height of the church tower, becomes intertwined, forms a center for the acoustic linking of intense sleep sounds, and wanders on. It spirals out from the city, as far as the borders of the province. All the rustling of this coming night will be wrapped up until dawn, when it will whirl through the breaking day as a happily colorful memory of the fair and fly sparkling into the coming week of hard work. How many of the stranded dancers will still be safe in the streets, and how many, perhaps not until tomorrow morning, will turn out to have been suffocated by the mountains of paper tailings that fell on them . . . ?

At one of the kiosks that haven't yet been entirely cleared away, you buy a few hip flasks of herbal liqueur for your churning stomach.

Then you head out of the city, in the hope of finding Comelli and Kalkbrenner again, and you almost fear that, having lost sight of the two of them, you have also lost sight of the last strands of the future that remained for you.

How sticky the light has become this afternoon, as you painstakingly push your way along the alleys leading out of the city, through the piles of paper plugging the streets. Isn't the light getting more and more solid, and isn't it already pushing you against the walls, so that you make hardly any headway anymore? Or has your shadow gotten caught on a hook in the wall, or a door handle, and is that what's pulling you back, like an elastic band attached to your body?

By way of contrast, the fronts of the houses, between which your shape forces its way through, stand easily and lightly, almost hovering over the patterns in the cobblestones. As if it had been understood that the walls should be painted pastel, they vibrate delicately in the air, quivering a little at every contact with the sunbeams, and the heat clouds flutter past somewhat faster than usual.

Your daily walk is precisely marked out. From here, it leads you out of the city for a short while, to a place where a bay of the plain glides into the city. You cross the bay on a narrow path that leads through wild cornfields. They were abandoned by the people who cultivated them, but they nevertheless continue to spread out farther and farther, growing luxuriantly. They are somewhat dried up this summer because of the heat, but they have withstood the worst drought astonishingly well. Sometimes their pattern is interrupted by little reedy places in swampy parts of the ground, and now and then they are decorated by blooming agaves that soar high up into the sky, their umbrella-shaped umbels casting unusual shadows on the path. Beside you on the left and right are the vertical green and yellow stripes of the walls of corn. They stand about two meters high, and have grown so thick that they're almost impenetrable. Songbirds are now rare in our landscape, but some of them have been able to rescue their nests into the places between the stalks of these tall plant fortresses. Through the bright white silvery cracks between the slats, one hears them hopping through the mostly dried-out leaves that hang down limply from the vines of the field wall, or on even rarer occasions, one hears them chirping, quietly, cautiously, so as not to attract the attention of any roaming city shotguns.

As you walk farther along the path, a strong wind blowing across the fields has begun to rummage through the stalks, and it intensifies as it runs along your path through the field corridor. Sometimes it sounds strange now, as if blown very deeply on an infinite number of panpipes. As it marches through between the poles, they bend away from it, more and more averse to its insistence. The dense panpipe murmuring, seemingly boomed forth from an infinite number of bass recorders, gets denser and denser to the left and right.

Yes, the corn fields have begun to sing madly from the chromatic depths of the earth, from the soil of the field. Closely snuggled together, the tone umbels of very dense deep woodwind sound surfaces climb extensively upward, sometimes patterned by the hissing of the dry leaves rubbing against the poles. This deep, close-meshed, gossamer-like humming fabric climbs upward between the corn stalks to your left and right and envelops you on your corridor between the fields. It seems indisputable to you that it is somehow not only audible, but is also starting to become visible, in the form of very dark, matt gray, shimmering, trembling scraps of sound cloth. They blow gently upward between the stalks, rising into the sky like droning, dense, hornet-tail-patterned flags, as if the tents of built-up piles of sound were pulling shadowy tone umbel wickerwork along behind them, sucking it slightly darkened out of the surrounding fields.

The sound increases steadily, grows louder, and almost threatens to force you out of the fields. Ever greater build-ups of sound-smoke come steaming up on either side of your swaying figure. It is a high blazing sound blossom fire glowing forth from the depths, blared upward ever more densely from the soil of the fields. Sometimes it seems to come from countless bass shawms pushed asunder, blazing upward in just as many little tone-fire tongues of flame. They sparkle up individually on every corn stalk, in ever-closer proximity to each other. Gleaming, they hover above from the top of the field and move out into the atmosphere. At the same time, the dense sound of foghorns from all the steamships sailing the oceans and rivers of the Earth seems to be gliding through the fields, like a hotly breathing foghorn choir, a spreading mushroom of musical smoke. It surges through the fields, giving off bass notes into the atmosphere of the planet. In the center of the mushroom's hollow stem, you now slowly work your way forward, taking a slightly diagonally uphill course out of the fields. You are pushed ever farther by the extensive blaze of the tone fabric from deep under the field. Its bright refractions almost cut you off from both sides of the plain, and it blows through everything around you, almost throwing you to the ground as it sprays around, smoldering and boiling, hissing past you, its light waves rushing and its airwaves blasting . . .

Fortunately, the wind goes into an intermission now for a while and takes its leave for an invisible hall of bedrooms, retreating into the upwards sloping vault of the firmament.

Finally you surface again, and the slightly exhausted field collapses behind you, almost limp on the ground in the abating wind. It hangs like a sponge on the soil, sloppily coagulated, in a not very controlled performance for the landscape audience that has in the meantime turned up to take a look. They stand on the shore by the cliffs at the edge of the plain. You climb the cliffs now, returning to the outskirts of the city that begins again right behind the colorfully painted wooden fences of the little gardens.

The people standing there are presumably some of the inhabitants who wandered out of the city during the fair, wanting to escape the continuing hurly-burly. To them, the city jammed with paper must have seemed not only unnavigable, but also dangerous, you could suffocate in it. Besides—the thought must have flickered through some of their skull vaults—what would happen if something caught fire there, or if someone out of malice intentionally played with fire? It's unthinkable. The drought has everything crackling like dry straw, and this has been the hottest of all summers in the past decades. Yes, you remember, right, when you returned to the square and found it emptied of people, the piles of paper on the Square of the Republic had seemed to you so disgustingly soaked and laden with lavatory stench, but people had probably intentionally started to dampen the paper snowstorm in the streets with fire hoses to make it rather more difficult for such a fire to get started, and thus to shift it out of the realm of the feeblest negligence . . .

At an appropriate distance, you join the group of people who have assembled here, presumably to observe the sound phenomenon. They look upward from a slight elevation in the ground. The many different people and groups almost always have opposing viewpoints about what they are hearing, and often get completely heated up as they present their counterarguments, sternly stressing their most basic theses. For example, one of them talks about the number of holes in a single cornstalk, whose distances, which should be measured from the ground, are just as significant as the respective thickness of the plant's cane for the pitch and also the volume produced by a single instrument. Now from the distance a breath of wind has blown over to us, it seems it will soon be blowing again full force, yes, and it does begin again, there is lively movement in the overgrown abandoned farmlands spread out before you. Already the quietly resounding deep blowing is working its way up toward us, at first very carefully, rolling slightly, tonguing through all the canes. It warbles out in all directions, traveling for kilometers through the entire plain. Then stammered bass notes pile up more and more densely over and beside each other, sounding deeply through all the forests. Finally they take the form of one of the musical rivers that is drawn like a line through the homeland and sprays laughingly into your face. In any case, over the confused sounds of the tonguing choir, the harsh buzzing of a marsh cane bass flute sounds out very sadly. And already, sound flower flames are opening at the tips of the hop-pole spears, while from the gently undulating foothill region, reciprocal cornstalk tongued kisses dart tenderly out, gliding inwards between the opened lips of the landscape's shore, their tone umbels shimmering.

It is a coyote skinned, jaw splitting, spirally accelerated spinning of light rolling machines, repeated with the systematic precision of a music box. Wasps buzz, wings swarm, and flashing note scraps tremble. It is a here and there, or out and up, a pushing off each other, or surrounding each other. Everything is spread out, like the sounds of an organ hitting the entrails of the atmosphere. Flashing pulsars emit bundles of melody, hidden by the papered walls that hover overhead. Their piercing echoing reaches us as hazy scraps that tip over to the side and roll away through the grass, roll ever farther away into the farthest distance. And at certain intervals a slightly splintering smashing-to-pieces banging can be heard on the horizon, dazzling its way here, and getting mirrored back again . . .

So that's it, you hear one of the inhabitants say, that's what people in the city are always talking about. They're anxious, they're worried. No, the thing is that they hardly speak about it, but rather are doggedly silent most of the time. Because, allegedly (that's what you maintain, not I), it's a disease! People are talking about some insects, worms or bacteria or fungi or lichen, as you will, that may have penetrated into the cornstalks and eaten all of them hollow from the inside, along with these holes, right, holes through which the wind blows in and out, and how bewitching that sounds, after all, we're hearing it. So that now is the dreaded singing and ringing of the cornfields, about which all the people in the city had sunk into such a deep silence.

Is it true that this year's entire crop was destroyed by these little creatures that are eating everything hollow or undermining it from the inside out, who incidentally exhibit a certain skillfulness in the manufacture of simply formed woodwind instruments? Yes, yes, that's as good as certain and was ascertainable a long time ago, and we continue to be absolutely powerless against it . . .

Not that one would have anything against the music from the fields, on the contrary, it's very beautiful, and it also sounds so strangely familiar, so refreshingly exhausted and happy, all through the country. It comes from the hollow canes of corn, and from other holes, everything has simply gotten full of holes, you understand. Because of these hollow spaces and holes the water and nutrients sucked up by the roots no longer travel upward in the plants, they'll never again get up to the corncobs on the cornstalks, but after all it's because of these corncob porridge meals that people plant corn in the fields, not so that the cornstalks can let themselves be hollowed out and have holes put in them so that the wind can blow through and immerse the land in wonderful sounds. So the cobs simply fall off, most have fallen off already, have come rustling down, naturally still in a completely unripe and unusable state, they have withered and dried out on the soil . . .

But and yes again and but, you now hear someone else take the words out of the former speaker's mouth and continue, if it were only a matter of the corn alone and nothing else, only the corn, it alone, that would be cause for a celebration, then the hens would simply not be fed any grains of corn for a year, if it were only just the corn, then I would invite all of you, and there's a real crowd of you here, think of that, and I'm a very parsimonious person and to a certain extent even a skinflint, but that doesn't matter to me at all, I would invite you without batting an eyelash, I wanted to say, just corn, I would invite all of you here on the spot to a bottle of champagne, and we'd get really tanked up here and be able to abandon ourselves by all means to this fantastic choral music of the cornfield singers, and we would have every reason to do without the corn harvest because the fields, instead of their yellow kernels, are giving us their marvelous concerts every evening, often during the day too, at noon, in the afternoon, depending on the location of the wind and the weather. And so that not only the people who always have time to come hurrying out of the city whenever a concert begins here to listen to these miraculous sound images—resounding there before our eyes they pass by out of the landscape, and having climbed high, they float away to the other side of the region, roll on, flooding away—so that not only those people could listen who can do so at any time, but also all the other remaining hard-working inhabitants of the entire country and of the city, I would immediately support having a radio broadcast van kept ready here at all times, and now and then also a train of television broadcast trucks, to broadcast this music to the other citizens as well, as soon as it starts, to record it live right away, without delay, or to broadcast it directly, from time to time also the images of the real landscape ballet dances, swinging around to the artistically waving force of nature, with images of the corn dances representing a chapter of their own, in my opinion, because if we had movement-translation keys handy, we could translate what these waving fields have to tell us, what news, messages or stories are being conveyed to us by the surrounding landscape. We had recently spoken of bottles of champagne, hadn't we, yes, I would invite you immediately to share those bottles, one per person, please note, so that the popping of champagne corks throughout the evening would have people nearby thinking there were fireworks going off, but unfortunately I feel no obligation at all to invite even a single one of you who are here together with me, enjoying the sound images performance, looking down at the plain and listening to the landscape presentation, to even a single small, not even to a baby bottle of champagne, because if it had been only the cornfields whose yield was destroyed, it wouldn't matter to me at all, but: the sugarcane fields planted nearby behind us on the other side are also destroyed, you understand, hollowed out, because these little creatures or bacteria have also scraped the sugarcane completely hollow, almost as if they've gone through the sugar stalk canes with tiny open razor excavators, completely clean inside, you know, neat work, but in doing so they have also eaten the sugar out of the canes, carefully, like they did here, and also the music that the wind creates there, actually considerably more intensely, more interestingly and more convincingly arranged than here, also more intimate and filled with greater desperation, squeezed out of the swaying sugarcane stalks, and apparently a sugarcane offers the wind a more advantageous swinging sound-box than the cornstalk here, the sound of the sugarcane flute was considered something very fine in former times, you know . . .

Oh yes, a third person begins his field complaint against these musical ballet performances whose choreographer and creator are the wind, the wind pushes its way into every individual hollowed out plant that presents itself, be it ever so small, and thus not only conducts the performance exactly and precisely, but also, as described, handles every instrument in person, it itself makes an extraordinary effort to blow into every hole as powerfully as possible, you know. But what I wanted to mention in addition: Nobody is talking about the sunflower fields? Their stalks too

have been hollow since yesterday, bored through by these gnaw-
ing bacteria that are worming their way around, patterned like
finger holes, as usual, as if we had to do battle against an army of
trained woodwind instrument makers.

Now, at dusk, do you hear all the rolled oats fields being chased
ahead or dragged behind someone through the blackly gleaming
varnished air? They hover past with a drawn out sound very like
a piccolo.

But already some people are talking about the individually hollowed out trees. Someday, as mighty wooden trombones, they
will make it that entire forests of the country cannot be entered,
because no one could withstand such tonal violence. When that
happens, the forests will no longer rustle as they do today; instead, a wood-splitting, screamed blaring will ring out through
the land. The choirs of tree tubas and wooden trombones will
boom through the hills, while the contrabassoon shrubs and clari-
net bushes get entangled in the undergrowth. No one could stand
it in such a forest, their eardrums would burst.

We should have opposed it right at the beginning, as it was getting going, someone says.

Oh dear, now we're hearing belated good advice again, is the
reply, and we're particularly fond of that, because with hindsight
everyone always claims to have known better! So do tell us, please,
what was the beginning, how did it all get started, what were the
telling signs you noticed back then?

We should have burnt down the first of the singing fields, but
now of course it won't do any good anymore, because the wind
and the sound carry the spores of these fungi or plants everywhere

with them in their flight, the spores are encapsulated in the chordal harmonies.

Now in any case the whole country is probably hopelessly covered by this sounding sickness, and sometimes one could think the whole continent was already stricken with it.

Somehow something has to happen soon, if anything can still happen at all.

Soon the entire country, the entire continent, the plant mantle of the planet will be completely hollowed out, and then, dried out, will crumble away.

Yes, in a few years at the latest, or earlier, the entire planet.

But it must have come from somewhere; or did it develop with us, come into being here?

No, of course it came from somewhere, you can be sure of that, and you still remember, one day or evening you heard something far away, very quietly and slowly coming nearer, from every direction . . .

Yes, right, that was something like a, something like, yes, like, yes, a sort of veiled cricket chirp blowing past through the air around us, extremely slowly, from high up, as if a foehn were blowing down to us from the sides of the high mountains. And having stopped here, hovering directly above us, it was barely audible. You could only hear it when you listened very quietly upwards, but even then you couldn't say exactly whether you had really listened upwards or whether the upwards listening was a listening into yourself.

That's approximately how it was, that's why people still know it so well, that's approximately how it must have all begun back then.

But to think that everything had to turn out so differently then from what we thought we had experienced at the beginning.

Yes, and one wouldn't have been able to believe it at the beginning.

But how were we supposed to know or have a presentiment that it would turn out like this, of all things? That everything has to turn out like this?

And today's generation doesn't do it any differently. Or any better. As we can see. Indeed, have seen. And did you notice how they kept cheering in the city this morning, keeping on at it until recently! What will come of it, and what will this turn out to be one of these days . . . ?

As if the plain were flooded by the ocean again.

What do you mean: doom? No one said anything about that! Quite the contrary. Because the landscape is spreading its music farther, listen, say others of the opposite opinion who have gotten very relaxed and happy from the sounds of the region, they say they can see it, hear it, like mist, the singing and sounding rises high up toward the sky from all the farmland. One day the entire planet will be enveloped not only by air, but also by sound, by music, we'll have an atmosphere of music. This will of course also lead to changing sound-weather over all the countries of the world, with precipitation, e.g., trickling like a flageolet, and then the light will be shrouded by shining sound clouds of great tonal heat, and the light will start to sound and the sound to give off light, it will hail down on us in choirs of air from all the cloud creases, a real music-weather will start to rule over us daily, every stray draft will spread cloud harmony colors through our days, and the darkness of night will start to sing to us comfortingly, illuminated like velvet. And does one not already see continuous sound vapors and melody fabric clouds rising up from the fields? The wind drives them on over the ocean, around the world and back, yes, is there not a beating of wings? It's as if, with trilled and ornamented notes, contrapuntally undersung, invisible or transparent flocks of birds were fluttering away from here to hot light. It is still silent around us, but not for long!

What nonsense that is, because common sense would certainly notice that the plants there, those hollowed out stalks, wouldn't last for long, but would soon burst from the pressure that the wind generates in their hollow columns when it constantly blows through and doesn't stop, doesn't one see, over there, how time and again one or the other corn stalk first bulges as if it's being blown up, doesn't it, right, look, and then bursts, yes sir, bursts, when the wind blows into a hole in the plant stalk, but can't find an exit anywhere, for example, can't get out of another finger hole in the corn, just look, did you see that now, and soon all the cornstalks there will have burst from the constant blowing through of this insatiable, indeed greedy wind activity, and sometimes it really seems to me, as it swings in and out over the plain, as if it is advising the landscape, how do you say, well, you know what I mean . . .

It has never been as strong as it is today, someone says, and that is cause for concern, because it seems to me that the whole plain is already overcome, is breaking up, listen, in merciless sounds, it's coming out of the ground, almost roaring already. Furrowed by the trade winds, it drones and glides. The swaying light beams glitter and tremble, making a fuzzy impression. And even the grass has now started to scream, as if in fear that it will burn in the transparent brush fire that is coming out of the ground in the surrounding fields and forests and starting to spread out in all directions, and is that so or does it just look like that? we ask ourselves. Everything has really begun to seethe; the withered meadow surfaces that make the brass band sound get thoroughly boiled. Individual swampy sound bubbles of cotton grass tufts take off, hover damply over the ground, and explode.

As if the plain were flooded by the ocean again.

The rushing ocean of sound soon flows on and arches over one of the landscape's tonal roof trusses. Its harmony walls cave in time after time, then recombine and expand again. With a sound pattern like the call of a cicada, the mountains of sound waves that carpet the region merge with the folds and fissures of the sunbeams, and bend far over the hills to the first suburban roofs. From there, a singing heat wave fabric is stretched as far as the first promontory ledges on the other side of the city. And from there, a skin of sound and light floods back over everything. It often splits or breaks open, quick as lightning, like a zipper over this district of the atmosphere, stretched tightly over the buttocks of our beloved region. Naturally, it also surges on, thither and yon . . .

A sea of sound starts running into the city, dripping through the eavestroughs onto the streets and squares, and getting stronger and more violent. It causes a real firedamp of music to break through all the roof trusses and lofts, and causes the melodies to flow down onto the alleys through all the gutters into the sewers. Of course, when such music torrents come flooding in, the sewers are immediately full to overflowing, and will undermine the houses so that walls crack and split. And some of the forgotten hopes that had started to go moldy resurface from the coal cellars and potato storerooms, deep under the first floor residences of the caretakers and odd-job men who watch over them . . .

Many of the people now seem to have started dancing to the rhythm of the landscape, to the surging of the undulating hills as they burst their banks.

The interlinking fabrics of grassy shrubs and melody waves blow through the girls' long hair.

The wild chordal calls from the strawflower gardens glide and reverberate through the huts on the outskirts of the city.

The longer you listen, the more strongly you feel that the sounding of the landscape is the introductory music to a fascinating annihilation you have almost wished for. It's the overture to the stunning beauty of a doom you have hoped for, when a hissing glissando will flash across the plain. You have longed for the exciting, moving destruction of nature by itself, and it will now continue destroying itself until the people have disappeared out of it. Then, freed from human beings, it can make a new beginning . . .

Or do you just feel this way about everything because it can't show itself to you in any other way, because you can only see it this way and not otherwise, although everything may be entirely different?

These veils of sound sink down around you. They cover the landscape like a skin, scaly with dragonfly wings, and flowed through by trade winds. Or are you just listening within yourself, is the listening into the plain simultaneously, or in reality, a listening into yourself? Indeed, doesn't it often happen that when you listen into the landscape of your surroundings, then you can often hear much more exactly what is going on in your own head, much more than when you only turn your ears inward, and turn into your head and learn less and less, soon you hardly understand anything anymore. These chords of veiled light hang down farther to you, you see, and feel, that you can be sure that all your inner thoughts and feelings are trickling down on you from the suburban sky as a fine, colorful pile of sound dust particles. They come gliding down from the shimmering sound powder dust of a shattered sheaf of light that covers this early evening, as if everything were hovering down from the atmosphere that turns out to be your own deeply personal, very secretly hidden structure of sensory perception. Until now, it must have been concealed somewhere in the airspace. And now it is enveloping all the outskirts of the city, as if, by extending your head over your environment, you had just now been able to recognize this region as the only distinctly discernible, clearly apparent reproduction of your state of mind. Or should your most intimate thought structure, which has now opened, and is spreading out in your surroundings, prove for your environment to be an exact likeness of its state?

Everything is so dry, so agreeably cool in this polished ray of sunshine. As if freshly painted, it makes a wickerwork shelter for the descending darkness, so agreeably uncertain . . .

Or for how long now have you been feeling that you're hardly a person at all anymore, but rather just a constantly evaporating and sometimes half reappearing state that is indicated to you by the surrounding landscape? Or perhaps that is one of the reasons why your surroundings apparently only show themselves to you as you see them, because you can't see them otherwise. This clock face of your presence in the plain, this means of calibrating the range of your state of mind according to the trembling of feathers and woven waves of sound, this backdrop, against which everything that is spread out around you takes place (or doesn't), has become more and more inexplicable to you and correspondingly more constrained toward you and increasingly blurred, immense. Because the land around you has already started to turn back at the edges, *to roll* itself *up* in your direction, toward you, in order to make any further deciphering, be it ever so fleeting, absolutely impossible. And now you have advanced to the point where the recently still facing horizon screens, the screens your tired shoulders brushed against now and then when you hid yourself behind them, have broken into each other and fallen over on top of you, so that the top of your skull knocks a hole through the airy canvas of the sky and your neck is completely enclosed by the frame of the firmament, as if by a ruff of the ether.

The wind draws back.

It lets all the notes it has sent whirling up from the fields of the plain fall into the steppe.

So as you continue on, the only remaining sound is the soft hovering and shimmering of the late afternoon wickerwork. It's just above the trembling, exhausted, weakened fields that have sunk in on themselves. As the sound shrinks back between the wall fabric of reeds, the branching, collapsed cornstalk ruins breathe a sigh of relief.

Or are those the chimneys of the apartment building up there ahead of you? They had previously started to play a stirring chorale, at first individually in very deep blasts from their blowers, puffed forth from the chimney hoods, breaking forth randomly from all the flues. And hadn't they soon gathered together to begin an astonishingly disciplined, darkly sounded fanfare? Or have all the apartment buildings of the city started blowing their strange funeral marches out of all the chimney pipes . . . ?

But then, when you get closer to the building, it seems to you more and more clearly to be an sea-going vessel, floating around in the melted airspace of this hottest of all summers. Its fog horns greeting you back from such a great distance, and calling out a friendly welcome for your long-awaited return to yourself.

The city lies ahead of you, surrounded by the already half rolled-up landscape, and you look down as if you were looking at the blurred outline of your own figure in the early evening fog of the battue's smoke blowers.

The opened windows are fluttering like flags, waving freely in your face, as if the walls, between which you squeeze your way through, had set sail.

When the edges of the gates push out from their frames, veils of mortar dust flutter crumbling through the alleys and envelop your head.

From the panes of glass, mirrored light mud flashes into your eyes.

Wooden huts rock away ahead of you through the wild gardens, like lifeboats that have been taken down, or broken loose, and gotten lost. They tip over behind the shrub grass edge of the sky. Leaning against its banisters, you brush along, exhausted, back into the most familiar home, the suite of rooms that in recent days has become almost unfamiliar to you again, your apartment, where nonetheless almost everything comes again and again to seem different to you, stranger and stranger, just as the greatest astonishment at the most unexpected surprise has started to seem suspiciously familiar to you.

I have jumped out of my skin so completely, you think, that I no longer care to think of myself as a person in me.

Rather, I see myself as a sort of subject that I'm observing, as someone walking along beside me, and I'm starting to have thoughts about my new companion, such as he is.

Is it because I then seem more important and worth seeing than if I thought about myself directly without taking a detour around myself?

Of course it's strange that you can think about yourself exactly the way you think about someone else, I think to myself, because you've never yet been able to think very much about anyone else.

But you've never been able to think about yourself either the way you do now, since you freed yourself from yourself as a sort of neutral person and made yourself independent.

All the same, you marvel at how much more important you seem to have become to yourself again.

Or, you ask, have I in reality completely overlooked the fact that I have turned my thoughts away from myself and toward someone else who has less to do with me than I might want to believe?

Why do you have the impression that you suddenly want to concern yourself with yourself more than before?

Is it possibly not so much you at all, when you see yourself now, but rather a memory of yourself, and is that what you're looking at instead?

Why does this house still seem like a boat to you? Is it because you believe you have already stood there so often, because everything gets solved in a more and more puzzling fashion? As if you had already tried countless times to throw this very evening behind you, but you were always thrown out of it and sank down at the shore's edge of its current hour limits, where the building you have been living in for some time has docked again. And you feel more and more intensely that it is a steamship plowing its way along between the cliffs of the suburban rooftops, up the hills and out of the city. And you just happened to catch it and walk on, right at the last minute before it cast off, just now, when you came back on board from the daily walk you've been taking for years, and climbed up the stairs.

Then on the top story you saw yourself appear once again, as so often, in that big mirror that covers the space on the wall between the door of your apartment and the door of the apartment across the hall.

Did you just now open the door to your apartment?

Didn't you open the door repeated beside it by the smoothly polished glass in the mirror? you ask yourself.

How should I be so sure of that, you reply, and even if you had opened the door in the mirror for yourself instead of the apartment door beside the mirror, you would enter the room as you are doing now, even if it was just the mirror room located behind the unlocked door in the mirror. From the room, you are offered, entirely reflected in the mirror, a sparkling, scenic view of this so late, sinking afternoon. Reflected by the mirror of the sky, or the sky of the mirror, it has flowed in by the open window, through this open mirror behind the entrance door, repeated by the glass wiped shiny beside the apartment door. You have now long since closed the apartment door behind you, and even if it appears a hundred times in the mirror behind you, you ask yourself politely not to mention it again . . .

Is it perhaps the small surface of the water falling elliptically over you, getting larger and larger at the edges of the glass? You held it in your hands recently as you were cooling your dry mouth, and could only choke down the liquid with difficulty as you put the glass back.

No, surely it was the contents of the hip flask that you emptied into your throat, and then put away, full of shame about your relapse into drunkenness, before you rinsed your burning mouth so that you wouldn't throw up?

But no, that's no hip flask standing there; it's an empty bottle that's been standing there for ages!

But perhaps it had always been empty, or there were only a few drops left over from a time you have long since overcome and put behind you, that may have been just now, or a few days ago . . .

Or what had that been that the pharmacist gave you this after-
noon? Was it that?

No.

But what is it then, if anything?

You hold the bottle up against the window, and when you look
through it, you can see into the distance, to a veil of mist over a
beach, a very extensive delta. It is wrapped up in a knotted pile of
clouds of smoke from the funnels of the river steamers. And floating
in the smoke, tied into bundles drifting out from the land, are count-
less broken off pieces of lighthouses.

On the bottle, all faded in capital letters, printed as if in a dream,
you see the name of a strong sleeping potion, when did you drink
it? Now?

No! Now the hip flask. That other bottle, that's from a long time
ago, probably several years.

And the bottle given to you today by the pharmacist you met
again after so many years on your walk through the fair, where is
that? isn't it standing there, entirely empty?

No, you can see it, the old label soaked off by the dish water of
years or months . . .

So where is the bottle from the pharmacist, did you drink it on
your way here?

No, it was a hip flask you drank.

You drank it just now.

Didn't you want to have a nightcap now, because you were so
exhausted from your daily walk?

And didn't you find that the bottle had already been drunk, was
empty, or did you put the empty bottle there now?

That's what happens when one allows one's own thoughts all-too-regular and-all-too close contact with each other. It would be better if you had a more formal relation with yourself, addressing yourself with an if I may, sir rather than a hey, you, so that one cannot impertinently suspect oneself in that manner and allow oneself to charge oneself with the meanest accusations. I will try to command my own thoughts to associate with each other from now on more and more frequently with an if I may, sir and no longer with a hey, you, either because it appears advantageous for a while to ensure a respectful distance or, what is entirely different, to elevate somewhat and prop up my completely burned down self-esteem. It may prove necessary to keep some distance between thought processes that suddenly surface or have long since surfaced and their conclusions. As it is now, you try to increase your own value by showing somewhat more respect for yourself and not accusing yourself suspiciously of such impertinently senseless gaps in your memory that are completely unfounded, you understand, my dear sir, and I have just drunk a glass of water, and there are two bottles standing there, and you, if I may, sir, want to accuse me of being so stupid as to have lost my self-control at this point of my life, in this boat of an apartment building that I occupy at the edge of the city. Though I really do feel like a talented young actor who got worn out at the beginning of his career. In his first and at the same time last casting, he had to portray a person of my name, but he wasn't up to the task, because the absence of useable scripts made it impossible for him to rehearse the role, so that I, especially to myself and not just to others, turn out to be the worst imaginable actor for the development of my own personality. But with that sort of single-mindedness I have not yet gotten lost, my dear man, which is what you, if I may, sir, continually standing in the way, getting stuck underway, want to accuse me of at the beginning of the trip. It consists of never leaving the place one has long since reached, where one has always been, and that one has already tried countless times to enter once and for all. Instead, one settles down here, as there, one stays to continue on at this point in one's life, my dear man, and if more people felt more obliged to themselves and conversed with themselves in their own heads with an if I may, sir instead of always feeling on intimate terms with themselves, my dear man, everything or much would be entirely different, but courtesy to one's own person is something that, in our part of the world, remains as completely unknown today as it was in the past, you know, sir, if I may!

Nevertheless, one should keep all communications on a formal basis, especially with one's own person, addressing it with an if I may, sir, but careless lapses still occur too often and the unsuitable hey, you is used, to which you thoughtlessly lower yourself time and again for the sake of simplicity, although especially in your case you are dealing with a You that bears only a faint resemblance to your own person, if I may, sir.

Yes, you're right, because you're so caught up in ossified self-observation that you would observe even your own downfall beside you or in you as an exciting experience that doesn't affect you. Or have you already downright turned to stone? It is a matter of indifference to you, whether or not you recently tried to put yourself permanently to sleep. Didn't you just now make the same attempt again, or only now, or again, or time after time, a minute ago, or a few hours ago, maybe a few days or even years ago? And has it become a matter of complete indifference to you if you're going to sleep forever now, without ever awakening again? And does nothing more about you affect you, because nothing more of you remains, hasn't for some time now, because you may already have killed yourself a long time ago? You closed off the interest of the people around you from yourself, letting it evaporate. Soon now the walls of your room will shut around you like book covers that enclose a story, and you will be caught in the middle of it, like an encoded word in a line standing at attention between two paragraphs, placed there to overcome invisible resistance from things beyond the written edges of the pages. And as the center of a story that, without your knowledge, has been written around you, and whose beginning is so far away, lost to you, that you will possibly never find out the beginning of the story, about the days immediately behind you, because you wanted to finally forget everything. Thus, you have already gone so far as to forget that your existence subordinates you to a story, whose beginning and cause are keeping themselves hidden from you, unknown to you; and because a story without a beginning is also always a story without an end, your story will perhaps have to remain an endless story forever, a story that can't stop and also will never be able to stop, because in the ongoing search for its beginning it never comes to an end.

And what about I, why don't you ever use the word I when speaking of yourself? Perhaps because in viewing your memory of a story about you, a story that you never succeed in writing to the end, and whose beginning you pretend to be looking for, but don't want to find at all, you are afraid that the beginning of this story simply consists of the fact that it had been brought to an end before the very beginning, before it had properly been able to begin. You had been just thrown into the middle of a story that was lost from the start. You can no longer find your way out of it and don't notice anything more about it, because it is your favorite story, in which you have gotten lost, because you are ignoring its lost beginning . . . and that's why you no longer say I when speaking of yourself, because your person loses all significance . . .

And what does I mean, can you tell me that, sir? No? Well then, you see.

Because one could perhaps only really say I if the sensations and perceptions, which are, after all, the most useful things we have at our disposal, were really fully able to sense and perceive everything that would be sensible and perceptible, if they were not dependent on and restricted by an anatomically middle-class, completely unusable body, which because of its amateurish construction unfortunately torpedoes their full development time after time. And one could get to such an I, if at all, only very slowly and tentatively, and of course exclusively using an if I may, sir. I do believe, particularly in this regard, that I may be on the right track. In any case, I won't be giving up again. What do you think, sir, if I may?

Hey you, I think you aren't interested in whether you tried to kill yourself a little while ago or not, or whether you're just now in the process of extinguishing yourself, because it's not just that everything around you had become meaningless to you, you have also become so meaningless to yourself that you don't even want to know if you are still alive or not anymore.

Yes, because it is finally plainer and clearer to me than ever before that I wouldn't be able to change anything about my condition anyway. Whether you are alive or long since dead amounts to the same thing, each state has become identical, both are fine with you, whether you are alive or not, because even if you are still alive, as you assume, you haven't felt anything in a long time, and you don't want to feel anything either.

Hey you, how long has it been since you really got satisfaction out of such feelings?

I mean, if I may, sir! since you, sir, still got any satisfaction from such feelings.

Nevertheless, right now, I'm inclined to think that one should not leave even a single stone unturned, one should try everything that might still be possible.

You, sir, are really getting on my nerves, carrying on like this.

Perhaps it would be best if we separated for a while, hey, you, you understand? If I may, sir, do you understand what I'm trying to say?

Hey you, listen, if I may, sir, listen, we'll simply, at first perhaps just on a trial basis, head in opposite directions from each other for as long and as far as possible, until, at the opposite edges of the horizon, we dwindle to the smallest dots and then completely disappear from each other's view.

Yes, and then suddenly, some day or night, we will have arrived at the shore of the sea, having completely overlooked the fact that it was somehow understood that, without any ado, light as a feather, we would be dissolved by the stillness of the ocean . . .

You see veils of air flare up there indistinctly over the distant forest, and trembling cracks and tears appear in the hazy sky. A shimmering, gray-streaked foehn races between the telegraph pole, organizing the flashing light into glistening, bewildered bundles of rays, and blowing them together into piles of light that roll away over the edge of the forest. The backlit trees seem to be polished black. Flocks of birds bump against the uppermost edge of the forest, they fragment

and are sucked up by the setting sun as it glides past, swimming away
with difficulty, with its last ounce of strength. Pale-skinned, it drives
its last storm of light in wisps of smoke past the edge of the city.

Thus the evening streams into the apartment building in which,
with utmost abandon, inwardly breathing a sigh of relief, you can
dissolve. A colorful, darkening mantle of light comes through the
window into the room, pushes its way toward you like a skin, and
coolly, pleasantly envelopes you up to your neck, so that only your
head still looks out, concentrating.

The rest of your body has pulled itself out of the cage of its skin.

The shrill ringing of the doorbell interrupts your concentration. Why
do you leap up frightened from your armchair?

Why the long, unnecessary way through the front hall?

Just stay sitting down!

Let it ring!

Why do you open the door to your apartment, although you neither want to know who is standing outside, nor are there any matters or demands that need to be dealt with?

Whom are you still expecting?

What are you still hoping will arrive?

No appointments have been made.

Haven't you known how to put a stop to visits without prior
appointment?

The only reason that you still opened the apartment door is probably to ask whoever is standing outside quite frankly: what do you
think you're doing?

It's not a person standing outside the door, but rather a three meters high wardrobe that is blocking at least half of your entrance, no, substantially more.

To think that one isn't even left in peace by wardrobes today could be cause for concern.

These are not very good times we live in.

The wardrobe is standing against the wall between the door of your apartment and the door of the apartment across the hall.

Presumably it hasn't been there long.

No longer than a few hours.

Probably minutes.

So where's the mirror?

The mirror, in which you had appeared just a while ago, used to hang on the wall where the wardrobe is now standing.

Perhaps it's behind the wardrobe, covered by the wardrobe?

Or is the reason you can't see it because you have dived so deeply into its surfaces, and they have meanwhile gone blind?

How long has the wardrobe likely been standing there?

You feel yourself observed by it, yes, it's a listening-post pushed in front of my door for the sole purpose of observing my existence uninterruptedly, you say, naturally one of the usual importune impertinences again; a grossly negligent disfigurement of the stairwell!

Just don't let yourself be provoked.

The best thing is to go right back into your room, where the sun will long since have drowned.

Yes, the darkness is scattering the evening's last piles of light.

Yes, through the crack of the door you still see a few wilted, sun-streak-cylinders rolling in from the corridor and being dashed to pieces on the edge of the wall.

Several fugitive bundles of light evaporate before the window and hop away through the steppe like burning animals.

In the undergrowth of the night that has broken in, flooding the plain, THE FOREST FIRE has begun.

Now, already flickering forth from distant hills, it pushes the glowing streets in front of it and quietly hissing nests of embers that flash around like misplaced signals, decorating the rolling clouds of smoke.

Slowly it moves closer to the outskirts of the city. Already it has reached the edge of the steppe.

As the crackling grassy bushes come gleaming toward them, the flocks of birds nesting there start with fright, flutter up out of the fire that surrounds them and try to rise up. But soon, even the last of them have lost their way in the darkness over the tongues of flame. They sink back exhausted, their singed wings folded together, and crash down, blinded by the fire, into the sea of sparks on the steppe.

The neighboring occupants have assembled at the gates and windows of the surrounding apartment buildings, disputing things in a lively fashion and gesticulating at each other: caught fire in the forest, a pity about all the wood, it really would have been much better to cut it all down beforehand and to use it ourselves as fuel . . .

Now even the river over there has caught fire. You hear that it has come to a boil and is letting off steam.

Countless flocks of butterflies of flame are blown upward from the burning bushes and poured into the red flashing rapids.

Somehow you must have fallen asleep for a short while. Because are you not filled with the silent suspicion that you are now waking up?

GERT JONKE is counted among Austria's most important authors and dramatists. Among other honors, he received the Ingeborg Bachmann Prize, the Erich Fried Prize, and the Grand Austrian State Prize for Literature. He died in 2009 at the age of 62.

JEAN M. SNOOK is an Associate Professor of German at Memorial University of Newfoundland. She translated Jonke's *Homage to Czerny: Studies in Virtuoso Technique*, published by Dalkey Archive in 2008.

PETROS ABATZOGLOU, *What Does Mrs. Freeman Want?*
MICHAL AJVAZ, *The Golden Age.*
The Other City.
PIERRE ALBERT-BIROT, *Grabinoulor.*
YUZ ALESHKOVSKY, *Kangaroo.*
FELIPE ALFAU, *Chromos.*
Locos.
IVAN ÂNGELO, *The Celebration.*
The Tower of Glass.
DAVID ANTIN, *Talking.*
ANTÓNIO LOBO ANTUNES, *Knowledge of Hell.*
ALAIN ARIAS-MISSON, *Theatre of Incest.*
JOHN ASHBERY AND JAMES SCHUYLER, *A Nest of Ninnies.*
HEIMRAD BÄCKER, *transcript.*
DJUNA BARNES, *Ladies Almanack.*
Ryder.
JOHN BARTH, *LETTERS.*
Sabbatical.
DONALD BARTHELME, *The King.*
Paradise.
SVETISLAV BASARA, *Chinese Letter.*
MARK BINELLI, *Sacco and Vanzetti Must Die!*
ANDREI BITOV, *Pushkin House.*
LOUIS PAUL BOON, *Chapel Road.*
My Little War.
Summer in Termuren.
ROGER BOYLAN, *Killoyle.*
IGNÁCIO DE LOYOLA BRANDÃO, *Anonymous Celebrity.*
Teeth under the Sun.
Zero.
BONNIE BREMSER, *Troia: Mexican Memoirs.*
CHRISTINE BROOKE-ROSE, *Amalgamemnon.*
BRIGID BROPHY, *In Transit.*
MEREDITH BROSNAN, *Mr. Dynamite.*
GERALD L. BRUNS, *Modern Poetry and the Idea of Language.*
EVGENY BUNIMOVICH AND J. KATES, EDS., *Contemporary Russian Poetry: An Anthology.*
GABRIELLE BURTON, *Heartbreak Hotel.*
MICHEL BUTOR, *Degrees.*
Mobile.
Portrait of the Artist as a Young Ape.
G. CABRERA INFANTE, *Infante's Inferno.*
Three Trapped Tigers.
JULIETA CAMPOS, *The Fear of Losing Eurydice.*
ANNE CARSON, *Eros the Bittersweet.*
CAMILO JOSÉ CELA, *Christ versus Arizona.*
The Family of Pascual Duarte.
The Hive.
LOUIS-FERDINAND CÉLINE, *Castle to Castle.*
Conversations with Professor Y.
London Bridge.
Normance.
North.
Rigadoon.
HUGO CHARTERIS, *The Tide Is Right.*
JEROME CHARYN, *The Tar Baby.*
MARC CHOLODENKO, *Mordechai Schamz.*

JOSHUA COHEN, *Witz.*
EMILY HOLMES COLEMAN, *The Shutter of Snow.*
ROBERT COOVER, *A Night at the Movies.*
STANLEY CRAWFORD, *Log of the S.S. The Mrs Unguentine.*
Some Instructions to My Wife.
ROBERT CREELEY, *Collected Prose.*
RENÉ CREVEL, *Putting My Foot in It.*
RALPH CUSACK, *Cadenza.*
SUSAN DAITCH, *L.C.*
Storytown.
NICHOLAS DELBANCO, *The Count of Concord.*
NIGEL DENNIS, *Cards of Identity.*
PETER DIMOCK, *A Short Rhetoric for Leaving the Family.*
ARIEL DORFMAN, *Konfidenz.*
COLEMAN DOWELL, *The Houses of Children.*
Island People.
Too Much Flesh and Jabez.
ARKADII DRAGOMOSHCHENKO, *Dust.*
RIKKI DUCORNET, *The Complete Butcher's Tales.*
The Fountains of Neptune.
The Jade Cabinet.
The One Marvelous Thing.
Phosphor in Dreamland.
The Stain.
The Word "Desire."
WILLIAM EASTLAKE, *The Bamboo Bed.*
Castle Keep.
Lyric of the Circle Heart.
JEAN ECHENOZ, *Chopin's Move.*
STANLEY ELKIN, *A Bad Man.*
Boswell: A Modern Comedy.
Criers and Kibitzers, Kibitzers and Criers.
The Dick Gibson Show.
The Franchiser.
George Mills.
The Living End.
The MacGuffin.
The Magic Kingdom.
Mrs. Ted Bliss.
The Rabbi of Lud.
Van Gogh's Room at Arles.
ANNIE ERNAUX, *Cleaned Out.*
LAUREN FAIRBANKS, *Muzzle Thyself.*
Sister Carrie.
LESLIE A. FIEDLER, *Love and Death in the American Novel.*
JUAN FILLOY, *Op Oloop.*
GUSTAVE FLAUBERT, *Bouvard and Pécuchet.*
KASS FLEISHER, *Talking out of School.*
FORD MADOX FORD, *The March of Literature.*
JON FOSSE, *Melancholy.*
MAX FRISCH, *I'm Not Stiller.*
Man in the Holocene.
CARLOS FUENTES, *Christopher Unborn.*
Distant Relations.
Terra Nostra.
Where the Air Is Clear.

FOR A FULL LIST OF PUBLICATIONS, VISIT:
www.dalkeyarchive.com

SELECTED DALKEY ARCHIVE PAPERBACKS

FOR A FULL LIST OF PUBLICATIONS, VISIT:
www.dalkeyarchive.com

SELECTED DALKEY ARCHIVE PAPERBACKS

FOR A FULL LIST OF PUBLICATIONS, VISIT:
www.dalkeyarchive.com